M.C. Vaughan is a Baltimore-based author of contemporary romance who doesn't sit still. Her stories are full of laughter, heart squeezes, dreamy locations and dreamier love interests. When she's not turning coffee into novels, she's dancing around her kitchen to new wave and '80s pop while whipping up an intimidating charcuterie board that she enjoys while deep diving into docuseries and feel-good television. Currently, she lives in Maryland with her husband and three delightful (mostly adult) kids.

Also by M.C. Vaughan

Romancing Miss Stone
Destination Weddings And Other Disasters

Discover more at afterglowbooks.co.uk

CODE NAME GORGEOUS

M. C. VAUGHAN

All rights reserved including the right of reproduction in whole or in part in any form. This edition is published by arrangement with Harlequin Enterprises ULC.

This is a work of fiction. Names, characters, places, locations and incidents are purely fictional and bear no relationship to any real life individuals, living or dead, or to any actual places, business establishments, locations, events or incidents. Any resemblance is entirely coincidental.

Without limiting the exclusive rights of any author, contributor or the publisher of this publication, any unauthorised use of this publication to train generative artificial intelligence (AI) technologies is expressly prohibited. HarperCollins also exercise their rights under Article 4(3) of the Digital Single Market Directive 2019/790 and expressly reserve this publication from the text and data mining exception.

® and ™ are trademarks owned and used by the trademark owner and/or its licensee. Trademarks marked with ® are registered with the United Kingdom Patent Office and/or the Office for Harmonisation in the Internal Market and in other countries.

First Published in Great Britain 2026 by
Afterglow Books by Mills & Boon, an imprint of HarperCollins*Publishers* Ltd
1 London Bridge Street, London, SE1 9GF

www.harpercollins.co.uk

HarperCollins*Publishers*
Macken House, 39/40 Mayor Street Upper,
Dublin 1, D01 C9W8, Ireland

Code Name Gorgeous © 2026 Mary Vaughan

ISBN: 978-0-263-42119-4

0426

Printed and Bound in the UK using 100% Renewable Electricity
at CPI Group (UK) Ltd, Croydon, CR0 4YY

To my pals – thanks for having my back
and all the belly laughs.

Girlhood never dies.

One

John Seymour paced his Georgetown apartment's living room. A honeysuckle-scented breeze wafted through the open windows. This morning's thunderstorm had mellowed into a golden June afternoon, a perfect backdrop for a storybook marriage proposal.

All he needed was his bride.

He patted the velvet box in his jeans pocket for the hundredth time since Jane had texted. Her flight had landed at Dulles an hour ago. Practical as always, she'd declined his offer to meet her at baggage claim. **Easier to Metro to Rosslyn and Lyft from there**, she'd typed.

She'd be home any minute.

Adrenaline surged through him as he surveyed the apartment. Shit, he'd forgotten the candle. After flicking his Zippo torch lighter, he held the flame to the wick of her favorite one. Theoretically it smelled like midnight in Paris. It definitely didn't. When he was there as a teenager, the City of Lights mostly smelled like river, garlic and bread.

Outside, a rumbling engine snagged his attention.

Jane?

Maybe. The idling SUV's tinted windows shielded its passengers. As he leaned toward the window, it took off, tires squealing. Stop signs interrupted this street every hundred feet, so there was no point in gunning it. Why in the world would—

"Ouch!" Pain bloomed on his thumb. The candle's wick had caught and flared while the SUV distracted him.

Ruckus, his rescue dog, raised his shaggy head.

"I'm okay, buddy." He slipped into the kitchen and ran cool water over his thumb.

He was okay? Lie.

He was a sweaty, jittery mess. Smart, funny, big-hearted, grounded, with striking eyes that saw his soul, Jane Marie Davis was the key to everything he wanted in life.

Please let her say yes.

A year ago, Jane sailed into the museum where he installed artwork. His museum's octogenarian director had consulted with her on an emerging voices exhibit. As they walked the space together, he informed both Jane and John that the show needed to be "well hung."

The smile she flashed had hooked him.

Two days later, over Filomena's triple chocolate mousse, he asked, "Want to come back to my place?"

"Yes, please. I need the end of your story about cracking the stretcher of a Picasso." She dropped her napkin on the table. "But FYI, I'm a black belt in Muay Thai, so think twice about getting handsy."

Then, much to his delight, *she'd* gotten handsy.

From that first date, they'd felt inevitable.

His phone vibrated against his ass. His younger brother, Thomas.

"Congratulations and best wishes!" Thomas's sweaty face filled the screen. "Wait. Where's my sister-in-law-to-be?"

"She's not home from her work trip yet. And I promise to call you first if she says yes."

"If?" Thomas widened his eyes. "Why if?"

John was ninety-seven percent certain she'd say yes. But the three percent of doubt was loud. Which he'd keep to himself. As the older brother, he always protected Thomas from emotional churn.

"Slip of the tongue. *When.*" The Washington Monument filled Thomas's background, which meant he was still on the National Mall's fields. "How'd we do?"

"We won in a sudden death shootout." Thomas grinned. "Expect Toulouse remains undefeated, even though you bailed on our clash with the brutal OMB Actuaries. Don't change the subject. Are you nervous?"

"Yes." He scratched at his beard. "But I'm ready. This has been on my mind nonstop since your wedding."

"You're welcome. It *was* the event of the season, wasn't it?"

"Don't be annoying, dear." Logan, Thomas's husband, leaned into the screen. "Where'd Jane go this time? New York? Barcelona? Casablanca?"

John lit more Midnight in Paris candles along the mantel.

"Casablanca was last month. This was a last-minute Rocksy appraisal in London. They dug it out of a warehouse last week."

The surprise work trip had given him the chance to pull out all the proposal stops. Rose petals strewn on their bed, chilled champagne, favorite meal in the oven because she was always exhausted after an international trip and wouldn't want to go to a restaurant. Hell, he'd even driven to Baltimore for the honey graham ice cream she often devoured in a single sitting.

"She has the coolest job." Logan sighed. "How's your setup? Will you have a good proposal story to tell approximately eight thousand times? And are you prepared to get mushy?"

"Jane doesn't do mushy." Jokes, yes. Incisive and cogent analysis and valuation of artwork, yes. Tirade of swearing when they lost at game night, absolutely.

But mushy? Never.

Thomas took the phone back. "*Everyone* does mushy. You may be older, but I'm wiser. Listen, you've got to tell her about it. Tell her everything you feel. Give her every reason to accept that you're for real."

John pinched the bridge of his nose. "You're the wrong generation to quote Billy Joel."

"Blame Mom for playing *Greatest Hits Volume I and II* on repeat when she drove us to school in France. Do you have a ring?" He bumped shoulders with Logan. "*Someone* didn't have one when he proposed."

Logan sighed. "So you could choose one with me. Your

taste—which some heathens call pickiness—is one of the many things I adore about you."

"Yes, I have a ring. Want to see?"

John creaked open the box to reveal the silver-and-sapphire art deco ring that caught Jane's eye in Old Town Alexandria last month. They were browsing for a brooch for his mother's sixty-fourth birthday. He'd doubled back the next day for the ring.

"It's *beautiful*." Thomas flashed him a smile. "Very Jane. Good luck!"

After the screen darkened, John clutched the back of a chair. Nerves buzzed under his skin. The loud three percent was more like five now. From day one, he'd felt a cosmic click with Jane. Like the universe had whispered *this one* to him. Every future he imagined, she was in it.

And that future would begin...

Ruckus rocketed from his bed with a joyful bark.

...now, apparently.

He calmly exhaled one, two, three as she exited the black sedan onto the dappled street. Her sundress fluttered around her knees while the bodice clung to the crescent curves of her hips, her waist, and her perfect breasts.

If she said no... *Stop that.*

John hurried into the hall, then down the front stoop's iron steps as the sedan eased away. Jane lit up with a smile as he approached.

Fireworks exploded in his chest.

"Hey, Gorgeous." Her ginger-and-lily perfume enveloped him as he kissed her hello, then took her bag from her. "How was your trip?"

"Fast, which is good." She squeezed his free hand three times, their signal for *let's go home*. "How's our boy?"

"Happy you're back. Like me."

She climbed the steps to the first-floor apartment of the townhouse his parents had bought in the nineties and converted to three units. In exchange for reduced rent, he handled the tenants' needs while his parents lived abroad.

Inside the apartment, Jane crouched to greet the wagging tan blur. "Who's a good boy? You are. You're the best, sweetest, goodest boy."

Maybe now?

He squatted next to her. "Jane, I have a—"

Ruckus nosed at him, knocking him on his ass.

Jane tugged her heels free. "Hey, can you work your magic on my neck later? The flight stressed me out. The woman next to me propped her naked feet against the seat in front of her. I swear she had a nail fungus."

The moment had disappeared. He couldn't follow athlete's foot with a proposal.

"Sorry, and yes." He rose from the floor, then helped her up. "Magic will be worked."

"I swear, everyone forgot how to share public spaces during the lockdowns. Dogs in restaurants, watching movies without headphones, eating chips from crinkly bags in museums… Oh! I got you something."

As he closed the apartment door behind them and flipped the dead bolt, his fingers prickled with adrenaline. *That* was his opening.

"I got you something too," he said.

"Me first." She rooted around in her carry-on. "Here."

She thrust a variety pack of Hula Hoops at him. When she said she was flying to London, he mentioned he'd eaten these crisps on a family vacation when he was twelve and wondered if they tasted as good as he remembered.

"Thanks." His heart stuttered in his chest. She listened to him *so* carefully.

"Welcome." She sniffed. "What are you cooking?"

This was it. "It's lobster ravioli from Filomena. I got carryout."

"Why? Wait." She knit her brows as she surveyed the tidy apartment, candles and champagne. "Did I mess up the dates? Isn't our anniversary in two days?"

His mouth was a desert.

"That's our first date." He clutched the bag of snacks. "But we met a year ago."

"Did we?" She laughed. "How do you remember?"

"Because I'm a meticulous note-taker."

He had been his whole life. Otherwise, it would've been impossible to keep track of where he and his State Department parents lived at any point in his history. He dropped the Hula Hoops on the coffee table, then picked up the journal he'd left there for this moment.

"Read this." He opened to the bookmark, then handed the journal to her.

She squinted at the page. "Your handwriting's atrocious. I need an Enigma machine."

"I believe in your ability to decipher it." He folded his arms to hide his shaky fingers.

"Okay, okay." In a low voice, she read, "'June 20. Hanging a new exhibit at the American.'"

He hooked his mouth up in a grin. "Is that supposed to be me?"

"Am I not nailing it?" She returned her sparkling green gaze to the entry. "'The art broker…who helped curate the Revolutionary Voices exhibit…is something else. Gorgeous. Smart. Funny. Extremely bossy.'" She glanced at him. "Gee, thanks."

"Keep reading."

Once she returned her attention to his journal, he dropped to one knee. His heart hammered against his ribs. Hell, he might faint. *No.* Him keeling over would *not* be part of their proposal story.

Instead, he took a deep breath.

"I'll… I'll marry her someday. Is that what it says?" As she looked up, the color drained from her face. "What are you doing?"

Jane hated surprises. Which he maybe should've factored into this proposal scenario.

"This." He opened the velvet box.

"But we've only been together for a year." She took a step toward him. "I wasn't expecting… This is so fast."

He lifted a shoulder. "Fast? Maybe, but why should we wait to start the rest of our lives together? I love the way you think. You're the first person I want to talk to in the morning and the person I want to wrap my arms around at night."

"We haven't talked about marriage." Her eyes shone as she took another step toward him. "At all. I… I'm so… I'm not sure what to say."

"Say yes." He pushed the ring toward her. "We love each other, don't we?"

Her eyes crinkled. "So much."

"Then let's get married."

Time stretched as she searched his face. Her eyebrow jiggled the same way it did when he answered a trivia question incorrectly at the bar. That wasn't good.

Except the jiggle calmed, and she smiled.

"Yes. An *emphatic* yes." She held her left hand out to him. "Let's get married."

If he hadn't already been kneeling, he might've collapsed with relief. He pressed his lips to the soft back of her hand, then slid the ring on her finger.

Her second knuckle stopped it.

"Damn," he said. "It fit my pinky."

She scraped it past her knuckle. "I'll get it sized. Now please come here and kiss me."

"Yes ma'am." He surged to his feet.

Jane's lips were as soft as sable under his. All he'd ever wanted was in his arms.

Jane caught a yipping Ruckus in a hug between them. "I guess he's happy for us."

"Everyone will be, Gorgeous." John tucked her dark brown hair behind her ear. "Everyone."

Two

Everyone will be happy for us, Gorgeous.

Hours after John had made that claim, she twisted toward him in their sex-rumpled sheets. He was wrong. Her boss, her boss's boss, and her flirty French ex would be decidedly *un*happy that John Carroll Seymour was her fiancé.

John would be too, when he learned the truth.

She squeezed her eyes shut.

There had been so many chances for her to come clean before today. When his parents flew into town to meet her, or when he'd asked her to be his plus-one at his brother's wedding. *Way* back in the beginning when he gave her a key to his apartment.

"Hey, John," she could've—*should've*—said. "Since we're stepping things up, let me be honest with you. I work for the CIA. Art brokerage is my cover. My real name's Vivian Flint."

But she hadn't because… Well, there wasn't one *good* reason why. Lots of little ones that added up to her being afraid he'd break up with her. Eventually she hoped if she kicked the can far enough down the road, he'd be hooked on her and stick around.

She ran her thumb over her ring's shiny sapphire.

The responsible choice would've been to say she'd consider his proposal. But the prospect of a love- and laughter-filled life with John was too tempting. *Yes* had tumbled out of her mouth before she could stop herself.

"Hi." He traced a circle on her shoulder. "I hear you thinking, Mrs. Seymour."

She kissed his hand. "I'm keeping my name."

Not Davis—Flint. Which he didn't know yet.

She flipped back the covers. "It's time for Ruckus's walk."

"I'll take him." As John stretched, the ripple of his body thrilled her. His job hanging hefty pieces of art kept him strong, but he loved good food, which kept his outer layer soft for comfortable cuddling.

"Don't be silly." Jane padded toward the dresser. "You've been on doggy duty since Wednesday, and I want to stretch my legs."

With his arm tucked behind his head, he said, "I can help with that."

"Not the kind of stretching I meant." She tugged on her favorite yoga pants, a sports bra and a T-shirt. Heaven after two days in tailored business gear and four-inch heels. She'd love to chuck every pair of stilettos she owned straight into the mouth of hell.

Alas, they were what her alias required.

Through a yawn, he said, "I'll wait up for you."

"You'd better," Jane called over her shoulder.

He would not. She could time a Swiss watch against John's biometric clock. At 10:15 p.m., unless he'd taken a nap, it was lights out. She adored his reliability, especially when it worked to her benefit.

Vivian closed the bedroom door, then called, "Need a walk?"

Ruckus bolted from his bed and sat next to the door, tail thumping against the hardwoods. She zipped herself into John's hoodie, then loaded its deep pockets with her keys, both her phones, a hot pink roll of dog waste bags and the flash drive she'd found in London.

She clipped the leash to Ruckus's collar. "Lead the way."

He tugged her into the night, then immediately slowed, sniffing every blade of grass along the stone wall dividing their quiet street from Holy Rood Cemetery. Technically, this neighborhood was Burleith, but the residents often referred to it as Georgetown.

As far as DC villages went, it was sleepy.

Her sneakers slapped against the sidewalk's crisscrossed bricks. Comfortable, reliable, useful…this was her favorite footwear. The number of heels she'd sacrificed so she could make a hasty exit without breaking an ankle was shameful. Those Louboutins deserved better.

She plugged in her headphones and dialed her handler.

Compared to her personal cell phone, her meets-SCIF-standards work phone was a clunker. Still, it was an improvement over the years when she was required to head into the office to brief him. Seven miles didn't seem like much, but in DC traffic, that translated to anywhere between fifteen minutes and an hour door-to-door.

MacColl picked up on the second ring. "Hope your shopping trip went well, Canvas."

"Total success. I bought a palette knife." In retrospect, she should've picked an easier code word than *palette knife*. It was a bitch to squeeze into conversation.

Ruckus paused to leave his mark on a hydrant.

"I expected your call four hours ago," MacColl griped.

"Couldn't isolate," she said.

Protocol dictated she call to brief him *if* she could do so discreetly. The airport was a nonstarter, as was the Metro, and the Lyft driver. Too many ears. Once she was home, she couldn't bail on John after he proposed. Or right after the glorious post-yes sex, the fabulous meal, and more enthusiastic post-dinner sex.

Another reason she'd said yes—she and John were *fire* in the sack.

"Should've tried harder," he said.

"Sorry, Boss. But I hope you had a good birthday."

Never hurt to kiss ass when she was in the doghouse.

MacColl humphed. "How'd you remember it's my birthday?"

"Special talent." More like muscle she worked hard to develop since she was a kid, when she couldn't rely on her ability to connect speech sounds to letters and words. Numbers, dates and art became her comfort.

"Your connection's shitty. Sounds like you're under water."

She looked at her phone. "Full bars. Might be a solar flare?"

"Whatever. Give me the latest on ZR/MONFUN."

The agency's digraph cryptonyms were often petty, but this one was just plain boring. MONFUN was short for *money funnel*, and ZR classified this as a Staff D operation. Staff D handled intelligence intercepts and worked directly with the broader intelligence community.

Collaboration was a specialized skill, and she excelled at it.

Some CIA—MacColl included—struggled with trust. He came of age during the Cold War and never recovered from suspecting everyone had an ulterior motive.

She, however, was from a different era.

Trust had its benefits. She wasn't naive—bad apples were out there. But dozens of her classmates from Georgetown's School of Foreign Service now worked for DoD agencies. So yeah, she'd go ahead and trust the NSA analyst who'd held her hair senior year when a half-dozen tequila shots caught up with her after the Diplomatic Ball.

"Canvas?" MacColl prompted.

"Here are the headlines. The painting Dilettante hired me to authenticate was legit."

Dilettante was their code name for Jean-Michel de Gramont, her, *blech*, ex-boyfriend and former mentor. Five years ago, after establishing herself as an art broker, she'd cozied up to him to build her street cred in black market art circles.

After their breakup a year ago, she advocated for turning him over to the local authorities. His money-laundering scheme had evolved into trafficking drugs via art. But MacColl overrode her. In his opinion, letting Jean-Michel continue to build his list of criminal activities would make the case against him stronger and more likely to lead to a conviction.

"Which painting was it?" he asked.

"*Boy Playing Trombone.* It's stenciled spray paint on plywood from a council estate in London. The sales history shows a shell company bought it in 2018, kept it in a free port, and sold it back and forth to another shell company, bumping up its value. Should fetch six million euros, give or take a half mil."

"Which shell companies?"

Ruckus led her to their usual destination—the Guy Mason Rec Center dog park. It was relatively deserted at night, and its walkways were well-lit.

"The seller's a familiar player," she said. "Gaizger Trading Company."

"Dragomir Mihailovic is at it again, eh?"

"Got it in one, Boss."

MacColl longed for his John le Carré days. Back then, the game involved dark alleys and dead drops. Now it was more spreadsheets and sanctions. Through those spreadsheets, though, they'd caught Dragomir Mihailovic's campaign contributions to pro-reunification politicians based in the Balkans. Otherwise, the Gonič family underboss was a mystery. Slippery. No photos had been uploaded to the DoD's shared systems for a decade.

"When's the auction tomorrow?"

"Nine a.m. GMT, 4:00 a.m. local." She'd wake up to watch the livestream. "There's more."

"I'm listening."

She searched the shadows. Nothing, and Ruckus was quiet. That was good enough for her to proceed with the briefing.

"Rocksy embedded a self-destruct device in the painting's frame."

"Does Dilettante know?"

"Doubtful. He loathes unpredictability."

MacColl sighed. "Does this stunt put you at risk?"

"No. Heightened emotions could work to our advantage. Angry people get sloppy."

"Agreed. We'll wait and watch. Anything else?"

"Yes, but it's personal."

Her heart kicked into overdrive. She'd been in tight squeezes and dangerous situations with barely a blip in blood pressure, but the idea of uttering this next sentence made her knees wobble. It would trigger a chain of events that would end with revealing her true identity to John. They'd either achieve a beautiful new relationship phase or break up. She didn't see an in-between.

"Canvas?"

"Brawn asked me to marry him."

Seconds felt like hours as her butterflies morphed into hornets. She never rocked the boat at work, had always followed orders without hesitation. Even as a little girl, she'd hated being a problem because it made her the center of unwelcome attention.

But John was worth it.

Finally, MacColl humphed. "If you said yes, you need to bring him in for a polygraph."

Her engagement ring gleamed in the park's overhead LED lights. Relief flowed through her. In more fraught times, MacColl might've told her to break it off.

"Then I need to bring him in."

"Tomorrow," MacColl said. "If he passes the poly, the wedding needs to happen fast."

Standard. Marriage brought legal protections that engagements did not.

"Roger that. One last thing, Boss. In addition to the self-destruct device, I found a thumbnail-sized flash drive."

"Christ, Canvas. You should've started there."

She ignored his irritation. "It's encrypted. Given the duty of care from warehouse to auction house, the drive could've come from anywhere. I'm leaving it at our usual place."

On cue, Ruckus squatted on a wedge of green grass next to the dog park's paved trail. She ignored the bag dispenser attached to Ruckus's leash. Instead, she ripped a hot pink bag from the roll in her pocket and stashed the drive, which she'd then shove into the bag she used to clean up after Ruckus. Then she'd dead drop everything in the park's waste station.

"Don't," MacColl said. "Bring it tomorrow instead."

Maybe this was a sign MacColl was finally starting to trust her capabilities. She pocketed the pink biodegradable plastic, then picked up after Ruckus with the normal green bag.

"Will do, sir."

He ended the call.

Sigh. Just once, it would be nice for him to say *nice work*. She'd heard his whole *your paycheck is your reward for a job well done* speech, but a pat on the back—even better, a promotion—went a long way.

At least he'd been decent about the proposal.

The overachiever in her laughed into the dark.

He wanted fast? She'd show him fast.

At home, as predicted, John was sawing logs. He slept in the ready soldier position, flat on his back, arms straight by his sides, ready to spring into action. Ironic considering she was actually the one who took middle-of-the-night calls from parts unknown.

"John?" She nudged his shoulder. "Wake up. I need to ask you something. John?"

"What? Who?" He bolted upright like Nosferatu disturbed before sunset. Unless sunrise or Ruckus's snuffling woke him, he greeted sudden consciousness with startled suspicion.

"Do you have any important meetings next week?" she asked.

"That's why you woke me?" He slapped at his bedside lamp, then grabbed his water to clear his groggy throat. "Jesus, Jane. Next week? No, there's nothing I can't move."

She straddled him. "Let's elope. Tomorrow."

John coughed on the water. "Why?"

"Because we can." She was telling the truth…but not all of it. "To Copenhagen. The weather's beautiful this time of year, the days are twenty hours long, and I have a boatload of points burning a hole in my pocket. Denmark's like the Vegas of Europe. Same-day licenses, and we don't need any special visas."

"You want to…" He rubbed his beard. "Go? To another country? Tomorrow?"

The agency preferred quick nuptials, true, but she also wanted to seal this deal fast. Otherwise she'd torture herself with legitimate reasons they shouldn't marry. Her subterfuge, his tense relationship with his parents, his unwillingness to travel.

But mostly her subterfuge.

"I promise we'll do a performance wedding too. But work's bananas, and I hate the idea of delaying because of logistics. I want to be married to you, John. Not in a year or two, but now. Your passport's valid, right? So there's no reason we couldn't—"

He cupped her face with his big rough hands and ran his thumb along her cheek. "Let's do it. Let's elope to Copenhagen and figure out the rest later."

Three

"There we go." Thomas unplugged the flash drive from his laptop. "Every stitch of wedding research we did is on this."

"Thanks." John pocketed the thumbnail-sized device.

Early this morning, John texted his brother, Thomas, and his brother's partner, Logan, to ask if they could dog-sit Ruckus while he and Jane celebrated their engagement with a spontaneous getaway. Once he arrived at their Capitol Hill townhouse, they demanded he stay for a cup of coffee.

"Any dates in mind?" Logan set Ruckus's water dish on the kitchen floor. "It took forever to nail down a weekend that worked for your parents' and Thomas's work schedules."

The hot mug irritated John's sensitive blister.

"The thing is…" He never lied to avoid friction. Better to face unpleasantness head-on and deal with the fallout than to keep secrets. "We're eloping."

"You?" Coffee lurched from Thomas's mug. "Why? Have you told Mom and Dad?"

"Not yet. I'll call them when I'm back." His parents had never done him the courtesy of announcing their big life decisions with lead time, so he didn't see why he should. "Jane's work schedule is unpredictable, so we're going for it. We leave for Denmark today."

Logan wiped up Thomas's spilled coffee. "But you still want to do something stateside? So all your nearest and dearest can celebrate you the way you deserve?"

"Yes, but we haven't talked about what we want." John lifted a shoulder. "I'd be happy with a potluck picnic in the backyard. Does one of you want to officiate?"

"Oh, John, *no*," Thomas said. "I won't let you downplay the biggest event of your life. And I can't officiate since I'm your best man."

"I haven't asked you yet."

Thomas dropped his jaw. "How dare you? And whom else would you ask? If you say Patrick or Timothée, I'll put you in a headlock until you recant."

John laughed. "I haven't talked to Timothée in almost twenty years. Pretty sure he'd turn me down."

"Patrick, I've met." Logan joined them at the table. "But who's Timothée?"

"My high school best friend," John said.

Thomas squeezed John's shoulder. "My first act of best-man-smanship is to demand you and Jane have dinner with us the second you return from this capricious-but-classier-than-Vegas elopement so we can plan your wedding. No brother of mine is getting married in a barn."

"I didn't say barn. I said backyard."

"Potato, potahto." Thomas waved his hand. "Rest assured, we'll help you find the perfect place to host a petite gathering of five hundred."

"I'm friends with like twelve people. Same with Jane." John had met a handful of her work friends, but her best friends lived abroad, and her parents died when she was in her early twenties. The rest of her family lived in Colorado. "We'd probably both prefer something more scaled down than your wedding. Which was great, but the National Cathedral and a splashy reception aren't my style."

Logan rested a hand on Thomas's drumming fingers. "Something more intimate, then."

Budget-conscious, more like.

Hanging exhibits wasn't a lucrative career, but John was happy. He'd quit corporate graphic design after three soul-sucking years. Since he'd always been good with his hands, he switched to art handling in his mid-twenties and hadn't looked back. His real talent lay in finding *the* perfect way to support and showcase an artist's work.

"Talk to Jane," Thomas suggested. "She might surprise you with what she wants."

"I will." He rose to empty his mug in the sink.

"I fully support this whirlwind romance, John." Thomas flashed him a smile. "Jane's good for you. You've been happier this past year than I ever remember."

He folded his arms across his chest and grinned. "Because she makes everything better."

"Aw, away with you." Logan shooed John. "Back to your bride and your international wedding adventure. We'll treat your pup to the best week of his life."

"Thanks, guys."

John drove his ancient Ford pickup across the city, then stopped for coffee and pastries. After unlocking the front door, he dropped his keys in the bowl on the console table. Jane's weekender bag lay next to the shoe rack. She'd be home from Muay Thai in ten minutes, enough time for him to pack and call his parents.

The bedroom door swung open. Jane appeared in a navy pantsuit and heels.

"Christ." He pressed a hand to his hammering heart. "I didn't know you were home."

"Sorry." Jane laughed. "You startle so easily. Are you okay?"

He set the coffee tray on the table. "Fine. Just shaved a few days from my life."

"They were probably shitty days anyway. Ooh, did you stop at Janti?"

"I did." Just like most weekends. He wiggled her preferred combination of drip coffee, a shot of espresso, and four raw sugars from the tray. "Here. Are you headed into the office?"

He loved her go-getter ambition. In an industry that risked becoming boring and dusty, she shook up norms with the artists she championed and exhibits she curated. But he preferred more of a heads-up that their plans might change.

"*We* are headed to the office." Her silver-and-sapphire ring winked in the sunlight. "I need to pick up a few things for our trip. We'll head to Dulles from there."

Relief thrummed through him. "Should I change?"

"Much as I love cargo shorts and movie T-shirts, maybe khakis and a button-down are better?" She sighed at her phone, which was buzzing like a hornet's nest. "Fucking Rocksy."

"What?" He unraveled the pastry bag and withdrew a croissant, handing it to her. "Did it set a record?"

"Big-time. It went for three times what I predicted."

"Isn't that good?" he asked. "You sound annoyed."

She ripped the horn from the croissant. "After the winning bid from an anonymous buyer was announced, a mechanism in the frame tipped some kind of acidic solution over the surface. It destroyed the painting. *Boy Playing Trombone* is now a messy swirl of goo, and people are losing their minds."

"The blank plywood's probably worth more now. Infamy is expensive."

She leaned her hip against the counter. "I bet you're right. The art world is so weird."

"Which is why you love your job."

"I don't love all of it." She dusted her hands as a shadow passed over her face. "But I love enough of it to stick around for a while. Let's load up the car. I already packed your bag."

"Yes, ma'am." Her decisiveness was *such* a turn-on. He glanced at the bedroom. "Unless you want to…"

As she kissed him, her ginger-and-lilies scent swirled around him. "Plenty of time for that in Denmark. I don't want to miss our flight. Now go change."

She nudged him toward the bedroom.

"Okay, okay." He raised his hands. "Can't blame a guy for trying."

His life was amazing.

★ ★ ★

While Vivian waited for John to lock up the apartment, she drummed her fingers on her Chevy SS's steering wheel. She was more of a supercar fan, but she purchased this model because it was (a) nondescript, and (b) had a beast of an engine.

Sort of like her.

John tossed his bag in the back. "Did you remember your EpiPens?"

Depends on what you mean by EpiPens. "Yes."

"Great." He buckled into the passenger seat. "I can't wait to see where you work."

"Don't get too excited," she said. "It's bland."

She eased into M Street's busy traffic flow. DC driving was tricky since she preferred *not* running over inattentive tourists. As cars pumped through the crowded intersections, she checked her mirrors.

All clear. No tails.

She swerved and laid on the horn to stop a minivan from hitting her in Dupont Circle, aka the fifth circle of hell. She used her defensive driving training more in DC's nightmare roundabouts than she did while navigating twisty Moroccan streets.

"Will your coworkers be there?" John asked. "It's like I already know Brady, Kyle, Alaina and Torrey from your stories. Oh, and Beverly."

"Not sure about most of them since it's a Saturday." Vivian chewed the inside of her cheek. He'd meet them soon…in a different context. "But Beverly definitely will be."

Because Beverly was their polygrapher.

"What about your boss?" he asked.

John sucked in a breath as she whipped a hard left across three lanes of oncoming traffic. She'd survived a white-knuckle drive on Switzerland's Furka Pass during a snowstorm, so maneuvers like that didn't bother her, but John's fear was reasonable.

"Sorry," she said. "And yes, my boss will be there."

A sudden move in the rearview mirror caught her attention.

Black Suburbans were a dime a dozen in DC. Diplomats, Feds, people who ordered Uber Black... Still, better to be cautious. Up ahead, the light turned yellow. She slowed to a stop, and the Suburban blew through the now-red light.

Phew, not a tail.

"Good," John said. "I'd like to meet the person sending you around the world."

The light turned green. After two blocks, she flicked her blinker and turned into her parking garage. It sat below a brutalist building in which the agency rented space. She reversed into a spot, then puffed her lips with an exhale.

This was it.

In minutes, John would learn she'd been lying to him for this whole year... But he'd get why, wouldn't he? She side-eyed him. Or would it be too much?

"Everything okay?" John settled a grounding hand on her shoulder. "You seem nervous."

"I'm great," she squeaked at a dolphin-level pitch.

What the fuck? Vivian Flint faced steely crime bosses across interview tables. Joked with them, threatened them and usually got what she wanted. She should have been handling this better.

"If you're having second thoughts, it's okay."

And *this* was why she'd fallen for him. His kindness, his lack of guile, handling her feelings like they were precious—an irresistible cocktail. On her bad days, when her worried heart got the better of her, she suspected he was too good for her.

"I've never been more certain of anything in my life." She opened the glove box, set her personal phone to airplane mode and deposited it inside. "Toss yours in there too?"

When they'd first started dating, she'd explained that she couldn't take her phone into work for security reasons. True, but not because of the bullshit she'd fed him about being discreet on behalf of their clients. Intelligence agencies didn't permit recording devices through the door. No phones, cameras, smart watches... Hell, even Furbys were banned.

John added his phone to the box.

By the time they reached the entrance to her office suite, the pit in her stomach had grown to a house-swallowing sinkhole. Oh great, now her hands were shaking. She should have had a better grip on her biometric stress responses.

"I've got a visitor," she said to Lawrence, the security guard who regularly worked weekends, as she laid her badge against the sensor. "Lots of people here?"

Hopefully not. She didn't want everyone to crowd John.

She passed through the metal detector. No beep.

"Not today." Lawrence flipped through the list of expected visitors. "Vacation season. ID?"

John handed Lawrence his passport. The security guard looked at it, then at John. After doing this twice more, he scanned John's passport into the system.

"Pockets?" Lawrence asked.

John dropped his wallet, Zippo and a flash drive into the waiting plastic basket, then stepped through the metal detector at Lawrence's signal. Vivian widened her eyes. What the fuck was he doing with a drive? While the security guard was busy with John, she palmed the drive and shoved it into her tote. Recording devices were problematic; tools for copying gigs of data were treasonous.

"Boss said you're in room five," Lawrence said. "Please escort your guest."

"Thanks," she said. "Follow me, John."

Their footsteps echoed as she led him to the room.

John caught her hand. "So this is your home away from home?"

Her stomach's sinkhole grew to an abyss. She'd been an excellent secret-keeper her whole life. First for herself, then for the agency and her country. *Revealing* the truth, however, was new territory.

She'd start simple.

"Yes," she answered. "When I'm not traveling or curating exhibits, I'm here."

"Huh. I expected to see your clients' work." He gestured to a hastily framed John Singer Sargent print a GS-4 staffer had bought at IKEA. "Not art posters."

"It sells fast," she said.

That was a half truth. Her clients' work never lasted long in a gallery. But he was right to question the decor of a supposed art brokerage firm. On the off-off-off chance civilians gained unescorted access to their suite, they'd lightly camouflaged their satellite office's hallways.

Not enough, apparently.

"Here we are." She opened the interrogation room's door.

This was it. Inside the room were a big wall mirror, a table on which the polygraph machine rested, and two chairs. What was he thinking? Nerves pinballed inside her harder than they had during weapons training at the Farm.

"Whoa." John entered. "Is this a conceptual piece?"

Oh God. This sweet, innocent man thought the polygraph machine was art.

"No." Fear clogged her throat.

If she didn't tell him the truth, she couldn't marry him. By telling him, she might lose him. Rock and a hard place? This was more like that *Star Wars* trash compactor thing, closing in on her from all sides.

Get it to-fucking-gether, Flint.

She cleared her throat. "You should sit, John."

The hitch in her voice caught his attention. "What's wrong, Gorgeous?"

Oh, nothing. I'm on the precipice of my life drastically changing, and there's nothing I can do about it except take a swan dive.

"I'll tell you after you sit."

"Okay." Warmth lingered after he dropped into the interview chair. "What's up? Are you sick? Married? About to break up with me?"

"What? No, never." She took a deep breath and notched her fists on her hips. Superhero pose, which should have boosted her confidence.

It did not.

"I don't know how to break this to you gently." She blew

out her lips. "So I'm ripping off the bandage. My real name is Vivian Flint. I'm an intelligence officer for the CIA."

The color drained from John's face. Nope, wait—some color stayed. Greenish yellow. Sort of a puce, edged in white.

"Am I under investigation?"

"No." She crouched in front of him and wrapped her hands around his. "Officers are instructed not to disclose their agency attachment until a relationship gets serious, and—"

"*Gets* serious?" John withdrew his hands. "We've *been* serious. At least, I've been."

She was fucking this up.

"Me too, but John, I couldn't figure out when I should—"

He pushed back in his chair. "Wait. You've been lying to me for *a year*, Jane?"

"Vivian. And it wasn't my choice." She backed up, allowing him room to pace, his preferred method of blowing off steam. "I was following protocol. Some people don't even tell their kids. But before we can get married, you need to submit to a polygraph. It's the final part of the background check the agency initiated when we started dating."

He shook his head. "What else don't I know about you?"

Her engagement ring bit into her knotted fingers.

"I'm from Baltimore, not Denver." With the floodgates opened, truth spilled from her faster than a swollen river. "My parents are alive. My mom's a bank teller. My dad's an HVAC installer. I'm one of five kids—two older brothers and two younger sisters, all overachievers. But you know lots about me. My favorite movies, my favorite paintings and my game night dominance—those are all real. And I'm really dyslexic, hate heights and can hold my breath for five minutes."

The wall clock's hands ticked like a bomb.

After the longest minute of her life, he blinked.

"I can't say it's nice to meet you, Vivian Flint." John's clouded expression was new to her. "Unlike you, I don't lie."

She couldn't breathe.

Four

John's world tilted. A knock interrupted the booming silence between him and the woman he'd thought he loved. Vivian Flint from Baltimore. Not Jane Marie Davis from Denver.

"Is your middle name Marie?" he asked.

She reached for the knob. "No."

A silver-haired Black woman strode into the room. The fluorescent overheads' gleaming reflection in her glasses obscured her eyes as she swiveled her gaze between him and not-Jane.

"I hear congratulations are in order?"

Vivian nodded. "Pending the polygraph."

John's brain cramped. "Pending nothing. You've lied for our whole relationship."

She folded her arms. "I wasn't permitted to disclose my identity."

Liars got under his skin. Which she knew. Just like he knew Jane didn't tolerate littering, line-cutting, or listening to phones without headphones in public spaces. Big public displays of emotion were also a no-go for her.

His stomach oiled.

But this wasn't Jane. This was Vivian, and he had no fucking clue what made her tick.

"Lean forward." The polygrapher snugged a band around his lower abdomen, followed by another around his chest.

"I'm not doing this." He tried to stand, but the surprisingly strong polygrapher pressed him back into the chair's squishy embrace.

"No need to be nervous." Velcro crackled as she adjusted

the blood pressure cuff on his biceps. "It only takes two to four hours."

"Am I under arrest?"

The woman laughed. "You were right, Viv. He *is* funny."

He locked eyes with Vivian. "What else have you said about me?"

"All good things," the polygrapher assured him as she capped his ring finger with a monitor, then stuck two adhesive circles to the back of his other hand. "Ready to start?"

"No," he said.

The woman chuckled again as the machine whirred to life. Paper flowed under gently undulating ink needles, then curled into a collection bin. He preferred to stare at the machine rather than Jane. Vivian, dammit. Because if he locked eyes with her, the sadness, anger and humiliation building within him would burst forth.

At the moment, numb seemed the better choice.

The polygrapher sat at the table's other side. "Did Vivian explain how this works?"

He shook his head. "I just learned she was Vivian a minute ago."

"Girl, what?" The older woman shot Vivian a look.

"I wasn't supposed to tell him, Beverly."

"You're Beverly?" John asked. Jane—not Jane, Vivian—had described Beverly as the office mom, the person who remembered everyone's birthdays and work anniversaries, sent them home if they had the sniffles, and kept their boss in check since she'd been on the job longer.

"The one and only." She gestured to the cables and cords wrapped around him. "Here are the basics. This machine is sensitive to biometric inputs. Pulse rate, perspiration, movements in the chair. It isn't perfect, but it picks up on strong reactions, which usually signal lies."

"I don't lie." He stared at the poster of a calm lake behind Vivian. "Unlike some people."

"Shots fired!" Beverly laughed again. "Listen, I'm not here to mediate. Let me ask my questions and get back to my weekend, and you two can figure out your wedding plans."

Wedding plans?

He'd asked Jane Marie Davis to marry him, not Vivian Question Mark Flint.

He clutched the armrests. "If we aren't engaged, can we stop this?"

Vivian flinched. "John—"

"Well, *that* spiked the needles." Beverly marked the paper with a red pen. "Since I've gone to the trouble to hook you up, let's ask a few questions. Vivian, mind stepping outside?"

"Okay." She opened the door. "Be kind to him."

Vivian slipped into the hallway, leaving him alone with Beverly.

"Okay, young man." Beverly uncapped more pens. "To start, I'll ask you three questions. Answer truthfully, yes or no, and don't get in your head about them. I don't ask trick questions. So here we go. Is your name John Carroll Seymour?"

"Yes," he answered.

"Are you thirty-four years old?"

"Yes."

"Do you live in Washington, DC?"

"Yes."

The temptation to add context tugged at him. He'd just turned thirty-four in May, which was how old his parents were when they got married. And yes, he lived in DC now, but had lived all over the world growing up.

"Good. Now I'll repeat those questions, but this time, lie so I can get a baseline for how your body responds when you're deceptive. Is your name John Carroll Seymour?"

"No." The needles danced wildly.

No surprise there. Lies made him desperate to move, to run, to outpace the discomfort building in his body. Always had.

Beverly whistled as she marked the paper. "Are you thirty-four?"

"No." More skittering needles.

"Might not even take a half hour," Beverly murmured. "Do you live in Washington, DC?"

The needles waved before he lied this time. "No."

"It's like you *can't* lie," Beverly said. "I've got my baseline. For the rest of these, I'd like you to answer truthfully. Are you an American citizen?"

"Yes." No noise from the needles.

"You were born in Belgium. Are you Belgian?"

"No." Could he shake his head? Better not. "My parents work for the State Department and were abroad when I was born. They didn't claim Belgian nationality for me."

Beverly's seat creaked. "Do you have frequent contact with any foreign nationals?"

"Yes." People he'd known for years through work, but he didn't offer details.

"Are these personal contacts?"

"No. Colleagues at the Smithsonian."

"Do you have reason to believe any of them work for foreign intelligence services?"

"No," he said.

"Have you ever committed a crime?"

That was a left turn. "Yes."

"Tell me more."

"I walk against traffic signals. When I drive, I speed, things like that. Sixteen years ago, I got into trouble in France for picking the lock at my high school. I'd forgotten a book I needed over the weekend."

He'd acquired the habit in rebellion against his parents' secrecy, but he'd never been able to crack into the safe they kept in their bedroom.

"Have you picked any locks in the past year?"

"No." The needles remained still.

"Are you engaged to Vivian Flint?"

The calm needles rioted. "Still wrapping my head around that one. Technically, yes, I'm engaged to Vivian Flint."

Her name felt strange in his mouth. Like a foreign phrase.

"Do you love her?"

"How is that relevant?"

"People aren't clear-eyed about their romantic partners. We need to ensure those partners aren't using agents for access to sensitive information. So, do you love Vivian Flint?"

"Yes." The needles didn't move.

Love had never been the problem.

But trust would be.

In the antechamber to the interrogation room, Vivian clutched the two-way mirror's sill. John was done with her. This hurt worse than pepper spray to the eyes, a pain she'd endured during training.

She pressed her forehead to the glass.

Since college, she'd let men go before they could leave her. Treated everyone as a fling to avoid rejection. She'd started with John that way, but he seemingly adored her and her love of art, game nights and sweary tirades. He'd introduced her to his family, invited her to move in with him and accepted it when she kept her Arlington apartment.

She swiped a tear from her eye.

No. There's no crying in spy craft.

A decade ago, during her first night in her chilly bunk at the Farm, when she'd been scared and exhausted from the training and close to breaking, she'd promised herself she'd never cry at work. She would *not* break her pledge over a man. Even one she was terrified to lose.

A shadow filled the doorway. "Flint?"

Great. Like she wanted to deal with her boss while her heart was shredding itself.

She turned to MacColl. "Hello, sir."

"That him?" He entered the room. "Looks short. And scruffy."

"He's six-three, and he's not scruffy."

MacColl favored suits, a high and tight haircut, and a shave so close it was more like exfoliation. For him, a bearded man in business casual was one step away from a hippie.

He flicked the eavesdrop switch in time to hear John say, "I can't trust her."

She tried to keep it together like a bomb disposal unit that barely quaked while chaos ate its insides.

"You good to give a mission update?"

"Yes, sir." Didn't matter if her personal life was imploding. Country came first, always.

"So, what the fuck with the Rocksy auction?"

"As expected, when the auctioneer gaveled the win, Rocksy remotely triggered it. My auction house contact said Jean-Michel repped both the seller and the buyer. Buyer's unknown. Best I could find is they're based in the Cayman Islands."

"Take that to Digger."

Digger, aka Anjali Patel, was a fellow Georgetown grad with a reputation for cracking codes and untangling twisty business ownership schemes. Other CIA officers snarked that their work wasn't real agenting, but Vivian and Anjali had snatched a ton of laundered money from organized crime bosses' and terrorists' pockets.

"Will Jean-Michel be a problem?"

"Affirmative. He's pledged to unmask Rocksy."

"That can't happen." MacColl leaned back in his chair. "You brought the drive?"

She reached into her purse. "Right here, sir."

Beverly's voice interrupted on the other side of the glass. "When did you and Ms. Flint begin a sexual relationship?"

Vivian's fingers stiffened around the drive. Her boss did not need to hear she happily jumped into bed with John on their first date.

"Can we…?"

"Sure." MacColl flipped the switch on the speaker.

"Thanks, sir." She dropped the drive in his palm.

MacColl turned it end over end while eyeballing her. "Your nonofficial travel request says you're heading to Copenhagen?"

If she couldn't turn this around, she might be moving her shit out of John's apartment. But she didn't need to involve Mac-Coll in her personal life.

"Correct," she said.

"How available are you while you're on leave?"

"Somewhat." Constant availability was another job reality. "Why?"

"There's been chatter about big ticket pieces coming up for auction on the European market. It's out of season, so I might need you to check into it while you're abroad." He flipped through pages in his notebook. "No one'll notice you poking around since you blend."

That was a compliment in their world.

When they'd distributed code names, *Canvas* had served a dual purpose. Art was her domain of expertise, and they could paint her any way they wished. For this particular operation, they chose neutral. Colored her red hair brown, tamed the curls into a sleek bob, clothed her fashionably—but not *too* fashionably—and encouraged a dull personality.

Perfectly forgettable.

Except she couldn't maintain dullness around John. Try as she might to keep it under wraps, her spiciness surfaced with him. And the sizzling way he looked at her, touched her, loved her from the start showed he didn't see her as the wallflower she tried to be.

Hence his nickname for her—Gorgeous.

She preferred it to Canvas these days.

"I'll give you more info when you're in Europe." MacColl pushed back from the table. "I'll grab the file and drop this with the techies for decryption. While I'm at it, I'll drop off your work phone. Based on the quality of last night's call, you might've damaged it."

She withdrew it from her bag. Normally she'd sign it over to the techies herself to keep the chain of custody clear, but MacColl might be cutting her slack given her personal circumstances.

He tucked the phone into his inner suit pocket, revealing his holstered firearm. She didn't carry one. Due to her frequent travel, guns would be a pain in the ass.

"I'll be back in five." He paused at the door. "Listen, a lot of boyfriends retract a proposal when they find out about all this. Marriage is tough—even harder when your partner doesn't get what we do. So if he's one of those types, don't torture yourself, kid."

Only someone twenty years her senior could get away with calling her *kid*.

After MacColl left the room, she hit the intercom button to listen to the interrogation.

"Do you love Vivian Flint, aka Jane Davis?" Beverly asked.

"You already asked me that."

"We ask questions several times to compare the responses for truthfulness." Beverly marked the sheet. "Do you love Vivian Flint? I need a yes or no response."

"I can't turn it off like a faucet." John sighed. "But I don't know her, so it's over."

There it was.

As soon as one person was done with a relationship, the whole thing fell apart. Her only face-saving option was to march in there, call his bluff and offer to return the beautiful ring he'd given her just twenty hours ago.

She tugged at it, but the ring was stuck.

Fuck.

Her theatrics would apparently require Vaseline. She stepped into the hall, then shrugged her tote higher on her shoulder.

After two knuckle-shattering raps on the interrogation room door, she barged into the room.

"May I help you?" Beverly asked.

"Stop the interview." She tugged at the ring again. No dice.

"All due respect, Viv, you don't have the rank to give that order. But we're finished." Beverly tore the curled paper from the machine. "I'll give you your privacy."

The door clicked shut. John pulled the sensors from his fingertip and the back of his hand. Silence thundered in her ears. When she wasn't wanted, she tried to be useful.

She took a step toward him. "Can I help you with those?"

"I've got it." He ripped the blood pressure cuff from his arm, then stood and twisted to try to remove the bands around his chest and waist like a dog chasing its tail.

"John, let me help. That's a two-person job."

"I said I've got it."

He definitely didn't.

"Stand still," she ordered in her take-no-shit voice.

John obeyed.

She pinched the plastic connectors that were lined up with his spine. The bands fell away from his body. She caught them and placed them on the table next to the polygraph machine.

Adrenaline prickled her fingertips. "I know you're upset, but can we—"

"Upset?" John stepped back from her. "I'm upset when someone steals the last open spot on our street and I have to park by Duke Ellington, or when I miss trash collection day, or when we lose trivia night. This is more."

"Angry?" she suggested. "Surprised? Embarrassed?"

He wrinkled his brow. "Not embarrassed. I'm not the one who's been lying for a year."

"Yeah, but…" She tangled her fingers together, and this fucking ring *still* wouldn't budge. "I mean… I'm good, but there were a couple of slipups where you might've caught—"

"I'm hurt." Pain flashed in his eyes. "Okay? That's what I'm feeling."

A familiar loud popping noise stopped her response.

"What's that?" John asked.

Her heart took a back seat to her protective instincts. She flicked the dead bolt on the door.

"Gunfire."

She surveyed the room. The one-way glass was unbreakable, so no getting through there. But damn, there was *nothing* in here weapons-wise. She could combine the discarded polygraph bands with her Muay Thai defensive moves, but if there was more than one armed assailant…

They needed to escape this dead end.

Another burst, further away this time.

John shoved himself between her and the door.

"What are you doing?" she asked.

"Protecting you." He braced his shoulder against the steel door.

"I appreciate the gesture, but we're sitting ducks. We need to leave."

"We can't go out there."

More shots. Were they closer? Hard to tell.

Oh, God—Beverly had just left the room. What if she—

No. Vivian closed her eyes. No spiraling. If she'd come here alone, she would have skulked around to find her colleagues. But she had to get the civilian, John, to safety. Every second they delayed was a second closer to capture.

Or worse.

"John, I'm a trained CIA officer. You need to follow my instructions. Okay?"

They stared at each other for five eternal seconds.

Something shifted behind his eyes. "Okay."

She tugged him away from the door. With him behind her, she'd be first in the line of fire.

"On the count of three, I'll open the door and scan the hall. If it's clear, we'll cross. Keep low and follow me. Got it?"

"Got it," he said. "But what if—"

"No time for what-ifs." She crouched, then quietly turned the dead bolt. "Here we go. One, two, three…"

She depressed the handle, then eased the door open. With her head low, she scanned the hallway. Clear. Heart in her throat, she scuttled across the hallway and into the alias assignment room. John's heat skimmed her back as he followed her.

Gold star to him for following directions.

She scanned her badge to gain entry to the alias room. The door auto-locked behind them.

"Officer Flint. Anyone here?"

No one returned her greeting. Odd. Saturdays were typically quiet, but not deserted like today. She'd been so grateful John wouldn't be overwhelmed by coworkers that she hadn't questioned the unusual lack of staff.

There was no such thing as coincidence.

"Where are we?" he asked.

"The alias assignment room."

An attack on a covert office was bad. Really bad. Until she knew who was responsible, who to trust, they might need to disappear. She opened a file drawer and flipped through folders until she found passports and pocket litter for a married couple who resembled her and John. She took the materials and shoved them into the inside pocket of her suit jacket.

"What are you doing?" he asked.

She rifled through a desk. "Working on a plan B."

"What was plan A?"

Aha—the nail file kit was exactly what she needed. Well, a screwdriver was exactly what she needed, but those were thin on the ground. Good enough would do.

"Plan A was celebratory preflight cupcakes at Baked & Wired after you successfully completed your polygraph. That's shot to shit, so we're activating plan B. Follow me."

The alias assignment room's most important feature had nothing to do with identities.

"Where?" he asked.

"Here." She knelt next to an air duct and worked the screws with the tip of the tweezers.

"Please tell me plan B isn't escaping through there."

"Okay, I won't." The final screw plinked against the ground. She pried the vent free. Damn, she wished she had her phone and its flashlight. "Let's go."

"An air duct won't hold me."

"This will, but be careful. There'll be screws and sharp pieces of metal. And it'll get hot."

"Why do you know so much about air ducts?"

"I told you. My dad's an HVAC installer."

On Saturdays, Dad would take the kids on side jobs to get them out of Mom's hair. Among her siblings, she understood blueprints the best because the shapes and patterns made sense to her. To this day, she looked up the duct work on any building where she was assigned. It had benefitted her more times than she could count.

More shots echoed outside.

"John." She squeezed his biceps. "You go first. It's a straight shot to the parking garage."

"But—"

"Go," she ordered. "I'm right behind you. I promise."

He furrowed his brow. "Fine. But if we fall through the duct, I get to say I told you so."

"Deal. Now, *go*."

As soon as John's feet disappeared from view, she slung her bag over her shoulder, then followed in reverse. Good thing she'd worn a pantsuit instead of a dress. Duct crawling was hell on the knees. From inside the metal rectangle, she reached for the vent and placed it in front of the duct. Anyone doing a quick scan might miss it.

A woman could hope, anyway.

Five

Sweat poured down John's face. Vivian wasn't kidding about the duct being hot.

"Fuck!" She sucked in her breath behind him.

No room to twist to check on her. "You okay?"

"Scratched my leg. Minor, but my pants are trashed. But honestly, they were trashed already. Dry cleaners wouldn't be able to remove the grime. From yours either, by the way. Sorry about your dress khakis."

"The state of my pants is not top of mind. Getting out of here alive is."

Light sliced through a vent up ahead.

"Look, everything you're doing, I'm doing too, and doing it backwards. This is perfectly safe. The duct will take us to the parking garage, but it won't kill us. The bad guys with guns, on the other hand…"

John closed his eyes. "Not helping."

"Which is why I focused on pants," she offered. "The mundane keeps me centered."

"You might not need centering if you had a normal job."

"I *have* a normal job. Lots of people do it." Her feet bumped into his. "Why'd you stop?"

"End of the line." He pushed at the vent. "It's stuck."

"Not stuck, fastened. You have to punch it."

"It's metal."

"Well, we can't go back." From behind him, he heard shimmying. "So either you punch through it or we live here now. Give me your hand."

"For what?" He shimmied his hand past his hip and wiggled his fingers.

She thrust a bundle of cloth at him. "My suit jacket. Wrap it around your fist and punch at the vent. The screws are a half inch, and the metal's flimsy. You'll win."

He didn't believe her, but they didn't have much choice. After wrapping the jacket around his hand, he backed his elbow up as far as possible and punched forward. The vent cover popped free easier than a Coors twist-off and clattered onto a car's trunk.

"Good job!" she cheered.

Pride pushed away the stress for a hot second. Her praise always gave him a bright burst of serotonin.

"Check to see if anyone's around."

Zero people and a handful of cars dotted this level. "Seems clear."

"Then go," she said. "I'll follow."

He crawled forward and stretched toward the car. With his arms braced on the trunk of the car parked under the vent, he wriggled free, then hopped to the ground. Vivian's sensible flats emerged, followed by shapely calves and thighs. Her legs hinged at the hips, and her feet touched the trunk. She yanked her purse from the duct, then jumped down from the car.

Dirt streaked her face. "Hi. You good?"

He had no idea. "Yeah."

"Great." She gestured for him to follow. "We're over there."

"What about your coworkers?"

The car beeped as she clicked the fob. "I'll check on them after you're safe."

Safe. Safe would be good.

If he thought about the past fifteen minutes for too long, he might have a breakdown. Unless he'd already had one and the man who emerged from the shadows in head-to-toe black was a figment of his imagination.

Just in case, he yelled, "Look out!"

Vivian switched into MMA fighting mode. When she connected with the man in black, something in the intruder's arm popped. A hunting knife spun across the parking garage.

"Get in the car!" she shouted.

As John dove into the passenger seat, she kneed the man in the balls. He dropped like an anchor. While he was on his knees, Vivian delivered a roundhouse kick to his face to finish the job.

Wait, nope, not finished. Three more men ran down the ramp.

John opened her door from the inside.

Vivian jumped into the driver's seat, hit the ignition, then peeled from their space. Gunshots popped around them. She hunched and shoved his head between his knees.

"Keep your head down," she said. "It's not safe."

He twisted under her grip. "But your head's up."

"So I can see."

"Why are people after you?"

"Stop talking. We might be bugged. I can't deal with everything at once."

"But—"

G-forces tugged his stomach as they squealed around a turn.

"I *promise* we'll talk later." She let go of his head and popped open the glove compartment. "Put your phone in airplane mode in case they're tracking you. Then put your head back down."

"Why would anyone be tracking me?" He adjusted the setting, tossed the phone back in the glove box and rested his head on his knees.

"Dunno. But if it's not me, it's you. We can't take the chance." She slowed at the exit, then swiped a parking key card. They sped out of the garage. She wove through the byzantine streets of Washington, DC, with the fluid skill of a Formula 1 driver.

"Where are we going?" he asked.

She shook her head and pressed a finger to her lips.

More turns. Then she stopped. "Okay, it's safe to come up."

Between crawling through ducts and spending the last ten panicked minutes in a seated fetal position, he'd developed a cramp, and his neck muscles protested. She'd parked in a deserted tree-covered lot. The lamppost flags displayed two letters—AU. American University sat in a calm area of DC that bordered Maryland.

He joined Vivian outside the car. "We should go to the cops."

"Not yet. Protocol dictates getting to a safe location, then contacting the chain of command." She reached into the trunk for her roller bag. "Involving local law enforcement can lead to unnecessary collateral damage."

She unzipped the suitcase and efficiently transferred items into her work tote. Passport, EpiPens, the travel jewelry case he'd bought her last Christmas, her glasses, a couple pair of silk underpants, an outfit, toiletries, first-aid kit, and…a phone he'd never seen before.

"Essentials," she said. "Anything you can't replace easily and need for a few days."

He stepped back. "Are we still going on a trip?"

She leveled a gaze at him. "Maybe, but we definitely have to go black. No car, no contacts, change in route. I'll figure it out, and we'll have a long, detailed discussion about everything when we're in a safe place. But right now, I need you to hurry. Please."

John shifted his weight to shake off the tightness in his ribs. He believed her, and he had infuriatingly few options. Despite everything, his instinct was to stick with her. From his carry-on, he removed toiletries, boxers, a change of clothes and his phone charger.

"Leave that—we can't take the phones. Too easy to slip up and turn them on, which means we can be tracked."

He clutched the charger. "But I need to be able to reach Thomas and my parents. Shouldn't I warn them?"

"It's safest if we don't contact them yet, but I can mention them when I call in to the office. On that note—when we're in public, vague is best. Like when we play *Taboo*. References to things only you and I understand." She freed an index card from a rubber-banded stack. "Copy important numbers from your cell, but do *not* take it out of airplane mode."

He yearned for his normal world from twenty-four hours ago. But that world was gone, and Vivian seemed to know what she was doing.

With an outstretched hand, he asked, "Got a pen?"

At the Tenleytown-AU Metro entrance, Vivian dropped their phones in the garbage. John cringed, but she had no choice. After three stops, she signaled for them to exit. Then they doubled back and took the train one stop in the reverse direction, getting out at Bethesda, Maryland.

The designated contact spot was three blocks away.

When they crossed Woodmont Avenue toward the Tastee Diner, John asked, "Hungry?"

"No. This place has a pay phone. It's old school, but it works."

She unzipped her tote and dug through its morass for her index cards of coded phone numbers. Gah, there was so much stuff in here since she'd grabbed the essentials from her suitcase. She needed to make room and organize this mess.

"Here." She thrust John's wallet, Zippo and flash drive toward him.

He handed the drive back. "That's not mine. The wedding one has an Apple logo on it."

Cold washed down her body. She must've mixed up the drives at the office. Dammit, her feelings for John were dangerous for her professional concentration.

Noted.

She slid the drive into the secret pocket in her bag. Silver lining—the drive she'd stolen from the Rocksy painting was safe from whomever attacked the office. Which she'd point out to MacColl when he lit her ass up for the mistake.

If he was still—*no*.

She had to believe her colleagues were okay. That they found ways out too, and they'd all regroup at a safe house to plan their next move. She refused any other possibility.

"Stay close." She plunked quarters into the pay phone and dialed MacColl's number.

Her stomach shrank with each unanswered ring. After ten, she hung up.

Protocol dictated she contact Deputy Director Janna Vandenberg next. The deputy director was an agency lifer who spent half her career in the field and had ascended the hierarchy without alienating the rank and file.

In other words, she performed miracles.

Vivian fed the quarters to the pay phone again.

"Vandenberg." The deputy director's soft, authoritative voice caught Vivian by surprise. "Who's on the line?"

"Canvas." Dammit. Her voice had wobbled.

"I hoped it was you. We'd like to talk to you."

"Ma'am, first, what about Boss, Earpiece, and…"

Lawrence didn't have a code name.

"I'll update you when you come in for a briefing."

"Where to?" Vivian fidgeted with the steel phone cord as she waited for Vandenberg to name a safe house in the area.

"Take the Blue Bird to HQ. And bring Brawn."

Vivian cut her eyes to John standing sentry by the booth. Head to Langley on the shuttle? John hadn't officially been cleared, so he shouldn't go anywhere near HQ. Plus the attack on the office wasn't a random break-in—assailants had followed her to the garage. For all she knew, her cover was blown. When that happened, you did *not* invite the officer to headquarters.

"Canvas?" Vandenberg prompted. "Can you do that?"

"Yes, ma'am, can do."

"Good. See you soon."

The line went dead.

Technically, she hadn't lied. She *could* follow the orders.

But she wouldn't. Things would be different if Vandenberg

had used MacColl's code word. Without that additional security, Vivian would listen to her instincts.

She worried the silver pendant on her ever-present necklace.

She'd figure this out eventually. Not this minute, not necessarily today, but her differently wired brain made her naturally good at reasoning. She stepped back from detail, sifted through huge amounts of information to identify patterns and saw the big picture.

That's what was missing—information.

She folded the door open.

"What do we do now?" John asked.

She rubbed harder at the pendant. "We'll start with the drive."

"Don't tell me you're a hacker, too?" John crossed his arms. "You always make me deal with the Wi-Fi when it goes out."

"Because it's annoying." She found her burner phone in her bag. "I dabble, but this one's beyond me. Fortunately I have a friend who can help."

An e-bike charging station stood a block away. The last time she and Anjali had hit the bars on Woodmont, they'd abandoned her car in favor of this mode of transportation. Not the escape vehicles she would have preferred, but beggars couldn't be choosers.

"Follow me. Our chariots await." At the station, she texted the service number and paid with a credit card in her sister's name.

John crossed his arms. This was his *look-at-how-easygoing-I-am* stance, but he only used it when he was being super judgy.

"You said no cell phones," he pointed out.

"It's a burner." She wrested a bike from the rack and presented it to John. "We're taking the Capital Crescent Trail. I'll lead. Keep up."

Six

As they biked under the shade provided by thick green trees, John shook his head. Jane was not an outdoorsy woman. Museums, fashion and board games, yes. Willingly dipping into a forest in suburban Maryland in the thick heat of June?

Big fat nope.

Except…she was? She held her arm out to the side, indicating a left turn. There was no trail in that direction. Vivian gunned up the emerald hill, her brown hair bouncing behind her.

Maniac.

His pulse hammered in his neck. He crested onto a street that ran parallel to the trail. After making sure he followed, Vivian delved into an alley bisecting a mixed neighborhood of modest homes and fancy architectural rebuilds.

Up ahead, she stopped next to a tall wooden fence.

"Where are we?" he asked.

"Friend's house." After she punched in a code, the back gate unlocked. Vivian scanned the neatly manicured half acre of land and the small cottage tucked within it.

"Have I met this person?"

"No." She shut the gate behind them. "Anjali and I went to college together. She's a coworker, too. We EOD'd—"

He picked an errant twig from her shoulder. "What's an EOD?"

"Sorry." She rubbed her forehead. "Federal government jargon. Entered on duty. We were in the same cohort. She's one of my best buds."

John's brow wrinkled. "But you said you didn't have local friends. That they live in Denver, London, Casablanca."

Shit. He'd paid *so* much attention to her, and she'd treated that like a problem, something to evade, instead of the total gift it was.

"Some of them do." She grabbed the knocker's brass ring. "But Anjali's here, and you'll like her. She's a real one. She'll like you too, because she loves me."

She knocked three times, paused, then knocked once more.

A short woman with golden brown skin opened the door, shook her head and slammed it shut. "Go away."

"Anjali, come on, open up."

"Fuck off, Flint. I don't want to see your face for six more weeks."

Vivian pinched the bridge of her nose. This was her self-inflicted wound gesture, like when she'd spent a full minute acting out a title to a movie he'd never seen during charades.

"Best buds, eh?" John asked.

"I begged her to access files I didn't have clearance to see. It might've landed her on swing shift for, uh, three months. She'll be done in six weeks." Vivian knocked again. "Anj, come on. I wouldn't bother you if it wasn't critical."

Silence greeted them.

Vivian sighed. "If you don't open up, I'll go say hi to Aunty Meena. I'm not responsible for what happens if she notices my engagement ring and asks me questions about your dating life. And *that* might force me to tell her about Winegrad."

John tried to lock in on the names, file them away for future reference. He riffled his hair. What the hell was he doing? There was no future with this person. She'd lied to him for a year, and as soon as she told him the truth, gunshots and goons descended on them.

Anjali opened the door and dragged them inside. "You're the worst. And you look like hell. It's bad enough my parents insist I live at home until marriage. Now I have to worry about you ratting me out?"

"You love me." Vivian shrugged.

"Not today I don't. Take off your shoes."

"You need to work on your *best buds* definition," John said.

Anjali turned to John. "And you must be John, aka the person who's been making Flint smile. I've heard a lot about you."

Second time someone said that today.

"Wish I could say the same," he said.

"She loves me, but she can't admit it." Vivian extracted the drive from her pocket. "This isn't a social call. What are the ears like here?"

"Daily sweep came up clean an hour ago. Honestly, my mom's the biggest security risk."

She held out the drive. "I need someone to decrypt this, and you're the best."

"No argument here, but why not take it to the office?"

"We did. The office got shot up, and MacColl's not answering. It might have something to do with whatever's on this drive."

Anjali darted her gaze among Vivian, her outstretched palm, John, back again to Vivian, then puckered her lips and snatched the drive. "Well, *that's* not good. But the phone tree hasn't been activated so we should assume they're okay. Let me see what I can do. Not like I had anything else on the agenda today besides taking my mom to the farmer's market."

Vivian's friend possessed the quiet calm of a paramedic handling an emergency. They must teach that at CIA school. He'd seen his girlfriend… fiancée…ex? hunker down the same way since the shots were fired at the office.

"Thanks, Anj." Vivian rolled her neck.

John blinked his dry, gritty eyes. This woman… Her gestures, her expressions, her voice were all the same as Jane's, but the things she was saying… She was this whole other person zipped inside the woman he loved.

"I need to sit down." He slumped on Anjali's loveseat before his rubbery legs gave out.

"Dude, you look pale," Anjali said. "Need a Coke or something?"

"He prefers water. Be right back." Vivian disappeared, then returned with a glass of ice water. "Drink that. You'll feel better."

She expected a lot from water.

"Might be overkill, but I'm black boxing this shit." Anjali opened the living room's armoire doors and revealed an evil genius level of tech, then unhooked a cable and flicked a couple of switches. "Where'd you get the drive?"

"From the frame of a Rocksy painting I appraised on Thursday in London—the one Rocksy destroyed at the auction yesterday."

Anjali glanced at her ceiling, brow puckered in irritation. "Bitch, why didn't you *start* there? That's obviously related to whatever went down at the office."

"I agree, but I need more evidence. FYI, the buyer's unknown but is based in the Cayman Islands. MacColl wants you to dig into them."

"That is literally almost nothing to go on. This drive might tell us more." Anjali plugged it into a hub adapter. "How'd you walk away with it if you were delivering it to MacColl?"

Vivian sighed. "I mixed it up with a drive of wedding plan info John brought."

"OMG, that's *hilarious*." Anjali clapped. "The star pupil is too pre-cockupied to do her job. Well done, Johnny boy!"

Heat washed over John's cheeks. Better to wander away from their conversation than get roped in further.

"Shut up," Vivian said through a laugh.

"I will not. And ooh, this is a mess. But nothing quantum computing can't solve." The screen filled with gibberish. Her fingers flew over the clicking keyboard, copying and pasting relevant alphanumeric text. "Ugh, Viv, grab a mint. Your coffee breath is rank."

While they bickered, John found a beaming Jane—whoops, Vivian—in a framed picture. He almost didn't recognize her with a riot of auburn curls. Must be from college since she wore a Hoya T-shirt. She stood in front of a kegerator and held what look like huge golden clock hands.

His chest tightened.

When they'd been dating for two months, Thomas and Logan invited them to dinner. During dessert, she'd pored over the family albums Thomas had inherited when their parents moved to Luxembourg. John assumed she didn't have childhood pictures, but he never asked.

How could he have been so incurious?

Anjali's whoop caught his attention. "I am a god!"

In the glow of her monitor, Vivian's and Anjali's twin victory smiles fell. This must be bad. Nothing threw Jane. Obstacles were puzzles to be solved, not to fear.

"Those are..." Vivian covered her mouth. "Those are staff lists, complete with home addresses and phone numbers, from BSL-4 labs around the world."

"What's a BSL-4 lab?" he asked.

"Biosafety level four," Anjali answered. "They contain pathogens that cause serious disease for which there's no treatment or vaccine, ostensibly so the scientists can study them. There are fifty-nine BSL-4 labs around the world, and the greatest concentration of them is in Europe. If any are compromised, it could trigger another pandemic."

The seriousness of this situation thudded into John. There was no good-for-humanity reason for anyone to buy that kind of information.

"Fuck," he said.

"Fuck indeed." Anjali leaned closer to the screen. "The README file says this is the first of three drives and left instructions for the next handoff at a charity auction in Monte Carlo."

"When?" Vivian asked.

"Three days from now." Anjali wrote digits on an index card. "Who sold the Rocksy painting in London? And why split up the delivery of the BSL-4 intel?"

"Dragomir Mihailovic's holding company sold the Rocksy painting. He's a Croatian underboss from an up-and-coming crime family. As for why they're split up, my bet is the full price for all the intel is more than a single auction can fetch."

Vivian worried her silver pendant.

She did that whenever she was deep in thought. Planning an exhibit, strategizing a *Settlers of Catan* win or figuring out the best route across DC at rush hour.

"Jean-Michel said he was headed there." She invaded Anjali's space again. "He's been trying to crack the Monte Carlo scene for years."

"Who's Jean-Michel?" John asked.

Vivian and Anjali exchanged an awkward glance.

"You want to handle that?" Anjali asked.

Vivian cleared her throat. "He brokers lots of Rocksy sales in Europe."

"Among other things." Anjali flicked some switches, then loaded an elegant website. "Is this the Monte Carlo auction?"

Vivian hit keys to magnify the page. "Yes. Shit, they've got work from one of my artists. In London he said he'd secured a Rocksy donation and several wet-paint pieces from emerging artists."

"That's your territory, isn't it?" John asked. "Wet-paint work?"

"Yes, and he'd like to take it over." Vivian twiddled her pendant. "Wet-paint works are ripe for exploitation. My operation leverages that to catch bad actors using art sales to launder dark money. *My* question is, why didn't I know my artist had pieces in this auction?"

John scratched the back of his neck. "Am I supposed to answer?"

"No. She does this a lot." Anjali rolled her eyes. "Like I don't have anything better to do than listen to her problem-solve out loud."

"You love it." Vivian bumped shoulders with Anjali, then at John, and grinned.

Uh-oh. That particular grin meant she was about to take decisive action. Which would excite him if they were at home and half-dressed. But, here, in this context it probably meant her next move involved something risky, like—

"We need to go to Monte Carlo," Vivian continued. "Mac-Coll said there's been chatter about auctions in Europe. Wonder if this is related?"

John's neck tensed. "You planned to work on our honeymoon?"

"No." Vivian twisted her lips. "Well, some."

"She's a workaholic." Anjali propped her hand on her fist. "We all are."

Vivian paced Anjali's living room. "There are lots of eyes at airports."

The answer was obvious to John. "We could go to the authorities and…"

"No." Vivian and Anjali shook their heads.

"I've got it." Vivian snapped her fingers. "Smalltimore to the rescue."

"Another one of your random high school friends?" Anjali asked.

"What can I say? I got along with everyone." Vivian flipped through her index cards, then punched a number into her burner. "And this person owes me a favor for keeping them out of the drunk tank after our last high school reunion."

When her phone buzzed, Vivian held up a finger, then answered.

"Hey, Konnie! Glad you called me back. Any chance you're flying internationally in the next twenty-four hours?"

She paused. Then her face split into a grin.

"Morocco? Tonight? Perfect. Where do I meet you?"

Nothing about the words *Morocco* and *tonight* equaled perfect in his opinion.

"Love that you still read comics. See you there." She hung up and exhaled. "This is better than I hoped. I filed nonofficial travel for Denmark. People might be watching for us in European airports, but not African ones."

"Us?" He backed away from her. "Jane—"

"Vivian."

"I can't run off to another continent with someone whose name I don't know!"

She winked. "Stick with Gorgeous like usual, and we'll be golden."

Yesterday, that wink would've made his heart skip a beat. He'd always loved her cheeky confidence when navigating annoying situations with grumpy neighbors, parking inspectors dishing out tickets, or boorish art patrons. But now? When their lives were in danger?

Her confidence was delusional.

"Oh, barf," Anjali said.

"Don't be jealous." She held out her hand, then wiggled her fingers when he didn't immediately clasp it. "John, please. You've got to come with me. You're not safe here. But I'll fix it."

He shifted his weight.

Until three hours ago, he trusted this woman implicitly. This was supposed to be the first day of the rest of their lives together, putting each other first, having each other's backs. But he couldn't trust someone who'd lied to him so easily.

Could he?

She *had* come clean. Plus, Ruckus loved her, and dogs don't love bad people. His brother adored her too. *John's* feelings were an unresolved question mark, but one thing was certain. Whether or not she was delusional, he'd never forgive himself if they parted and something bad happened to her.

"I'll stick with you for now."

Vivian dropped her pendant. "Good."

"If you two are finished, here's your code." Anjali handed the index card to Vivian. "The README file indicates the code works for all three drives involved. It also says an executable file fires when you enter the code. There's a self-destruct routine built into it. Enter the wrong code twice in a row and it'll wipe the drive."

"Noted." Vivian took the drive back from Anjali.

An urgent knock sounded at the door.

"Beta," Anjali's mom said through the slim gap of the door. "Why are bikes in the garden? And why do you have the security chain up? Do you have a boy in there?"

If Vivian stayed, she'd dissolve into giggles. Anjali was thirty-two as well. Her mother's vigorous policing of "boys" when her daughter defended democracy on the daily was hilarious.

Anjali flipped her the bird and pointed toward her bedroom. "Bikes, Amma?"

Vivian blew Anjali a kiss, then grabbed John's hand to guide him to their escape route. *Whoa.* The rightness of their joined hands neutralized her giggles. The last hour caught up with her like a freight train colliding into a wall. The very real possibility of leaving her, then getting him out of the crossfire, then dissecting the reason they were attacked…she'd been laser-focused and in her head.

But his simple, warm grip had her back in her body. This—John—was everything she needed, He was her safe harbor, and he said he'd stay with her. It wasn't a lot, but it was enough. A spark.

She'd take it.

"Through here," she whispered as she unlocked the window and climbed outside. John followed. The slow metallic slide of the front door's chain reached them through the open window. She pulled John down so they'd be out of sight.

"Come in, Amma," Anjali said in an exaggerated voice. "Want some chai?"

Once the cottage door closed behind Aunty Meena, she and John crouched and circled around to the front, then quietly wheeled their bikes through the gate.

"That's not the first time you've snuck out of her house, is it?"

"I used to crash here after boozy nights blowing off steam."

John cocked his head. "But you don't drink much."

"I'm not a kid anymore. Tough to stay on my toes if I can't feel my feet." She shrugged the straps of her bag onto her shoulders. "Ready to roll?"

"Where are we headed?"

"To meet up with a friend and catch our ride to BWI Airport. But first, we need to change."

They rolled back out to Bethesda proper, then docked their bikes. In an Exxon convenience store, she changed in the bathroom. A sleeveless jumpsuit to catch a lift in a cargo plane to Morocco was a better option than a shredded pantsuit.

She handed John the bathroom key attached to a hubcap, then shopped for durable snacks while he changed. As she paid for the protein bars with cash, she glanced at the news onscreen. Nothing about the attack on K Street. Casually she added a giant pair of sunglasses and a baseball cap embroidered with a faded DC flag.

Not entirely inconspicuous, but it would do.

John threw a Twix on the pile. "For when your sugar's crashing."

She swallowed the lump in her throat. Harshness she could take. Easier to push back against his judgment if he acted like an ass. But his kindness would undo her.

"Anything else?" the cashier asked.

"No." In the small four-pump parking lot, she handed the hat to him, then popped on the sunglasses. "Basic disguise. People mostly pay attention to hair and eyes."

Their conversation during the walk to the Bethesda North

Metro station was muzzled. Too many ears. At Union Station, after a quiet food court lunch, they boarded the MARC train. She busied herself with booking her off-the-grid place in Morocco.

The quiet between them was killing her, but it couldn't be helped.

How could she be great at her job—well, *jobs*—and a complete relationship disaster? Undercover government assignments required more than the average amount of trust from a partner. Most officers either married other CIA people or waited until they transferred home to start serious relationships.

That had been her plan when she first joined up.

Run around the world being fabulous and smart, save the country a few times, freeze her eggs at thirty-four, punch out of field work at forty, then boom.

Settle down.

But the universe gave her John about a decade too soon. For his sake, she should've stiff-armed him. But she'd been swept up in how *easy* John was compared to the operatives she'd dated over the years. No brooding dark soul, no middle-of-the-night startles, no quiet disappearances she needed to have faith were work-related missions.

Nope.

John, with his broad shoulders, soft beard, kind laugh, and straightforwardness, was the antidote to her cynicism about a complicated world. Best of all, he wasn't competing with her. He was a support, not a siphon. She'd learned to be a support for him, too.

Then she'd wrecked it by clinging to agency guidelines like a life raft.

She'd kicked the honesty can so far down the road it had disappeared. John was understandably pissed. She couldn't ignore the wary look in his eyes as the Lyft they'd caught at BWI Rail Station dropped them at Cosmic Comix.

"This is where Konnie told me to meet them," Vivian said.

John faced down the life-sized Superman cutout.

He held the door open for her. "Surreal day gets surrealer."

At the store's far side, three guys shot the shit. Vivian's oldest brother, Brady, was a die-hard comics fan, so she was familiar with these shops and their luscious papery ambience. Personally, she'd always been drawn to the art. Comics' influence in pop and street art, from Roy Lichtenstein to Andy Warhol to KAWS, was undeniable.

Rocksy, too. But she expected that, since—

"Hey, Viv. You brought a friend?" Konnie thrust their bodybuilder arm at John. "Konstantin Sollon. Friends call me Konnie."

"John Seymour." They shook hands in a way that tested each other's strength.

"Rusty, Dave, catch you next week." Konnie collected their comics stack. "I'm this way."

As the three of them climbed into the unnecessarily tall Ford truck, Konnie asked, "How do y'all feel about dogs?"

"Love them," Vivian and John said in unison.

"Wow, did y'all practice that?" Konnie laughed. "The flight manifest just has me and my copilot. I can skirt around passengers by saying you're escorting an animal, and we have two high-strung Pomeranians on board."

"We'll be your dog whisperers," Vivian said. "No problem."

Six hours and the entire Atlantic Ocean later, she had regrets. John sat in the jump seat across from her with Bijou the barker in his lap, while she tended Bonbon the biter. They'd calmed the dogs with constant belly rubs, the same kind they gave Ruckus when exuberant neighbors set off fireworks on the Fourth of July and New Year's.

"Sorry," she mouthed.

John shook his head and looked away.

Shame and guilt slithered inside Vivian. The love of her life was disgusted with her, and she couldn't blame him. Not one bit. She'd lied to him about almost everything and had convinced herself it was the right thing to do.

Because agency rules. His safety. Her cover.

More lies.

The truth was…falling in love was terrifying and she'd used her alias as emotional Kevlar. If John dumped *Jane Davis*, she could tell herself he hadn't rejected the real her. Ego protected. But he'd stayed and entwined himself so deeply in her heart she couldn't tell where she ended, and he began.

A jostle startled her out of her swimming thoughts.

As did Bonbon nipping her hand.

"This is your flight captain." Konnie called over their shoulder. "It's a beautiful day in the seaside city of Casablanca. Local time is 2:00 p.m. Today's high will be twenty-six degrees Celsius with eighty percent humidity. Thanks for flying Personal Favor Airways."

After taxiing down the runway, they crated the Pomeranians.

"This make us square, Vivian?" Konnie asked.

"No," she said. "Now I owe you one."

"I'll take it." Konnie grinned. "Good luck with this one, John. She's a pistol."

"I'm aware," he said without a hint of a smile.

Between her dry throat and clenched stomach, she felt like she'd swallowed cement. But she'd figure this out, too, and win back his affection. They were meant for each other, and nothing bonded people better than travel.

And light espionage.

Konnie handed them noise-blocking earmuffs. "When we pop the door, a luggage truck'll take you straight to the terminal."

"Thanks, Konnie," she said as she slipped on the earmuffs.

With a wink, they shot Vivian a finger gun and mouthed, "Here's lookin' at you, kid."

Groan. Like she hadn't heard that one before.

The cargo door popped open with a whoosh, and humid

air swirled through the cabin. As she stood, she regretted not pregaming the flight with pain meds. Between the air duct crawl, hand-to-hand combat, hustling across town, and sitting for hours in a jump seat soothing a prickly Pomeranian, her muscles protested.

Judging by John's stiff gait, he was in the same situation.

The luggage truck driver waved, and she and John hopped on the back. After he ferried them to the terminal, they handed him the earmuffs. They dipped inside the terminal's welcome cool dryness. Finally, familiar territory.

"Follow me." She slithered through the streaming crowds. Some travelers wore Western-style clothes, while others wore long loose robes. She nodded toward a glossy wood door up ahead. "That's our pit stop."

She withdrew her plastic membership card and dipped it in the scanner.

The lock tumbled. She pushed the door open, delivering them into a calm, hushed oasis. Businessmen had twisted modern red, purple and beige barrel chairs to enjoy the back wall's unobstructed tarmac view. Personally, she preferred the art above the buffet. She'd convinced the manager to purchase her artist Amina Hassan's work. The oversized painting added much-needed vibrancy to the space.

She led John past the prayer room and to the stairs at the back.

"Bienvenue au Salon Rubis," the front desk clerk greeted them in French. "How may I help you feel better today?"

Unless this attendant had a time machine, she'd have to settle for the bag she'd stashed here.

She slid her key card across the counter. "My suitcase, please?"

The attendant inserted the card into the reader. "Ah, Ms. Davis." She switched to French-Moroccan-accented English. "Would you and your guest care for your usual spa treatment?"

She ignored the tension wafting from John.

"Yes, please."

"One moment." The attendant slipped into the storage room

behind the desk, then reappeared with Vivian's Zero Halliburton black aluminum carry-on. "Here you are. You'll be in room three today."

"Thank you," she said.

John reached for her bag. "I've got this."

Vivian considered resisting. She shouldn't receive relationship privileges if they weren't actually in one. But she ached, and it was heavy.

Let him wheel the thing. It was a small sign that not all hope was lost.

At door three, she knocked, then entered the low-lit room.

"Helluva time for a massage," John said.

"We're not getting a massage." She sat on the padded table. "I have an arrangement here. Can you lift the suitcase up on the table?"

He thumped the bag next to her.

"Thanks." She rotated the numbers to her three-digit code—620, their anniversary—and popped the case wide. A tidy collection of dirham, prepaid debit and phone cards, a tablet, and breathable layers of clothing more suitable to the local climate waited inside.

"Here." She handed him an outfit. "Change into those."

He stared at the pile. "Why did you pack men's clothes?"

"In case I travel with a man," she said. "Unless I'm taking a routine action with known players, the agency prefers sending two agents into the field. Couples raise less suspicion."

"How often do you—" John closed his eyes. "Never mind."

"You can ask, John. Part of the reason I waited to tell you about my job is you'd naturally want to ask a lot of questions. Not all the answers are reassuring, so it's not a great early relationship conversation. But we're a year in and have ripped off the bandage. Ask away."

He waved her off. "No, I'm good."

"I'm ready if you change your mind." She winced as she attempted to unzip her jumpsuit.

"Turn around," John said, then hissed. "Jesus Christ. You've got bruises everywhere."

"Do I?" She glanced over her shoulder.

"Yes." He slammed through the cabinets. "There's no medicine here. It's all lemongrass essential oils and—aha. Tiger Balm."

"I'm fine." She gingerly wriggled into her balloon pants. "I'm a fast healer."

He gently laid a hand on her shoulder. "Stop arguing. Stand still."

John's rare bossiness emerged when she wasn't taking care of herself. Skipping meals because she was too busy, not drinking enough water, trying to work long hours despite a massive head cold that turned out to be walking pneumonia.

After the plastic snap of a bottle's lid, John smoothed the nose-awakening cool cream on her back. A few tears she'd been holding back escaped. Camphor and menthol were partially responsible, but in her exhausted state, John's kindness reduced her to a messy bitch.

Because it drove home what she'd lost.

Seven

It took all of John's willpower not to punch the wall. Vivian held her own during the attack in DC, had barely broken a sweat, so he'd thought she was fine.

God, he was so stupid.

She wasn't a superhero. She was an ordinary human person who'd taken a beating while he'd spent the last day simmering in his hurt feelings. He would've treated a stranger better than the person he wanted to be his wife.

"I'm sorry I didn't ask if you were okay."

"I'm fine. Peachy." Her voice's levity was forced. "I've had worse."

"I can't believe you put yourself in danger like this." He rested his hand on her shoulder and smoothed more cream on a greenish bloom at her nape. "The bruises you blamed on Muay Thai class… Was that true?"

"Sometimes." She stepped away from him. "Let's get dressed and go."

"After you take ibuprofen." He swiped a short bottle of water from the fridge hidden in a cabinet. "Here."

She took it while strategically clutching her clothes. "Privacy, please?"

He pivoted.

Behind him, fabric rustled. Soon she tore a packet and glugged water.

"Okay," she said. "I'm officially drugged and dressed, so you can turn around."

Even bruised and exhausted, she was gorgeous. She'd changed

into an ivory V-neck dress and draped a Mediterranean-blue patterned scarf around her shoulders. Sensible sandals replaced her normal sky-high heels, and the humidity had turned her chin-length hair into beachy chestnut waves.

"More modest than my normal clothing." She hooked aquamarine teardrops into her ears, then lifted the scarf to cover her hair. "But it's best to blend."

"You think you blend?"

"Yep."

That might be the wildest thing she'd confessed in the past twenty-four hours.

"I'm naturally a redhead, but I do this—" she gestured to her brown locks "—to be less noticeable. My mom and sisters are gingers, too. Not the boys, though."

Before the polygraph, she said she had four siblings. "Where do you fall in the birth order?"

"Middle of the pack. Two older brothers, two younger sisters. My psych profile says I'm a classic middle child. Rebellious, sociable, independent, on-the-go, feels overshadowed. Do your clothes fit okay?"

Like they were made for him. "Yeah."

"Good, I hoped they would. Let's go."

John grabbed the suitcase and followed Vivian. At the front desk, Jane withdrew ten orange one-hundred dirham notes from her wallet and slid them across the counter.

"Merci beaucoup pour votre aide et votre discrétion."

The attendant pocketed the bills. "Bien sûr, mademoiselle. Toujours heureux d'aider un ami de la Couronne."

In the main terminal, John murmured, "She called you a friend of the crown. What's that about? Do you know royalty?"

After a beat, she said, "I can neither confirm nor deny."

Oh, but that glimmer of a grin meant she absolutely knew a royal. He'd always loved Jane's confidence, but Vivian's humble deflection was undeniably sexy. Who *was* she? Curiosity edged out his frustration as they took the stairs to the lower level.

"I'll be able to help you better if you tell me more about who you are here," he said.

"Agree to disagree. And definitely not in a crowd." She paused at a ticket machine and swiped a credit card. After poking her selections, she collected the tickets it spit out. "Our platform's over there."

He tapped his impatient foot. Helluva time for his sleepy curiosity to finally wake the fuck up. Who was this woman? What had she done during her career? Where had she gone every time she kissed him goodbye? All the questions he should've been asking over the past year, but couldn't until they were alone together.

So they waited in silence.

When the train arrived, they found empty seats in the last car. After placing the roller bag in the luggage rack above their heads, he dropped into the seat across a small table from her.

"How about now?" he asked.

With a smile, she answered, "Later."

As the train whisked away from the airport and into the palm-tree studded city, an older gentleman sat next to Vivian, while a teenage boy sat next to him. Across the aisle, a family of four was sharing an aromatic kebab lunch. Nothing about them screamed spy to him.

His stomach grumbled.

Sometimes, he resented his body's regimented needs. He was mostly easygoing, but if he didn't get eight hours of sleep, eighty ounces of water, and meals by six, noon and six, he was a basket case.

"What time is it?" he asked.

"Three," she said. "Nine a.m. our time. Want a protein bar?"

No judgment in her voice, but he felt like a baby.

Grudgingly, he said, "Yes."

She handed him his favorite—chocolate chip cookie dough.

As he ate, Casablanca whirred past them in a green, blue and tan blur. He relaxed his shoulders. Since he'd switched careers, he'd focused on building his résumé and hadn't traveled much. Trips for work, sure, but those were all in the US.

He'd forgotten how much new places made his blood hum. If only they had the time to see it like leisure travelers rather than a spy and her wayward maybe-fiancé.

After twenty minutes, Vivian tapped his knee. "This is us—we pick up the tram here."

More tickets, a brief wait, then a tram ride through increasingly dense neighborhoods. When Vivian stood, he readied the roller bag. Off the tram, the street energy was instant and intense. Motorbikes wove around donkey carts and cars clogging the stone road.

John took the sidewalk's outside lane. "Is it always this crowded?"

"On the main drag, yes, but not where we're staying. Turn left."

The suitcase vibrated as they walked. Sweat beaded and rolled down his back. Uncomfortable, but DC's swampiness had taught him to tolerate humidity.

Vivian stopped at a humble wooden door. "This is us. Before we go in—while we're here, I'm Jane again. You're Jason Jones, according to the passport I swiped from the office. We'll work on your backstory later, but be sure to respond to the name."

She creaked open the ancient door.

The inside was like crossing into Narnia.

He tipped his head back. "This is unbelievable."

Three stories of thick tan walls wrapped around an open courtyard fringed with lush greenery. Intricately laid gold, blue, red and green tiles decorated the floor. A splash pool lay in the courtyard's center, surrounded by pockets of chairs, tables and loungers.

"It's my favorite place in Casablanca," Vivian said. "The person who owns this place, Mariam, ran it with her husband for twenty years. When he died last year, she took it over since women are finally able to own property."

"Jane!" A woman in desert-colored robes crossed the courtyard, then wrapped Vivian in a hug. When they separated, their hands remained clasped. "There's no one else here, per your request. Is this the young man I've heard so much about?"

Vivian nodded. "Yes, that's my fiancé. You can stop begging me to bring him now."

What had she told this woman about him?

"Hello." He stuck out his hand.

Vivian shook her head slightly. Ah, right. That likely wasn't done here.

Mariam smiled. "While I congratulate you both, unmarried couples do not room together in Morocco. After I lay out dinner, I'll stay at my sister's for the evening. What you two do with that information is up to you. Now, let me show you to your rooms."

The dark wood banister, made satin by centuries of use, steadied him as he followed the women to their rooms on the second floor.

"Mademoiselle will stay there, and, Monsieur, this is yours." Mariam gestured to two rooms that faced off across the hall. "I'll leave you to settle in."

The older woman brushed by him in a haze of fine flowing garments.

"Here." He rolled the suitcase toward Vivian. Despite his desperation to get her alone to talk, he'd wait until Mariam left. He wasn't sure how the conversation would go, but they had a better shot at unvarnished honesty without extra eyes and ears around.

"You can come in." She took the bag. "We'll leave the door open."

In her room, she lifted an orange cookie from a crystal dish on the desk and moaned as she chewed, sending a bolt circuiting through his incorrigible body.

"Want one? They're my favorite—orange blossom and almond macarons. Mariam makes them fresh every day."

Macarons had also been his favorite when he lived in Marseille as a teenager. His girlfriend's parents had run a café that specialized in the light and chewy cookies. But pride demanded he not indulge in the things Vivian had kept from him.

"No thanks," he said.

"Suit yourself." She reached into her large purse and withdrew her tablet.

He hovered at the window, trying to ignore her moan as she munched another macaron. Most nearby buildings had converted their upper levels to entertainment areas. TV antennae and satellite dishes bloomed like flowers among the hopscotch of roofs. In the distance stood a clock tower with Moorish windows.

"Good news." Vivian tapped her nails against the tablet. "We can catch a bullet train to Tangier tomorrow. I have a friend there. Then we'll take the ferry to Gibraltar, and boom, we're in Europe."

"What about trying your office again?" he asked.

She popped another macaron. "I will, but I've gotta see what I can do to get intel on my boss's boss without attracting attention. My gut still says something is off with her."

"Your gut's full of macarons."

"True, but irrelevant." She swiped away the train schedule, then logged into...a coffee shop website? "Macarons heighten my ability to solve mysteries."

"Jane." He relished being able to use her alias. "I could do with more information."

Pulling her attention from the screen was like peeling apart stubborn Velcro.

"Okay." She sighed, relenting. "Some of my artists help me with my government job. They get perks as a result."

"Is coffee the perk?"

She laughed her first genuine laugh with him since the interrogation room in DC. He was surprised the sound soothed the tension knotting his shoulders.

"No, placement in exhibits is the perk. Coffee is my communication system. I give my artists gift cards. Each is attached to an account to which we both have access. I check the balances daily. If anyone needs to talk to me, they buy a coffee. It saves us from having digital communication trails." She flicked her attention to the screen. "Oh, balls. Amina purchased a coffee yesterday. How do you feel about a field trip?"

"Not great. Staying put seems safer."

"Too late. I replenished the amount."

John crossed his arms. "And that means…?"

"She'll be expecting me."

"Then why did you ask?"

"I was hoping you'd say yes." She tossed the tablet on the bed. "It'll take an hour, maybe two. It's a good time to go because we're between calls to prayer. Maghrib's not until 8:45. But you can stay here if you want. There's a security code on the door, so it's safe."

John shifted his weight. He didn't want them to leave this oasis, but he doubted he could stop her. This was her element, and one of her most attractive traits—her capability—was on full display. True, she'd done this all day, every day, without his knowledge, help or protection. As long as he was here, he'd stick with her wherever she went.

"I'm coming with you. But no more side quests, okay?"

"Deal." She held out her bag. "Gimme your stuff. The pickpockets here are world class. I should try to take the ring off, too."

Vivian tugged at the silver, but the band didn't budge. "Ugh. Between the humidity and travel, my fingers are sausages. I might have to cut this off to give it back to you."

The tension returned to his shoulders. Take the ring back? He'd rather dive into broken glass than return this ring that so clearly belonged to her.

"I don't want it back. No matter what, it's yours."

"Uh, it's a symbol of how you hate me, so no thanks."

He sighed. "Don't be dramatic. I don't hate you."

But there was a chasm between not hating her and trusting her, and he was still figuring out where loving her fell in the middle of it all.

"Glad to hear it." She sighed and ran her fingers through her hair. "If Amina notices the ring, though, play along. We're a happily engaged couple, okay?"

"Okay." What else could he say? *No, I'll tell her everything.*

On their way out the door, Vivian stopped by the kitchen.

"Need anything from Marché Central?" she asked Mariam.

"Non." The innkeeper dusted her hands together. "Ah, wait—I'm low on ras el hanout, if you'd be so kind. And I'll be leaving soon. Do you remember the door code?"

"Yes," Vivian said. "Have fun at your sister's."

As they stepped onto the street, noisy life swirled around him. Diesel exhaust, too. Vivian donned movie-star-large sunglasses, then handed him the DC baseball cap.

"Here," she said. "Blend."

When Vivian didn't know what to say, she buried herself in work. As the crowds, noise and scents thickened on their way to the souk's colorful chaos, she flipped to the data page of his fake passport.

"Jason Jones lives on Clarendon Boulevard in Arlington, Virginia, and was born on August 7, same year as you. So he's a…"

"Thirty-four-year-old?" John offered.

"Bzzt," she said. "We were looking for Leo."

"Do you put stock in astrology? Jane thought it was silly."

She scrolled on her phone to the astrology app. "Jane and I differ on this topic. Which makes sense since she's an Aries. Anyway, I use it to shape a personality."

"I already have a personality."

She agreed, and he was a steady, loving, goddamned delight, which fit his Libra sign to a T.

"Wait, you said Jane's an Aries," John said. "So is your birthday *not* April 12? We hosted a dinner party to celebrate."

"And it was lovely," she answered. "Jane needed to be an Aries because she's ambitious and possesses a strong work ethic. Traits I share to some degree because I'm an Aries rising."

"What does that mean? Nope, never mind." He lifted his cap and riffled his hair. "When's your actual birthday?"

"It's…" Talking about herself was strange. "Don't laugh. It's July 4."

"Why would that be funny?" he asked as they passed through wrought-iron gates. Buckets of fragrant flowers lined the walkway. "Can I call you Yankee Doodle Dandy?"

"You may not." She closed the passport and shoved it in her bag. "Although I *did* think the fireworks were for me when I was little."

A kid careened past them on a twenty-inch bike.

"That's adorable," he said.

This was…surprisingly enjoyable. Her secrets had stung—no doubt about that. But he had a chance to discover the woman he loved all over again, and this time, he knew her tells. When she hesitated, he'd be able to coax her to tell him more. To reveal. Something about that stirred things inside him.

"If you're not an Aries, what's your sign?"

"Cancer." She turned left in front of the food hall. "We're big on family, communal activities and patriotism. Our memories are strong, so we hold grudges, and we wear our hearts on our sleeves."

"That definitely sounds like you. Except for that last part. I've never seen you cry. Not even when we watched *My Girl*."

His misreading of her hurt was like a paintball to the heart.

"I'm not a robot, Joh-Jason." Whoops. "I don't cry because my siblings teased me *mercilessly* for it as a kid. I actually have big, huge, sometimes-I-can't-breathe feelings. But I wait to feel them until I'm alone and preferably in the bath so no one can hear me if I cry."

She widened her eyes.

She'd just…barfed that right out, hadn't she?

The unvarnished truth in her mouth felt weird. Like when she'd sipped a can of Fanta at a family picnic and something solid landed on her tongue. She spit out the soda and a fucking *bee*, but it didn't sting her. Nope, it fidgeted its wings, then flew off, unbothered. Much like that bee, honesty with John hadn't stung like it had when she was a kid.

"Sorry," he said. "I didn't mean to hit a sore spot."

She hid her gasp with a cough.

She'd worked so hard to cultivate Jane Davis's image as a self-reliant, unflappable woman with zero childhood wounds. But Vivian Flint? Oh, she flapped. A lot. And when she showed that version of herself, she expected to be teased. Even by John. Instead, because he's the best, he apologized and made her big emotions feel safe.

"You couldn't have known. Besides, the teasing was good training for my career. Toughened me up. So it's okay."

He made the humph noise that meant he disagreed but didn't want to argue.

"You get all the points for figuring out how to use a past hurt to your advantage, but that doesn't mean it was ever okay."

She stumbled and dropped her phone.

Fuck, John was right. She was a well-adjusted adult, but that didn't excuse the way her siblings treated her, or that her parents let it happen. Although arguments could be made about the well-adjusted thing since she'd spent years pretending to be someone else.

John scooped up her phone. "Here. So what's a Leo like?"

Grateful for his gracious topic change, she scrolled to hide her shaky fingers. "They're full of primal creative energy and are associated with visibility, attention, courage, generosity and creative impulses."

"Not sure if I can pull off the visibility thing. I prefer life behind the scenes."

"You'll do great." She returned her attention to the screen. "The lion needs be the center of their partner's world, and centers their partner as well, making them feel seen, possibly for the first time in their lives. Ew. Zodiac descriptions aren't normally this sappy."

"I'm more concerned that your reaction to centering your partner was *ew*."

"It's just that if your partner sees the truth of who you are and rejects you, it cuts deeper."

Oh, God. She clapped a hand over her mouth. Again with the emotional barfing. Operating mostly on adrenaline and protein bars meant she wasn't filtering properly. One benefit of her line of work was keeping a part of herself protected with the excuse that it was for the job. Not anymore.

John caught her elbow. "Jane—"

She held up her index finger. "Pause. We shouldn't be talking about this out here. We can build a personality later. Just don't go wild with details or try to be too interesting."

He searched her gaze. "I'll probably stay quiet."

"Good plan." She broke eye contact. A beat too late, she realized she'd reached for the warm anchor of John's hand. "Is this okay? I don't want to lose you in here."

"Yes, it's okay."

They were silent, but the souk was loud.

Shopkeepers hawked everything a person might need, and the unpredictable arrangement matched her jumbled thoughts. Colorful shoes, fabrics and ceramics brightened the path. Pungent spice shops interrupted the diesel fumes wafting from the roadway. Weavers intertwined vibrant threads to create patterns on their looms, and the rhythmic clang of metalworkers' hammers matched the rapid beat of her heart.

Soon they arrived at a stall plastered with wild paintings.

"Jane!" Mehdi Hassan, Amina's husband, greeted her warmly. He leaned behind a tapestry and called, "Amina, Jane Davis est arrivé."

Her friend emerged and kissed Vivian on both cheeks. "It's good to see you, my friend!"

Jane hugged her. "It's been too long."

Amina turned to John. "You must be Jane's young man friend."

Vivian covered her mouth, but it didn't stop her giggle. Young man? John was six years older than Amina.

"Bonjour," he said. "Sorry, I speak tiny French."

Incorrect. John spoke excellent French, but Vivian let it go. Espionage required a *yes, and* improv philosophy. Never call out your partner's lies.

Amina inspected John with her artist's eyes, then nodded. "Jane was correct. Your eyes are the color of the sky at dawn, a miracle of azure flecked with gold."

Heat whooshed into Vivian's cheeks. "All I said was your eyes are blue."

"Nice to meet you. I am—" he mini-paused "—Jason. Jason Jones."

"Welcome, Jason Jason Jones," Mehdi held a curtain aside to invite them in the back.

"Please, join us for tea." Amina slipped past her husband.

The modest table in the back held a steaming pot of tea and a ring of doughnuts. Vivian's stomach cheered. Sfenj were delightful treats. Not too sweet and perfect for dunking in tea.

"What's new?" Vivian prompted. "Any shows on the horizon?"

"Always so impatient." A cloud of mint enveloped them as Amina poured tea into small cups. "Tell us, Jason Jason Jones. Is this your first time in Casablanca?"

According to the passport she swiped from the office, this was Jason Jones's first time here. It had recently been stamped in Canada, Mexico and, inexplicably, Djibouti.

"Yes," he said. "And it's just Jason."

"Will you stay for dinner?" Mehdi asked.

Jane blew on her tea, then sipped. "Not this trip, but maybe the next one."

"I'd like that." Amina laid a paint-spattered hand on hers. "We haven't properly chatted in ages."

"Umi!" A curly-haired boy flew through the curtains.

Mehdi caught Omar, their eight-year-old son, in a hug. Vivian spoke enough Darija, aka Moroccan Arabic, to travel confidently, but couldn't keep pace with the boy's excited babbling.

"In French, please." Amina tapped him on the nose, then smiled at Vivian and John. "We're teaching him French to haggle with tourists."

The boy restarted, this time in perfect French. "Coach Daouda showed us a move called the Elastico. Baba, come. I'll show you."

He slid from Mehdi's lap and tugged his father's hand.

"Not now, sweet boy," Mehdi said. "After our guests leave."

Mehdi had left Vivian to catch up with Amina dozens of times. Unsurprisingly, he did not want to leave his wife in the company of a strange man.

"It so happens," Vivian said, "that Jason is an amazing footballer."

Omar's eyes widened.

"It's true," John said in halting French. "I play both of you? But sorry, my words is bad."

Omar spun the soccer ball. "We can practice talking, too!"

"Okay with you, my love?" Mehdi asked Amina.

"Indeed. Jane and I have much to discuss."

Omar held the curtain open. "Let's go! The field is this way!"

Something about a man happily playing with a kid hooked Vivian's heart. Brady, Kyle and Alaina all had kids. As cute as her niece and nephews were, Vivian held babies like a sack of potatoes that might shit on her. Her siblings teased her about it—because of course they did—but that's why she planned to start a family with someone who was already good with kids.

"This is new." Amina's fingers grazed Jane's ring. "Has the young man with stars in his eyes asked you to marry him?"

Vivian nodded. "He wants to call it off, though."

Assets shared more if *she* shared more. Made herself vulnerable. Secrets were seeds that sprouted into intimacy.

"Bah." Amina swept her hand through the air. "He adores you."

"Not anymore." Vivian sipped her tea. "I lied about my job. Now he doesn't trust me."

"When Mehdi was courting me, I kept my painting secret. I worried he'd tell me to stop or lose interest in me. But I could no sooner stop painting than I could stop breathing. If we were to be married, he needed to know."

"And he accepted it?"

Amina tipped her head back and laughed. "Absolutely not! He ended his courtship as soon as he saw them. He worried about the danger they would pose to any family we created."

Amina had never shared this part of their story. Vivian's heart ached for her friend and what she must have felt. Now she understood the crushed-soul sensation caused by the person you loved pulling away so quickly.

She prompted, "So what happened?"

Amina sipped her tea. "He yearned for me. We talked, and talked, and talked again. Moving away from Rabat helped. Here, we can be our own people. Our families love us, but it's difficult to fit within their restrictive frames. So, we stopped trying."

A lump rose in Vivian's throat.

If Mehdi could accept Amina's calling and career, could understand his then-fiancée's initial deception, maybe John could accept hers. Forgiveness was possible, but it would take time and effort on her part. She needed to loosen her grip on protocol. Agency rules were agency rules, but to hold onto John, she needed to figure out how to bend them. "Cheers." Vivian clinked her teacup against Amina's. "Now that there are no extra ears around…why'd you signal me?"

"I thank Allah every day for you. Since my Dali Museum exhibit in Paris three years ago, my online sales have grown rapidly. It's improved my family's quality of life. Omar is at L'ecole Française Internationale de Casablanca, and Mehdi was able to reduce his hours. Even those in my family who do not approve of my venture happily take the dirham I send home each month."

"I'm glad to hear it," Vivian answered.

Conversations with Amina always involved lots of backstory, but eventually they'd get to the point if Vivian didn't push.

"As a result of your efforts on my behalf, I am accustomed to interest in my work. But yesterday was unusual."

Amina tore a sfenj in half and bobbed it in her mint tea.

Patience.

"Tourists come through often, but yesterday, a woman entered the souk to speak with me specifically. She was tall, blonde, and looked as though she'd been cut from ice. She offered me twice my normal rate for a painting."

Prices were rarely posted in the souk. The vendors shared them verbally to kick off Morocco's national past-time—haggling. If Amina had the transaction on paper, the provenance for this particular work could increase her entire portfolio's value.

"What did you sell it for?"

"Oh, you misunderstand. I refused to sell to her."

At this stage in an artist's career, each increased price is a rung on the ladder to a bigger stage. Few can afford to refuse sales, but Amina was built differently.

"Why?" Vivian asked.

The sfenj's sweetness combined with the tea's mint was heaven in her mouth. Her stomach rumbled. Maybe John was on to something with his regimented schedule.

"This woman was rude to Omar. Called him a little shit

in Croatian when his ball bumped into her fancy outfit. Who wears Chanel to the souk?"

"Hang on—you speak Croatian?"

"No." Amina shook her head. "My Croatian great-grandmother spent her last years with us and frequently swore. She made me laugh. Mehdi urged me to reconsider, but I would not."

"Do you know anything else about this woman?"

"Yes." Amina rose from the table and flipped through a stack of paperwork on a small desk. "She gave me her information in case I reconsidered selling a painting to her."

She handed Vivian a business card. Simple yet elegant, it read *Lola Vorlicek* in embossed gold. No title, no business listed. But there was a +377 number—Monaco.

Once again, there was no such thing as coincidences. A Croatian art broker based in Monaco approached one of Jane Davis's clients. A Croatian crime boss is the painting's seller in which she'd found a drive. This was related—she could taste it. But how?

Not enough information to see a pattern, but she'd get there.

"Thank you." She pocketed the business card. "This has been helpful."

"My pleasure. And you'll stay for dinner next time," Amina declared.

Vivian leaned in to kiss her friend on the cheek. "Yes, next time."

Eight

John and Vivian cut through the thinning crowds. The tangerine fingers of Casablanca's late afternoon sun reached through the marketplace and picked out the reddish undertone of Vivian's curls. The color matched the spicier personality that had surfaced since she'd revealed her true identity.

Was that just yesterday?

It felt like a lifetime ago, but minus six hours for the time zone difference and…yup. It had been only a day.

Vendors busied themselves with closing up shop, trying their best to finish the day with a sale. His stomach grumbled, but Mariam had said she'd lay dinner out for them. Probably safer to eat what she prepared than street meat from a tourist area, anyway.

"This is my favorite time of day in the market." Vivian stretched out her arms, the same way she did when a soft breeze blew through Burleith as they walked Ruckus together. "After the stalls close, the plaza turns into a carnival. Storytellers, dancers, musicians…"

As if on cue, a guitar riff pealed through the air. A European musician with silver hair that carried the light yellow of his former blondness played "La Grange" by ZZ Top. The thick bluesy beat competed with the shrill, reedy wind instruments played elsewhere.

Tension ballooned in John's chest.

From day one, conversation had flowed between them. He wanted to say he would've expected romantic songs in Casablanca, not a rock song about a Texas brothel. But they weren't in a jokey, comfortable place. He was stoppered. All he wanted to ask were questions about her, her job, their safety, and what he was supposed to do with the bigness of all of this.

"Is Omar any good at soccer?" she asked.

Her simple question had stopped his mental tailspin.

"He's good but needs practice. Learn anything from Amina?"

She paused to admire a flower stall's offerings. "Can't say."

Roadblocked again. "Can't, or won't?"

"Sea lilies are my favorite." She handed fifteen dirham to the hijab-veiled woman running the stall, then lifted a bundle of white flowers into her arms. Away from the gathered crowd, Vivian murmured, "*Can't*. I swore a secrecy oath, remember? I can't divulge anything without written consent from the director."

"I doubt US government officials are here." John gestured to the tourists and locals circulating among them. "But I respect your adherence to the rules. I guess I'll save the juicy tidbit I learned from Omar and Mehdi for written consent from the director."

She elbowed him gently. "You, sir, took no such oath. Spill."

"Can't." He was being an asshole, but this was what happened when he didn't eat on his normal schedule. "Shouldn't talk shop on the streets."

To their left, a seated man played an ululating tune on a clarinet-like instrument. Cobras wavered, trance-like, in the air.

"Holy shit." He paused in his tracks. "Snake charmers are real?"

She tugged on his biceps. "Yes, but keep moving or—"

A man wearing a striped fez stepped in front of him and raised his arms. Something heavy, cool and smooth wriggled around John's neck.

He froze. "Is there a snake around my neck?"

Snakes didn't bother him in theory. But he wasn't a fan of fanged reptiles suddenly cuddling his jugular.

Vivian sighed. "Yes."

The man in the fez mimed taking a picture. "Camera?"

As Vivian waved the guy off, John calmly plucked the snake from his neck and handed it back to the man in the fez. Several more men surrounded them in a circle.

"Pay," the man said. "Four hundred dirham."

"For what?" John asked.

"It's a scam." Vivian sighed. "For the nonconsensual privilege of wearing a python for a hot second, they expect to be paid." She reached into her jumpsuit's zippered pocket, then shoved bills at the man. In French, she said, "That's all I have. Forty dirham."

The man gestured for more money.

Vivian shook her head. "No more."

They pointed at John, and he turned his pockets inside out. After snatching the dirham from Vivian and yelling at them, the men jostled him as they disappeared into the crowd. He reached for Vivian's hand.

"I'm impressed," she said as they headed toward the street.

"Yeah, getting scammed is impressive."

"No, the snake. Most people would freak out."

"The men yelling at us worried me more than the snake." He glanced over his shoulder. No one followed them. "Thomas had a python growing up. That thing was a garter snake compared to Mike Tythop."

Laughter pealed out of Vivian. "Excellent name. I didn't figure Thomas for a snake guy."

"We wanted pets, but my parents were allergic to pet dander. So Thomas, always the lawyer, looked for the loophole. But I had to wait 'til I had my own place to get a dog."

"Doesn't that mean your parents can't visit you?"

"If they actually are allergic, yes. But I'm not convinced they are. My high school girlfriend had a dog and a cat, and they never sneezed when she came over. I suspect they didn't want pets but didn't want to argue about it either."

"I'm sorry." She squeezed his hand.

Much as he liked the comfort, they weren't on hand-squeezing terms. He let go and stopped at a baseball cap stall. The logo for Raja Casablanca, which Omar had declared to be the best football team in the world, was embroidered on several of them.

"I want a hat," he said.

What he actually wanted was a few feet of distance between them to process this new reality before they glossed over it. The tug toward this woman, toward forgiveness, was undeniable. They were already slipping into their familiar, comfortable patterns. And as much as he loved who he was with her, he needed breathing room. Could he just...be okay with all the lies? Vivian Flint was a stranger. A stranger whose hip fit the curve of his hand like she was made for him.

Confusing, which was why he needed space.

And the hat was a good excuse.

"You're wearing a hat," she said.

"With a DC logo. These blend better." He turned to the person running the stall and gestured toward a simple black cap with the green eagle logo. "How much?"

"Five hundred dirham."

No way was a baseball cap worth the equivalent of fifty bucks.

"Two hundred," John said.

The vendor laughed and shook his head. "Four-fifty."

"While you haggle, I'll buy spice for Mariam," Vivian said. "Back in a second."

Goddammit, he only wanted a few feet of space, not to lose her in the crowd. He twisted toward her, but she'd already disappeared. Where had she—wait, there. Her blue scarf flashed amidst the shoppers.

"Four hundred!" the hat seller called after him.

No sooner had he caught up with Vivian than a curly-haired small man wearing a gold crucifix necklace blocked her path.

The man's gaze roamed from her feet to her face. "Very nice."

"Hey." John grabbed her hand again. "Back off."

The guy raised his hands in apology, then melted into the crowd.

She slipped her hand from his grip. "Unnecessary. Our goal is to gather info and blend. Not fight with locals."

"So we accept shabby treatment?"

"Sometimes." She fiddled with her necklace. "Often, actually. But I can handle myself."

His protective instinct unfurled in his chest. If she wouldn't take his hand, he'd boost his shoulders and do his best to project a menacing vibe.

"I believe you," he said. "I saw it yesterday. And the resulting bruises."

"Bonjour!" she said to the man who had finished with his previous customer. Her hand hovered over one of the dozens of powders mounded into wooden bowls. "May I have fifty milligrams of ras el hanout?"

The vendor shoveled spice into a plastic bag and knotted its top. Vivian exchanged the dirham for the spice bundle, then dropped it into her bag. As they distanced themselves from the market, the noise dimmed.

"I should bring some home," she said. "I make a mean chicken tagine with it."

"But you don't cook." Over the past year, if they weren't dining or carrying out, he'd been the one in the kitchen.

"I don't have time. Two jobs, remember? Speaking of which, what'd Omar say?"

He laughed. She was relentless.

"Fine, I'll tell you. Omar asked his dad if Amina found out he'd sold her painting to the mean lady. Mehdi hushed him. That's all."

Vivian worried her necklace. "That might be important. It's hard to tell without all the pieces. Sometimes you only know what matters in hindsight."

She could say that again.

By the time they'd landed in Morocco, his anger had burned

off. She'd lied to him, yes. But he understood her logic, even if he didn't agree with it. The thing that troubled him was that he'd missed every clue she was leading two lives.

Either she was excellent at spy craft, or he was thick.

Both things could be true, too.

"Mariam's gone," Vivian said as she punched in the code. "We have the place to ourselves. Dinner should be in the courtyard. Feel free to start eating, but I need to freshen up—it was hot as balls out there."

Before he could agree, she was gone.

Vivian pressed her forehead to her closed door. She hadn't lost him yet. He'd held her hand and defended her honor against smarmy men in the street. And done it in perfect French with an accent that sounded like singing and sunshine.

A shuddery breath escaped her.

Get it together, Flint.

She woke her tablet, then flipped to the keyboard and reverse-searched the number from Lola's business card, and... nothing. Next move...call Anjali? No. Unless she was life-or-death desperate, she wouldn't involve her friend more than she had.

Vivian blew out her lips. She'd take a break, then come back fresh.

From her suitcase, she extracted her emerald one-piece bathing suit. The splash pool in the courtyard provided guests a means to rinse the street dust from their bodies. A quick dip and she'd feel more human. She tied a blue sarong at her waist, then padded down the cool tiled hall and wooden stairs.

When she reached the courtyard, John broke the pool's surface.

She licked her lips as water sluiced down his body. Strength wrapped in softness, and the very definition of the Golden Ratio. Broad shoulders, narrow waist, thick thighs, and enough meat on his bones to create the most comfortable cuddle she'd ever enjoyed.

Exactly her catnip.

"You could've started eating without me. It's past your dinnertime."

"I'm not a toddler." John looked up from the pool. "I can skip meals."

He could not. Any time he missed one, he turned into Mr. Crankypants.

She ventured toward the pool. "Where'd you get a swimsuit?"

"I didn't. You said we're the only ones here."

Oh. *Oh*. She averted her gaze. "I'll head to the lounge."

She beelined toward the table. Naked, wet John was unfair. Splashes behind her meant he'd launched himself from the pool again. She would *not* imagine him naked, she would *not* imagine him naked, she…dammit. Her imagination was working overtime.

Mariam had left them a feast. Baked quinces, meslalla olives, couscous, and a chicken-and-almond pastilla garnished with sugar and cinnamon. Hopefully she could focus more on the delicious food than the naked man hovering behind her.

Correction. Half-naked. John had wrapped a towel around his waist.

She plated her dinner and tried not to get more distracted.

"Looks good," he said.

"Yeah, Mariam's the best." She slid the napkin from its intricate gold ring, then draped it on her lap. "Don't let me forget to put the ras el hanout in the kitchen."

They would eat, go to bed, and she'd simply ignore the fact he was across the hall.

"Hey." John touched her elbow as he sat opposite her. "Can we talk? Like, *really* talk."

The eat-bed-ignore plan was officially out the window. Her heart rattled her ribs. Despite her resolve at Amina's that they'd need to talk this through, words curled up and died on her tongue. The importance of the conversation they needed to have about her job, their relationship, the world and everything in between froze her brain.

All she could manage was, "Yes."

John took a deep breath. "You've read my file. I want to read *your* file. Metaphorically."

Hope sparked inside her. His curiosity was a bridge-builder. If he was done with her, he wouldn't give a shit.

"I'll tell you anything that's unclassified. Where do you want me to start?"

"Your family." He tore into the pastilla, and the shredded chicken, egg and almond pie's aroma wafted toward her. "Where you grew up, schools, best friends and boyfriends, why you joined the CIA. I'll ask questions along the way."

She sighed. "That's a lot of backstory."

He leaned against the pillows and spread his arms wide. "I'm not going anywhere."

You might.

"Vivian, please. I need to know who you are."

He didn't know what he was asking of her. Cloaked in her Jane Davis alias, she'd shed parts of Vivian Flint that she'd rather forget. To explain who she was, she'd need to dredge it up and hand it to him on a platter. But if that's what it took to win him back…

She poured lemon water. Whiskey would be better, but Mariam didn't stock alcohol.

"Specific questions are helpful," she said.

"What are your parents' names?"

"Frank and Kim. Dad worked overtime a lot when I was a kid—"

"Installing ducts."

"That's right." She nodded. "So Mom took us to free museums. She had a deep appreciation for art that I've inherited.

If my grandparents had had money, she would've gone to art school. Instead, she mostly paints rooms and redecorates."

That came out wrong. Her parents were warmer and more vibrant than her sad, babbled description. She rubbed her eyebrows.

"You frowned when you mentioned your mom. Do you not get along?"

"Are you kidding? My mom's amazing. I love her."

She fiddled with the napkin ring. That was all true, but not the *whole* truth. So she would tell him something she'd never admitted to anyone.

"I don't want to be like her."

Jane Davis's dead parents were easier to deal with than Vivian's living ones. Jane put her parents on a pedestal. Vivian had to grapple with her parents' flaws, like Mom's inability to put herself first and Dad's love of Natty Bohs.

"Why?" John asked. "I mean, I don't want to be like mine either, so we've got that in common. But I'm curious."

Vivian rolled the napkin ring. "My mom defines herself through caregiver roles. Crossed a lot of boundaries, too. When we grew up into fiercely independent adults and didn't need her, she fell apart. She's better now because she helps my siblings with their kids. There are five little ones. Ezekial, Elijah, Gideon, Mark and Eve."

"Very biblical," he said.

She saluted him. "Irish Catholic, at your service. My parents are also good friends with the parish priest, so they'll pressure us for a traditional wedding mass."

Oh, Christ. The Great Babbling continued. She steamrolled over her gaffe.

"Anyway, I promised myself I'd never base my self-worth on the role I played in other people's lives. How much they might need me."

John ran his hand through his hair, which made his chest ripple.

More unfairness.

She scooped up a forkful of couscous. Her appetite had disappeared, but she needed a plausible pause in conversation to calm her mouth and flaring libido down.

"Tell me about your siblings," he said.

"I have, remember? I just pretended they were coworkers."

That should have been her first clue that John was different. She'd never disclosed an ounce of truth about her family to anyone she'd met through the job. Too risky. But with him, she'd opened that door, hungry for him to know some part of her real life while staying within the agency's protocols.

John leaned forward. "I'm glad they're actually your siblings. I thought you had an unhealthy attachment to your coworkers. Are you all close?"

"Very." She nodded. "We bicker and blow up at each other, then meet for dinner and Uno at my parents' about twice a month. But I have to warn you, they're intimidating. They're all smart, successful and confident. Good-looking, too."

"Like you." John dug his spoon into a baked quince.

Warmth flowed through her like honey. She worked hard to achieve those qualities. John knew about her learning disability, but she'd spoken only casually about it. Framed it as an interesting quirk, like being able to fold her tongue. Digging into it with him would require her to trot out her raw less-than feelings.

But wasn't that the point of this conversation? For him to know the real her.

Insecurities included.

"I wasn't always that way," she said. "Big families label their kids—the funny one, the athlete, the artist, the tenderhearted one. I was the 'special' one because I'm dyslexic. They'd all help me with my exercises, provide visual supports, color codes, things like that. I was like a family group project. They still see me that way. Like I need their help. I kind of hate it."

John let her continue, uninterrupted.

She sipped her lemon water.

"It started when I was eight and my grades were terrible except for math, art and phys ed. My teachers suggested I repeat third grade. My parents disagreed because they thought I was smart, so they had me tested. Voilà—dyslexia. They enrolled me in an expensive private school for kids with learning disabilities like mine. I felt guilty about the expense, the carpooling, and the disruption to everyone else's routine. So, I learned to hustle."

"Hustle? In third grade?" He locked gazes with her. "Vivian, you needed something different—not extra—and they did right by you. You didn't need to make it up to them. You were worthy of it."

She couldn't breathe.

Worthy. She'd strived for academic dominance and then devoted herself to using her skills and talents to making a positive difference in the world. All to prove her parents had made a good investment in her.

And here's John, the first person to whom she'd spilled her guts, telling her she didn't need to prove anything. That couldn't be true.

John leaned forward. "Dyslexia is just how your brain's wired, like being right-handed. It's nothing to apologize for. You get that, don't you?"

Emotion clogged her throat.

"I know it here." She tapped herself on the temple, then moved to her sternum. "And I'm working on knowing it here."

He sipped from her glass. "Where did your art career come from?"

Bless him for understanding she needed a topic change.

"Art was always my solace. Shapes and patterns and colors never flipped around in my brain. But Torrey's the truly artistic one, so I let her have that label and focused on becoming the smart one. During my senior year, I scored enough scholarships to go to Georgetown."

"*That's* why you were wearing a Hoya T-shirt in the photo

at Anjali's house." Understanding dawned on John's face. "You didn't go to University of Denver. Was art history your major, like you said?"

She swallowed a sticky bite of honey-drizzled baked quince. "No. Culture and politics. I minored in international econ and worked at the Smithsonian. After graduation, I'd planned to go into finance. But then the terrorist attacks at the museums in France happened."

John set down his fork. "I remember that. We'd just moved back to the States from Marseille. We were all horrified."

"This might sound obnoxious, but I was mad I wasn't involved in a solution to prevent that from happening again. So instead of applying to jobs at random J.P. Billionaire & Sons finance firms, I applied to Georgetown's security studies master's program."

"And got in, obviously. Is that how you ended up at the CIA?"

She nodded. "During my first year of grad school, I wrote an algorithm that was a spookily accurate predictor of where people would loot antiquities. It's a national security concern because looted items are sold on the black market, and the sales revenue is often funneled into organized crime or terrorist activities."

John thumbed his chin. "I'd like to revise my earlier statement. You're *the* smartest person I know, not just one of them."

He meant it as a compliment, but too much attention made her uneasy. Sigh. To be an overachiever who eschewed the spotlight was a special kind of hell.

"My paper caught the attention of the CIA recruiter based at Georgetown. They wanted me to take on the alias of an art broker. I'd tap into black market funnels—fences, dealers, private sales, shady auction houses—to shut them down and decrease the flow of the IMF's estimated $67.4 billion per year to criminals and terrorists."

"You must've been such a kid. I mean that in a good way,

but that's a lot for a young person. How old were you when you started there?"

"Twenty-two and a student when they recruited me, twenty-four when graduated and I went full time. Not to brag, but I was kind of a wunderkind. It was all very Bond. Travel, risk, luxury, lovers, all to establish myself as a name in the field while learning how auction houses sell art. The rules vary from country to country."

"Lots of secrecy." He nodded.

"Which allows people to game it. Anonymous buyers and sellers, cash deals, manipulating taste. So I find emerging artists around the world, build them up, and watch who uses their work to make a killing at an auction."

"Like Amina?"

"She's on the cusp. Rocksy's a better example." Vivian hid a yawn. This conversation was weirdly exhausting. "Which brings us to today. So there you go. That's the blitzkrieg version of my life's story. From academic underdog to tenacious scholar to Department of Defense operative in the art world."

He tilted his head to the side. "Have you killed anyone?"

"No. I'm not that kind of agent. Gunplay and explosions are not my norm. The goal is to get information and get out. Not to be noticed."

"Who wouldn't notice you?" He leaned back in the pillows again. "Thanks for sharing all that. I feel like I know you better."

She dropped her head into her hands. "Ugh."

"Ugh?"

"Yes, ugh." She shoved back from the table and paced the courtyard. From the sound of his footsteps, he followed her. "We *know* each other, John. That was basically my transcript and CV."

"It was more than that, Vivian." He caught her waist.

They stood in a fragile bubble of silence.

Until he pressed his lips to hers.

His kiss was like coming home. This familiarity, this intimacy, was precious.

"Does this…" she breathed "…mean I'm forgiven?"

He pressed his forehead to hers. "For the lies, yes. I understand why it was necessary."

She backed away. "Why do I feel a *but* coming?"

"This is a me thing." He riffled his hair. "I've told you that I always came second to my parents' jobs. I've made my peace with it because that's what public service requires. But…"

"There it is," she said. Sometimes she hated being right.

"I don't want to shape my adult life around it, too. Your job will come first, and I get why. It's important. But as long as you're a part of the CIA, I can't be a part of us."

Her stomach squeezed. "Are you asking me to quit my job?"

"No, never. I respect your choice. But I'm sorry, I'm not cut out for this life. I hope you can understand and respect that."

He left her in the courtyard.

Once he closed the door to his room, she choked her sob on a jewel-toned pillow.

Nine

John rolled over in the dark.

Three a.m. Anxiety must've shaken him awake. Was he off base for telling Vivian he couldn't get past her job? He'd thought Jane's passion for art brokerage was attractive. The way it lit her up, made her fire on all cylinders as she paced his apartment and excitedly chatted with artists and buyers on the phone.

This last day, though?

Vivian was breathtaking. She'd rescued him from harm's way, spirited him to Morocco, then navigated Casablanca like she'd been born there. And she'd done it all like it was no big deal, cracking jokes along the way.

This was what she was meant to do.

He loved that for her.

For him, not so much. Growing up as an afterthought to his parents' careers had been hard. He didn't want that dynamic in his adulthood. But he might make peace with Vivian's calling if the last twenty-four hours were a sign of how they could be. It was too soon to tell, though, and he didn't want to give her false hope until he'd had a chance to— A click caught his attention.

Probably nothing. Old bones were bound to creak in a centuries-old house. Except with Vivian, "probably nothing" stood a decent chance of being *something*.

He scanned the room.

He couldn't see shit through the picturesque netting that draped his bed. Another noise—a thump this time. Definitely something.

He concentrated.

Hang on—was Vivian crying?

Another loud sniffle from across the hall. Ah, hell. She'd said she cried when she was alone. This was his fault. He shouldn't have kissed her. Mixed signals were cruel, and despite their relationship's murky state, he didn't want to hurt her.

He couldn't let her just sob over there.

He dragged on his T-shirt, then slipped his Zippo in his pajama pants. Light pooled from underneath Vivian's door, interrupting the hallway's inky dark. As he padded across the hall, movement in his periphery caught his attention.

A black-clad figure stood outside the second-floor patio door.

A door that was locked—he'd double-checked before heading to bed. Man-in-black had attached suction cups to the glass. They were the heavy-duty kind John used when setting objects under glass displays at the museum. It was an effective way to install or remove panes of glass without leaving fingerprints.

Pretend you don't see him.

More easily said than done, because he wanted to run screaming from the riad.

Not without Vivian.

He tapped on her door. "It's me."

She eased it open. "What's wrong?"

He slipped inside, locked the door, then turned to her. "What are you holding?"

"Same thing I always hold when someone knocks on my door at 3:00 a.m.—a collapsible baton." She wiped away shiny tear tracks with her pajama sleeve. "Trouble sleeping?"

"No." A billion words stuck in his throat, all competing to escape. "There's a guy."

She straightened her spine. "In the hall?"

"Patio. He's trying to break in."

"Well, shit." She eased open the armoire and dove into jeans, socks and sneakers, then thrust the riad-supplied slippers at him. "Here. Best I can do."

"Best you can do for what?"

"Our escape. I don't have a fight in me tonight."

After extracting a bundle of nylon from the armoire, she crossed the room with the precision of one of Degas's ballerinas. She eased the window up, then hooked two carabiners onto anchors hidden behind the curtain.

Ah, a fire escape ladder.

With one foot out the window, she beckoned to him.

"Don't rush." Vivian's whisper tickled his ear. "It makes the ladder wiggle."

She shimmied down the rungs. With adrenaline pumping through him, he followed her into the night. When his slippered feet hit the ground, Vivian gestured for him to follow her to the yard's edge. She reached into a wall of leafy green plants and tugged, and a secret door swung inward. They slipped through it and into the alley.

Quietly she closed it behind them.

They were in the alley that ran next to the riad. Despite his eight inches of height advantage, he had to hustle to keep up with her as they hurried toward the street. The slippers didn't help. At the alley's end, Vivian held up her hand to signal him to stop.

She peeked around the corner.

"Shit." She pinched the bridge of her nose. "Black SUV on our six. Green neon underglow. Terrible music. It's the snake charmer."

"This is a lot of effort to collect the forty dollars we didn't pay."

"Doubt that's what this is about." She withdrew her baton. "Get low. We'll crawl across the street, then run for it down the alley."

Before he could ask questions, she speed-crawled across the road like a horror movie villain. He shot after her, knees be damned. Once he joined her, she straightened, tightened her backpack's straps and sprinted.

The alley brightened as they closed in on the next block.

Vivian circled her arm around his waist. "Pretend we're a couple."

Muscle memory took over as his protective arm met the familiar shape of her shoulders.

He glanced behind them. "Why did he follow us to the riad?"

"Beats me, but I'm pissed I thought the snake charmer was doing the tourist trap thing. He targeted us. It's a trick that hired goons pull. They interact with a target, and the person who hired them watches, then confirms they have the right person. Skeezy guy too, I'd bet. The one who ogled me. We need to get to a safe place."

"The police?" he asked.

She shook her head.

"Does that mean the police are the bad guys?" he asked.

"No. Well, sometimes, but the ones here are good guys who ask a lot of questions. I know a place where we can crash. A fortress. Ooh, and there's our chariot."

A teenager sat on a retro motorbike near the club, smoking.

"That bucket of bolts?" he asked.

"We need wheels. I don't steal from civilians. Loom over my shoulder and look like a tough guy in case he tries to mug me." She approached the kid. "Excusez-moi?"

Thus began a very brief negotiation while John did his best to menacingly loom. The kid's attention perked up at the words *two thousand*, and he immediately demanded five hundred more. Vivian nodded and exchanged dirham for the key.

As the kid walked away, a plume of smoke curled into the air above him.

Vivian wrinkled her forehead. "Can you drive this?"

John's stomach sank. "I—"

"I'm kidding." She nudged his shoulder. "You looked like you believed me."

"I always believe you. That's kind of the problem."

"You're right, sorry." She swung her leg over the motorbike's duct-taped seat. "No helmets, though. Here." She shrugged her backpack free. "Wear this and hang on to me."

The black SUV from the riad slithered into view.

"Fuck," she said. "Get on."

She dropped her foot on the kick-starter and…nothing.

The SUV crept closer.

Vivian pumped the kick-starter again. Still nothing.

"Third time's the charm," she said.

The bike finally rumbled to life, and Vivian gunned it. John held tight.

Letting her go would be the end of him.

Vivian's instincts took over as the SUV bore down on them. The therapy podcast she'd been listening to lately said typical trauma responses were fight, flight, freeze, fawn or flop.

Her particular trauma response was *fuck you*.

Because honestly, how dare these guys target her and John at the marketplace, break into their riad, then chase them in the middle of the night? Alone, she would've happily thrown hands at the patio guy, then dropped on top the SUV like a spider to take out the snake charmer and interrogate him. At the very least she would've called the police to report a suspicious loiterer.

But with John in tow, it was safety first.

"They're gaining on us," John shouted.

Not in a panicky way. He was loud, but this was the same matter-of-fact tone he used when quoting an interesting article in the *Post*.

"Roger that," she answered.

His grip on her tightened as she sped through middle-of-the-night Casablanca. Shame she couldn't give him a proper tour of one of her homes away from home. The place was beautiful, especially at night, with all the pale buildings lit up in a golden glow.

The bike coughed and backfired.

"Hang on," she shouted.

Ignoring how much she loved the feel of his arms around her, she hairpinned into a narrow alley that the SUV's fat ass couldn't fit within.

"That was close," John said.

Close? Nah. This was easy. Close was when she'd been pinned in a blind alley and had parkoured her way out of it. But she'd keep that story to herself. After several sharp turns, she stopped at a set of steel double doors.

She cut the engine. "We're here. Can you let me go?"

"Oh. Yeah, sorry." He released her, then slid off the motorbike.

The doors vibrated with the *unce-unce-unce* club music they'd play until closing. Pain shot through her knuckles as she knocked three times. She paused, knocked three more times, paused again, then gave two more knocks. She shook out her fist. It had been a minute since she worked here, but hopefully they hadn't changed the code.

A moment later, the lock on the other side thunked. The unoiled hinges squealed as the door opened. The club's candy-colored lights spilled over a familiar figure.

"Bonjour, Tonton," she said.

"Jeanne d'Arc!" He picked her up and swung her around, the only man on the planet besides John whom she allowed to do so. He set her back on her feet with as much grace as a trained ballerino. "What's the deal?"

"Trouble," she explained in French. "May we come inside?"

Tonton appraised John before complying. Good for him. As the head of security for Café Americain, he was responsible for the employees' and club-goers' safety. After five long seconds, he gestured for them to wheel the motorbike inside.

"Park the bike," he said as he bolted the doors. "You can have the office."

"Thanks, Tonton," she said.

"None needed." He waved a hand. "I'm still in your debt. What else can I do for you?"

As they followed the French expat, the increasingly loud music thumped her chest.

"Pants and shoes for my friend?" she yelled.

"I'll see what I can do."

Tonton pivoted and opened the first door on the left, then ushered them inside his soundproofed office. He spent no time in here. He preferred to be on the floor, keeping watch, while his staff kept eyes on a wall of security monitors.

Tonton shut the door behind them.

"Tell me—you are truly okay?" This beefy tattooed man had a reputation for being merciless with miscreants, but he was a marshmallow to the people under his care.

"Fine," she said. "Assholes tried to break into our riad. I don't want trouble from them."

Tonton smirked. "If my memory's intact, you're the one who dishes out trouble."

"Flatterer," she said.

"I need to get back on the floor, so I'll leave you here." The old softie's eyes twinkled. "Unless you want to dance? Earn a few dirham? Learn a few secrets?"

She shook her head. "No thanks. I have plenty to do back here."

"As ever. Lock up after me, eh?" He pointed at John. "And you—be good to my Jeanne."

John nodded. "Yes, sir."

After Tonton stepped into the hall, she flipped both dead bolts. A long breath escaped her. This place smelled the same as always. Cocoa butter, cash and fog machine.

"Bathroom's over there." She pointed to the door opposite the couch. "Backpack?"

He slipped it from his shoulders and handed it to her. "When did you work here?"

"Six years ago." She sat at Tonton's desk and slipped her tablet from the bag, then unfolded the case to access the keyboard.

"Did you buy art, or…"

She broke her gaze from the tablet's smooth surface tablet and locked eyes with John. "Dude. Does this *look* like a place where art buyers gather?"

He lifted a shoulder. "I don't know how things are done here."

She sighed. "After living in Europe for a few years, Jane Davis was a go-go dancer in Casablanca. It fit her student-loan-debt persona and put me in touch with sketchy people. Everyone loves an art broker with scandal in their past."

"But you don't dance."

"That doesn't mean I *can't* dance. For example."

She lived to tease John. For ten seconds, she shimmied and twirled in the way that earned her an obscene amount of tips and coaxed intel from stubborn lips back in the day.

"See?" She abruptly stopped, then returned to her seat.

John's wide eyes, which stayed glued to her as she typed, told her she still had the goods. Even better, his eyes darkened the way they did when he was about to toss her over his shoulder and head to the bedroom.

He might not be back to love, but lust was a start.

"Who *are* you?" he asked.

"Vivian Flint." She logged into her Canada-based VPN. "Dancing like that was all part of the job here. Café Americain does a brisk secondary business learning people's secrets and cashing in on them."

"Aka blackmail."

"Correct." She shot a finger gun at him. "Tonton's grateful because I learned something that kept this place from being shut down. Pro tip—if you're the chief of police, never tell your entertainer you fathered the mayor's youngest child."

"How did that come up in a nightclub?"

"You'd be surprised what people brag about." She cracked her knuckles. "Let's see if we can connect some dots. Want to be my sounding board?"

He leaned back against the couch. "Shoot."

She typed *Lola Vorlicek* into her search bar. "Is it a coincidence that Amina recently turned down a handsome offer from another dealer, and after we visited her, we're targeted by goons in the Central Market? Maybe."

"That doesn't sound like a sincere maybe."

"It isn't." She filtered the search results for images. As the thumbnails filled in, her stomach dropped. "Oh, shit."

"*That* sounded sincere." John circled behind her.

"That's Lola Vorlicek. And that—" she moved her finger from the blonde woman to the fashionable man standing next to her "—is Jean-Michel de Gramont."

"The infamous ex." John's heat radiated her back as he leaned forward. "Is he a model?"

"No, but he acted like it. Vain, prissy and enamored of extravagant lifestyles."

"What's the connection between him and the woman trying to buy Amina's work?"

She paged through photos. "My best guess is she's the new me. An assistant/lover he mentors in his grift. He's limited in where he can travel due to drug offenses, so he farms out pretty young things to the places he can't go. He actually sent me here to assess Casablanca's reputation as a burgeoning hotbed of visionary art."

She left out that she'd also fallen a tiny bit in love with Jean-Michel.

Which was a huge no-no because it could compromise the mission. She'd offered to resign from the operation. MacColl talked her out of it, said bailing would do more harm than good. So instead of quitting, she'd planned to break up with Jean-Michel.

Then she met John.

Wonderful, reliable, funny, uncomplicated John. The man who'd shown her that love didn't have to be difficult to be real. The man with whom she wanted to build a life. The man for whom she'd burn the world.

A loud knock shook the office door.

"Stay back." She grabbed Tonton's gigantic stapler.

"The hell I will." John followed her.

"At least stay out of my striking circle." Once she peered through the peephole, relief flooded through her. "Oh, shit."

"How bad is it?"

"Zero bad." She flipped the dead bolts.

"Jeanne!" Her squealing friend wrapped her in a hug and a cloud of Chanel No. 5.

"Coco!" Vivian let her friend go. "Coco, this is John. John, this is Coco."

Fuck, she'd used his real name. Another slipup.

"Jeanne has her John!" Coco peppered him with cheek kisses. "Are you in town long? There's a fantastic new boutique you'd adore."

Vivian lifted a shoulder. "We leave at dawn, sadly."

"In trouble again, eh?" Coco reached into the canvas shopping bag slung over her shoulder and offered Vivian a cigarette from a half-empty pack.

She declined. "I quit."

"You smoked?" John asked.

"Like a chimney," Coco answered. "Tell me about your troubles."

"We were in the Central Market earlier, and a snake charmer dropped a snake on John," Vivian said. "Striped fez, scar from his eye to his mouth. Shorter than John, but not by much. An hour ago, someone tried to break into our riad, and the striped fez guy was waiting outside in an SUV. Know anyone who fits that description?"

Coco had an uncanny memory for the faces, names and predilections of Café Americain's clientele, which was basically every man in a fifty-kilometer radius.

"That sounds like Baaka Adlani," her friend said. "The snake charmer scam is a family business, but he does a little of everything so he can do mostly nothing. If he was hired to break into your riad, he might've brought his burglar friend, Raphael Dubois."

Vivian wrote the names down on the scratch pad on Tonton's desk.

"There *was* another guy at the market," John said. "Short, curly haired, wore a crucifix necklace. His jewelry choice seemed weird because he was being gross to Jane."

"Marry this one, Jeanne." Coco placed her hand on his chest. "For many reasons."

"Coco," she warned.

"Okay, okay." Coco removed her hand. "That sounds like Raphael. He brags about his thieving. Says it's not breaking and entering if people leave windows open."

John furrowed his brow. "They sound…not smart…if they told you all this."

"Men reveal much to a pretty face they underestimate." Coco fluttered her false eyelashes. "When my tits are out, men confess like it's Easter."

Vivian choked back a laugh as she stepped over to the desk to grab her tablet.

"Recognize her?" She flipped the Lola-filled screen toward Coco.

"No," Coco said. "But she has style. Shall I keep an eye out?"

Damn. She was hoping for more intel.

"Yes, please." Vivian made a mental note to send Coco a gift basket.

"I need to get back. Mustn't worry Tonton. But before I go…" Coco thrust a bag toward Vivian. "All the normal send-off gifts for running away with a man."

She took the bag. "You shouldn't have."

"But of course I should. Always celebrate romance, eh? Good luck to the both of you, and I hope your next visit is longer."

After a flurry of kisses, Coco departed.

"Here." Vivian tossed the bag to John on her way back to Tonton's desk.

"Check out the contents—see if there's anything useful?"

John sat on the couch. After rustling in the bag, he tossed something in the garbage. "Some friend she is. Those were peanuts."

She'd have to confess her allergy-free status to him soon.

"Money, pain pills, lipstick."

She bet it was the signature color she'd worn when she worked here—Parisian red.

He held up a citrine cloth. "Last thing's a scarf. A big one."

"That's a pashmina. Those are very handy, actually." She tapped at her keyboard. "You have time for a nap if you want to use it as a blanket."

"What about you?" he asked.

"There's too much happening in here." She whirled her finger at her temple. "I want to check on connections among Lola, Baaka and Raphael. Then I'll sleep."

John stretched. "Promise me you'll be here when I wake up?"

It hurt that he'd asked. Of course she would be. They were in this together. The important takeaway, though, was he still wanted her to stay with him.

"I'll be here, I promise."

"Okay then." He draped his body over the too-small couch and spread the pashmina over his torso. His ritual fidgets and fusses made her smile. They were comforting, and after a year of sleeping next to him, triggered her own desire to rest.

But there was no risk for the wicked.

Her fingers quietly flew over the keyboard. She messaged Mariam to warn her about the attempted break-in, and not to go to the riad without security or police. Next, she wired her a hefty payment to cover any damage and soothe any heartburn their stay had caused.

With that completed, she turned to the internet.

There must be a connection among the events of the past forty-eight hours. She wasn't seeing it yet, which meant she needed more information. Gather, gather, gather until the pattern clicked in her differently wired brain.

"One more question," John said.

She startled. She thought he'd dropped off.

"What's that?" she asked.

"How'd you get so good at this?"

"I…" Warmth swirled through her like the honey she'd drizzled into her mint tea at Amina's. "You think I'm good at my job?"

He twisted on the couch to face her. "No, I think you're great at it. You always know what to do. Doesn't matter if it's bullets or goons or snakes or being chased. You've got backup plans for your backup plans. Resources stashed everywhere. Friends falling over themselves to do favors for you." He flipped onto his back. "You're just really good at this."

Thank God his eyes were closed—no witnesses to her second sob fest today.

Embarrassing for a seasoned CIA officer.

Ten

"John, we need to go." Vivian's gentle voice sifted through his deep sleep.

He bolted upright. Instant regret as his brain thudded inside his skull. He pressed the heels of his palms to his scratchy eyes. "I feel like ass. What time is it?"

"Five. And here—these'll help." She handed him Tylenol, a tumbler of water, and a disposable mini-toothbrush.

"Where'd you get these?" He chased the pills with a gulp of water.

"My go-bag. I stuff it with whatever I need when I'm on the run."

"What's the most useful thing in there?"

She peeped in the bag. "Honestly? The binder clips."

He chuckled. "Not the collapsible baton?"

"Nope. Binder clips. A-plus in the handiness department."

This exchange was strangely comfortable. Yeah, they were hiding out in a Moroccan club. But they were still themselves, shooting the breeze while getting ready for the day.

He ripped open the toothbrush's packaging. "Learn anything after I fell asleep?"

"Not much. I tapped into the prefecture's criminal database. Nothing on Lola, and both men have a run-of-the-mill history. Assault and battery, theft, fraud. Real gems. But no obvious connections to me, Jean-Michel or the art world." She laced her fingers together and cradled the back of her head. "There's something underlying all this, though. I can feel it."

"Did you get *any* sleep last night?" he asked.

"Yes, but I woke up with my face planted on the keyboard. Can I have the pashmina?"

He handed it to her, and she stepped into the bathroom.

"Remember when I first moved in and you were frustrated that stuff wasn't where it's supposed to be?" she called through the open door. "Water bottle's in the fridge instead of on the table, shoes on the rack, shower curtain closed instead of open?"

"I wasn't frustrated." He scrubbed his teeth.

"You definitely were." She laughed. "Anyway, that's how I feel when there's a connection I haven't found in a case. Mental itchiness."

A hefty knock at the door startled him.

"That'll be Tonton." Vivian emerged with the pashmina fashioned into a hijab. She peeked through the peephole, then twisted the dead bolts. "Everyone gone for the day?"

"All but me." Tonton thrust a bundle at John. "Best I can do, Dauphin."

"Dauphin?" John took pants, a shirt and leather slip-on shoes from him.

"If Jeanne d'Arc fights for you, are you not the dauphin?" Tonton folded his arms. "Jeanne, a private word before you go?"

She nodded, then twisted to John. "Meet us out here after you change?"

As the door closed, he shed his pajama pants.

Tonton's desk phone beckoned. One call and John's parents would fly him out of here.

Did he want that? Two days ago, he'd been ready to elope. To entangle his future with hers. Her problems were his problems, and vice versa. And oh boy, did they have problems.

Despite everything, though, his adrenaline-fueled ass had stuck with his sort-of fiancée.

He was in this with her.

Delicate loose-end tendrils tickled his brain. The mental itchiness she'd described—he felt it, too. Not about the attack or black market art or money funnels or whatever the fuck.

About Vivian. He'd learn more about her if he stayed, like he did during dinner yesterday.

And he was curious about her, like he'd been with Jane.

Wanted to know everything about her.

John patted the pockets of his too-big pants to check for his good luck charm. His grandfather had given him the Zippo on his eighteenth birthday, saying, *"A man can always use a steady flame."* Ah, there it was—in his left pants pocket.

He flipped it open, flicked the flint, then flipped the lid down.

Time to go.

"Does either of you have a belt?" John asked as he opened the door.

"Non." Tonton lifted his shoulder into a shrug.

"How about a binder clip?" Vivian reached into her bag, folded the loose inches at his waist, then secured the material with the clip.

Her touch sent an inconvenient shiver up his spine.

"There," she said. "That'll hold 'til we get to Tangier."

The binder clip lightly scratched his back as they walked toward the steel doors, but he preferred it to his pants around his ankles.

"Stay back," Tonton said. After opening the doors, he surveyed the street, then gave the all clear. "Be well, Jeanne, and go fast."

"Always." Vivian kissed Tonton on the cheek. "I owe you."

John extended his hand to Tonton. "Thanks for helping us."

The older man crushed his hand like a frat boy with a beer can, but John held his own.

"She's tough," Tonton grumbled. "But look out for her."

"I will," John promised.

The motorbike's engine growled to life. "Let's go!" Vivian tossed her backpack to John. "À tout à l'heure, Tonton!"

The rumbling rust bucket sank under John's weight. As he belted his arms around Vivian's waist, her ribs expanded with a sigh. Under Casablanca's lavender sky, homeward-bound club kids crossed paths with vendors headed to market.

In this section of the city, new glass-and-chrome buildings stood beside older structures with peeling paint. As they merged onto a busier road, Vivian pointed to an enormous gleaming structure up ahead.

"That's the Hassan II Mosque. It's the second largest mosque in Africa. It's breathtaking up close." She breezed past an idling bus, leaving the mosque behind them. The road they traveled curved along the coastline. "Up ahead's the El Hank lighthouse. It opened up Casablanca to development."

She spoke about this city like he did when he gave tours to friends visiting DC. He dragged his bottom lip through his teeth. She'd *lived* here, not just visited like he assumed. How often had he filled in blanks that she didn't correct?

He needed to be better about asking questions. Specific questions whose answers would tell him more about Vivian.

"What's your favorite place in the city?" he asked.

"That's a tough one." Vivian revved the engine. "Ooh, I know. Mohammed V Square. It's nearby, actually."

"Show me?" he asked.

After a few turns, she slowed to a stop. "A lot of people call it Pigeon Plaza."

At Mohammed V Square's center stood an enormous fountain. The rest of it was filled with Alfred Hitchcock–level flocks of pigeons. The bored birds barely moved out of the way of the handful of human souls moving among them.

He laughed. "I can see why. But why do you like it?"

He'd expected a museum or a mural, but instead she picked pigeons.

"They remind me of people," she said. "Everyone trying to go through their normal routine, blissfully unaware of emergencies around them."

In the distance, a rich voice sang over loudspeakers. The

birds couldn't be bothered, and continued cooing and flapping as they meandered across the plaza.

"Shit," Vivian said. "That's for fajr. We need to go."

She gunned it, and within minutes, they parked at L'Oasis Train Station.

"What should we do with the bike?" he asked.

"I'll leave the keys." Vivian slid from the seat. "Someone's about to have a lucky day."

In the station, they crossed the marble-patterned linoleum to the ticket booth. After purchasing tickets for the high speed train, she handed him one.

"The Al Boraq's boarding." She swiveled her gaze, then pointed. "It's that way."

They took an escalator down to the bullet train's platform.

"We're in car two," Vivian said.

They walked until they found secluded seats with a clear view of their car's door.

Vivian paused in the aisle. "You take the window. Just in case."

"In case what?" he asked.

She lifted a shoulder. "Fights, pigeons, runaway trolleys of food. All the above?"

He sank into the plush velour, and she dropped into the seat next to him. Vivian yawned through the departure announcements. He'd bet she didn't sleep more than five minutes. This woman was the *worst* at taking care of herself.

As the train glided away from the station, he asked, "Why don't you take a nap?"

"Can't." The dark circles under her eyes argued otherwise.

"More like won't. You know, you make fun of me for needing eight hours of sleep per night, but shortchanging yourself and coping with coffee until you lose your mind over TikToks of babies getting glasses and seeing their parents for the first time isn't the picture of health."

She crossed her arms. "It's a beautiful testament to science and human connection."

"I agree, but sobbing?" He bumped shoulders with her. "If anything exciting happens, I'll wake you up. I promise."

"No." She kneaded her neck.

She had a stubborn knot that flared when she spent too much time at her desk. Or, now that he knew the real her, hand-to-hand combat might be the real culprit. Either way, she was in pain. And she had saved his life several times recently.

"Do you need a neck rub?" he asked.

"You don't have to," she said.

"That's not a no. Face the aisle."

She turned without argument, and he dug his thumbs into the troublesome knot. After a couple minutes, the knot unclenched. Her quiet moan made his cock twitch.

Which was bad. Very bad.

"Better?" he asked.

She rolled her neck. "Oh my God, much."

"Then you should nap."

"I told you, I ca—" A jaw-cracking yawn interrupted her. "Okay, fine. Here are some dirham to buy breakfast if the food trolley comes through. Wake me up in thirty minutes."

Before he could say okay, she was asleep against him.

Vivian sucked in a breath as she awoke.

"…terminus." The speaker crackled. "Once again, our next stop is the Tanger Ville Railway Station, the main train station in Tangier and the Al Boraq line's terminus."

The seat next to her was empty.

Impressive and annoying that John had climbed over her without waking her. She checked her watch. Nine? Christ, he'd let her sleep for two hours. She'd bet he was in the dining car to satisfy his clockwork body's breakfast demands.

Unnecessarily risky.

She marched down the car with her backpack tight to her

shoulders. Several passenger cars later, she'd arrived at the glass doors dividing her from the dining car.

Yep, there he was.

Tonton's red shirt aside, she'd recognize his back anywhere. He turned with a stack of sandwiches, pastries and bottles of water. Before she could hit the button and lecture him on the bad, bad idea it was to separate himself from her, two men blocked his path.

Twin forks of fear and anger skewered her heart.

Based on the fez and the curls, the goons from Casablanca had found them. Goddammit, kidnapping was not on her agenda. She ducked, then opened her phone's camera and angled it so she could watch their interactions.

Baaka, the one in the fez, pointed to the dining car's other doors.

They marched John away from her.

No. They were not taking him. Not today, not ever.

She slipped on her sunglasses and followed, remaining one car behind them. The train slowed, allowing a nonblurry view of houses clustered atop the green hills surrounding the station. She undid the safety pins from the folds of her hijab/pashmina.

As the doors opened, she hopped down the steps.

People of varying shapes, sizes, and styles of clothing poured onto the checkered platform. The red flash of Tonton's shirt was her beacon. She kept pace as they marched John through the palm-tree-filled train station and toward the glass-fronted main entrance.

Outside, the train station's plaza was the length of a football field.

She blinked against the sunshine bouncing off the skyscraper across the street. Turquoise taxis circled the station's roundabout, hunting for passengers.

She *could not* let them put John in a car.

This would need to be quick, stealthy. Raphael first, since he stood intimately close to John, likely holding a weapon to his ribs. Then Baaka, who might be slow to catch on because of the phone at his ear. She dropped her sunglasses in her bag, then withdrew two EpiPens. She flicked the caps off with her thumbs.

She was not lethally allergic to peanuts, and these pens didn't contain epinephrine.

They were loaded with two hundred fifty milligrams of propofol each, enough to knock out a big man for five to ten minutes. More than enough for these guys. Even better, they weren't highly trained professionals. Otherwise they wouldn't have their backs to the station.

Advantage—Vivian.

She went low and plunged the pen into Raphael's thigh. He yelped and backhanded her. The pain registered a second later, blunted by her rush of adrenaline. But fuck, he knocked the other EpiPen from her grip. On the plus side, he dropped his knife, too.

He lunged for the blade, staggered and dropped. Propofol for the win.

The other guy, Baaka, charged at her.

"John!" She dodged Baaka's meaty fist. "Get the EpiPen!"

"The what?"

Another dodge. "EpiPen. Near the curb."

She whipped the pashmina from her shoulders and wrapped a few inches of the ends around each of her hands. When Baaka's next fist rounded toward her, Vivian looped the scarf around his arm and redirected his momentum. He stumbled, but recovered quickly.

"John. Pen."

Another swing. She caught Baaka's arm with one loop and his neck with another, then tightened. A crowd had gathered, and fuck, phones were out and filming.

The big man struggled against her grip.

With her knee on his back, she demanded, "Who sent you?"

"Fuck you," he ground out.

"Wrong answer." She tightened the loops. "Who's your boss?"

"Fuck you…twice."

An unruly crowd meant police would arrive soon. They had to run. But she couldn't have this guy following them.

"Jab him," she said to John. "You have to. My hands are literally tied."

John stuck him in the leg, and a few seconds later, the large man dropped, taking Vivian down with him.

A bullhorn-amplified voice shouted at the crowd to move. The onlookers shifted. Yep, police had arrived.

She dropped the pashmina, then grabbed John's arm. "Run."

With her hand tethered to his, she bolted through the circle's traffic, then veered right. Tourist-heavy locations were the best places to blend, and in Tangier, that meant the beaches. Handy, since her friend Lisa's museum was near the beach.

Her bag slapped against her back as they ran.

"Vivian, wait."

"No," she called back. "Hustle."

They had to get off the street and into a crowded area. She steered them from the Centre Commercial, aka the shopping mall. Too much security there, and too many cameras. The road delivered them to a palm tree–lined corniche overlooking the beach.

Glass-enclosed elevator stations would take them down to the waterfront.

As soon as she and John were inside one, she leaned against the wall.

"Are you okay?" She fought to catch her breath.

"I lost my shoes, and my pants are falling off." He clutched at his waistband. "Other than that, I'm fine."

"Good. Because I'm furious with you."

The elevator doors opened, releasing them to the beach. She kicked off her sneakers and stomped away from him. The tide was high, so few people were swimming. A wave thundered to shore, obliterating a sandcastle.

"Me?" He jogged after her. "What did I do?"

Happy couples caught less attention.

She reached for his hand. "You put yourself at risk."

His grip was as warm as the sand between her toes.

"If I hadn't been in the dining car, wouldn't they have gotten the drop on both of us?"

A volleyball rolled in front of them.

"Probably not if you'd woken me when I asked." She scooped up the ball and threw it back to the kids playing on a roped-off section of beach.

"I'm the bad guy because I let you sleep?"

"No, because you let me sleep *and* you left me alone for a fucking sandwich."

"For *both* of us." He stopped. "Vivian, wait. Are *you* okay? Did he hurt you?"

Her cheekbone might be bruised. "Not as much as I hurt him."

"Good." He paled and leaned in close to her ear. "Did we… did I…kill them?"

"No. We hit them with enough propofol to knock them out for ten minutes. No killing."

"Propofol?" John asked. "So those aren't real EpiPens."

"No. I'm not allergic to anything. We've got to keep moving." She restarted their walk. "My friend's expecting us by ten."

"Not allergic?" He linked hands with her again. "I gave up peanut butter because I didn't want to murder you if I kissed you."

She couldn't stop her smile. Death by peanut butter smooch was absurd.

"That's sweet."

"It's not sweet. Not accidentally poisoning someone you love is the minimum."

His stomach growled.

"You really wanted those sandwiches on the train, didn't you?" Boats bobbed in the marina up ahead. "We're almost at the Villa Harris Museum. It's an unofficial safe house where I've stashed euros and clothes—my college roommate is the executive director. Dr. Lisa Devon."

"Are she and Anjali friends?"

"Yeah." Vivian paused to put her shoes on. "We all lived together senior year."

"You must not get to see her as often."

"Three or four times per year. Both of us are in Europe a bunch for work."

"Christ, that's how often I see my college roommate Patrick, and he's in Fairfax."

"I prioritize seeing them. My friends keep me sane. So do you." Her cheeks heated. Hadn't meant to say that. "How about you? Are you staying sane? Global shenanigans and subterfuge and waking up in strange places…" She gestured toward the beautiful Italianate mansions lining the road. "It's a lot to take in."

Dear God, the babbling had to stop.

"It sure is, Gorgeous."

She stiffened. She could be cool and ignore what he just said. But…nope.

"Was that *gorgeous* about the scenery?" she asked. "Or did you mean…"

"You. Sorry, it slipped out."

A smile bubbled her cheeks. She'd take it.

"Not much further," she said.

In this older part of the city, crowded buildings shadowed the narrow streets. They fell silent as they passed mothers with strollers, teenagers, and tourists dipping in and out of shops lining the path. As they rounded a corner, her friend stood on the steps of a repurposed Portuguese mansion, waving madly.

"Vivi—no, shit, I mean Jane! Jane Davis!"

The exhausted giggles bubbling from Vivian turned into

guffaws. Stress had clearly gotten the better of her. Lisa was the *worst* secret-keeper, but she tried so hard.

"Oh my God," Vivian wheezed. Her sides ached. "I'm going to pee my pants."

"Me too," Lisa croaked.

John stood helpless between them. "You're Lisa, I take it?"

Which caused Lisa to shriek-laugh again.

Vivian thumbed tears from her eyes. "Yes, that's Lisa. Let's go inside. We had to ditch some fanboys at the train station."

"Sorry to hear that." Lisa dabbed at her eyes with the ends of her scarf. "And sorry I can't get myself together. John, did Viv—shit, I did it again."

More giggles streamed from them.

Finally, Lisa asked, "Did *Jane* tell you we revert to teenagers every time we see each other? I'm normally more composed and intimidating."

Lisa locked the entrance's intricate wrought-iron gate behind them.

"Here." She picked up a sturdy-handled aromatic paper bag and thrust it toward Vivian. "You never remember to eat."

"Right?" John asked. "I don't understand it. And now you're my favorite friend of hers."

"Ooh, who else have you met?"

"Anjali, but she didn't give me food. Just water."

"Technically, *I* gave you water," Vivian said.

Lisa pumped her fist like she'd hit a home run. "Yes. I'm winning."

"Holy shit, Lisa, when did you get a Zakaria Ramhani?" Vivian stopped at the gallery off the main entrance. A six-by-eight foot portrait overlaid with Arabic calligraphy stared at her.

"Last month—thanks for turning me on to him." Lisa side-hugged her. "But let's keep moving. Staff arrives soon." Lisa led them through the museum's courtyard and into the storage area. She swiped her ID and entered a code, then held the door open for them. "Not to style shame, but you could use a change of clothes, yes?"

"Desperately." Vivian gestured to John. "FYI, his alias is a fashion-forward influencer, so take that into consideration. I also need hair dye, and he needs a razor."

"I do?" John palmed his jaw.

"We've been made," Vivian said. "We need to change our look. It's a safety issue."

"Okay then," Lisa said. "Clothes, dye, razor, maybe some cosmetics. John, you're, what? Waist size thirty-six, shoe size twelve?"

He rocked on his feet. "That's scarily accurate."

"I flirted with fashion as a career, but I like to wear clothes, not make them." Lisa pocketed her ID. "The door code's the same as our dorm door if you need to leave."

Her bestie slipped out the door and locked them inside.

"She seems nice," John said.

"She *is* nice." Vivian punched her six-digit code into the locker Lisa had reserved for her and withdrew a fat stack of euros. "You should eat whatever's in the bag."

"You too." He held out a paper-wrapped sandwich. "Don't say you don't have time."

"For these I'll make time." Her mouth watered as she unwrapped the tosta mista, a Portuguese ham-and-cheese melt and her favorite sandwich. The grill-pressed bread's crunchy corners were heaven.

"Not to be crass," John said. "But do CIA officers make a lot of money? Or does the government supply your cash hoards, too?"

She slowed her chewing.

Like any serious couple, she and John had talked about money. John and Jane knew how much each other earned and what their expenses were.

Vivian's revenue streams, however…

She shook her head. "The amount of paperwork required for

a cash advance is ridiculous. I've got two jobs, remember? And during the years I lived abroad, the government covered my housing and living expenses. I saved a ton of money."

There was some additional truth she couldn't share.

"Does my money change anything?" she asked. "Some guys are touchy about it."

By touchy she meant steeped in patriarchy so they believed their only value was being the primary breadwinner. Which meant they couldn't handle a woman out-earning them.

"Are you kidding?" he asked. "I'm happy for you. And based on the last couple of days? They should double whatever they're paying you."

He handed her an orange juice. It was hard to sip around her smile.

She *knew* he was one of the good ones.

Eleven

John finished his breakfast in four bites. "So Lisa's your college roommate Melissa?"

Vivian nodded as she devoured her sandwich. Good. Her outlook on life improved tenfold when she sat down to eat for five minutes.

"So she's the one who comforted you after your bad freshman-year breakup. And she was homesick until you took her to a late-night bistro and stuffed her with brie and merlot."

"Yep." She thumbed a curl behind her ear. "She's a good example of me telling you the basic truth while changing the window dressing. I'm surprised you remembered those details."

"Why? I hang on everything you say."

She tilted her head. "Really?"

"Really. Lisa's also the friend who took you on vacations with her family, right?"

"Yes. I'm impressed. She brought me as a buffer so her parents wouldn't grill her about grades. It was educational for me, too—their wealth showed me how the one percent live."

"I get that. My parents—and sometimes Thomas and I—were invited to ceremonies and dinners that obviously cost a fortune. So I'm comfortable with people with power and wealth, even though it's not anything I'll personally have." He swigged his orange juice. "Did it bother you to be around money since you had to scrape to get by?"

"Are you kidding? Down with capitalism and all that, but I loved skiing in Vail and yachting in Cannes on someone else's dime."

"Patrick took me to go-karting once. Basically the same

thing, right?" He crumpled his sandwich wrapper and pitched it into the trash bin.

"Obviously." She finished her sandwich. "Anyway, those trips were excellent training for what I do today. The luxury, but also understanding what motivates people, how they tick. Not to brag, but I had you figured out after a month."

The hair on his nape rose. He'd wanted to figure her out, too. Normal couple stuff, though. How to make her laugh, relax, which parts of her body to stroke to make her sigh with pleasure. But a spy had been analyzing him, assessing him…

"Never mind." She wiped the air between them. "Shouldn't have said that."

"Oh, no you don't." He wiggled his fingers like Bruce Lee inviting an opponent to fight. "Out with it. What'd you figure out?"

"You've got abandonment issues." She lifted a shoulder. "Most people do."

He knitted his brows. "No, I don't."

"John, you invited me to move in after six months and proposed after a year."

His skin prickled. "Because I fell in love."

"I'm not saying the timing was wrong." She touched his knee. "But it *was* fast. I'm guessing it stems from moving around so much as a kid. You crave routine. The same coffee shop every day, same route to work, laundry on Sundays."

He rolled his shoulders to shake off feeling like he was a painting under a museum's picture light. No, not a picture light. Those were low wattage. More like a spotlight.

"Routines are efficient," he said. "People thrive on them. Is there more?"

She closed one eye and contemplated him. "Sure you want me to continue?"

He folded his arms. "Yes."

"Okay. You think you're easygoing."

"Because I *am*. When do I argue with anyone?"

"You're arguing with me now."

"Because you accused me of being an asshole."

"Oh my God, you're so dramatic." She rubbed her forehead. "The opposite of easygoing isn't asshole, it's rigid. Meal times, sleep schedules, pillow quality, arriving five minutes early to everything—as long as those needs are met, you're happy. But if they aren't, you lose it. Therefore, not easygoing."

He clamped his jaw to stop an automatic denial.

"If I'm so terrible, why'd you say yes?"

She tossed her balled-up sandwich wrapper at him. "Add hyperbolic to the list."

He squeezed the sandwich wrapper ball. "But you didn't list any *good* things. My nurturing side, my sense of humor, my ability to fix anything. Where were those?"

"You're impossible." She giggled, then covered her eyes and peeked through her fingers. "You might also have anxiety."

He tossed her crumpled ball back at her. "That *you* caused by noticing things about me."

Grudgingly, he could admit he'd hit the gas on moving their relationship to the next level. She'd seemed too good to be true, and he'd wanted to make them permanent. When someone *gets* you, sees you, from the start, it's pure magic.

He'd gotten her, too.

Or so he'd thought. The cold shock of her confession had numbed him. But over these last couple of days... He'd thawed as he rediscovered her. The reasons he fell for her in the first place were there, just wrapped in this new layer.

"You never answered my question." He reached for her left hand, then rubbed his thumb along the sapphire. "Why'd you say yes?"

"For the same reason you asked. I was in love."

The past tense stung. "Was?"

He shifted closer to her, pressed his thigh to hers.

"Am, John. All of that—us—is real."

He brushed his lips against hers, then sighed. Her familiar feel, taste and tiny moans... His heart pulsed in his chest, his ears, his hips. This was like coming home. He didn't know how he'd explain their situation to his family, but he needed to keep Vivian in his life.

Light blazed into the room.

"Whoops!" Lisa closed her eyes and walked forward. "Sorry. I come bearing clothes."

"Lis, stop." Vivian took a bag from her outstretched hand. "You'll give yourself a concussion if you walk around with your eyes shut. Here, John. This bag's for you."

"We'll give you privacy," Lisa said. "Vivian and I need a girl chat."

Lisa grabbed Vivian's hand and dragged her toward the door. "Jane" had told him subtlety was not her college roommate's strong suit. Looked like that was true, too.

"I can't believe you picked red." Vivian sat on the toilet's closed lid as the hair dye seeped into her strands. "That's like, the *one* color I should avoid."

"It's not red. It's Ruby Rush. And with your coloring, platinum's the one to avoid. Now, what's up with John? I saw the ring and the kiss, but you have super weird vibes."

"On Friday he asked me to marry him—"

Lisa squealed and pumped her fist.

"Don't get excited." She tugged the pashmina around her shoulders. "He broke up with me when I told him everything about my job and who I really am."

"Then he's a fool. You're amazing. I'll leave him in storage while you skedaddle."

"I appreciate the false imprisonment offer, but no thanks." A sigh shuddered from Vivian. "I don't know what that kiss was about, or the one at the riad, or what's going on between us."

Being around her bestie meant she could be squishy, so she let the tears flow.

"Oh, honey." Lisa gathered her in a hug. "What about the riad? No, never mind. We'll put a pin in that. But he can't be serious about a breakup."

"He is. He says he can't be with someone who works for the CIA because I'll always put the job before him. That I lied to him for a year. Can you believe him? Twenty-two thousand people work there, and that doesn't even include contractors. Are we all untouchable?"

Breakfast was a brick in Vivian's stomach.

She wasn't quitting. The importance of the work made *her* important. Without it, she'd be... Normal. Like her former mentor, Ann, a mother of five who'd taken early retirement after a suffering a heart attack. Six months later, over lunch, Ann moaned that punching out of the inner circle was torture.

Message received.

But then Vivian met John. Over the past year, her vision of her future changed. Every version, every universe, every plan—he was her partner, her safe harbor.

Except he hated her career, and she couldn't have both.

"To be fair—" Lisa rubbed her shoulder "—he's probably not opposed to dating, like, a human resources manager. Your work's mission-driven. And lying to someone—"

"I wasn't *allowed* to tell him."

Lisa handed her a tissue. "I say this with love. Cut the bullshit. You were scared to tell him and withheld basic truths about yourself for a year. That's not great."

"This is a shitty pep talk."

"Real friends are real. But here's the peppy part. He loves you. He'll come around."

Vivian laughed into her tissue. "Now who's bullshitting?"

"Not me." Lisa shook her head. "The way he looks at you? Please. That's how I look at a charcuterie board. True love. But...does he know about Rocksy?"

Vivian bit her lip. "No."

"Then that's the final frontier. Tell him."

"I'll consider it." Vivian eyed the stiff shopping bag in the corner. "What'd you get me? It's not a Chanel sheath like last time, is it?"

"No, I was much more practical. How do you feel about a *Golden Girls*–esque caftan?"

"Terrible." Vivian dug into the bag and withdrew cerulean linen.

"Someday you'll understand the caftan's allure. Today's outfit is a wide-legged halter jumpsuit with pockets deep enough to smuggle a baby and your beloved Hokas."

Satin shimmered from the bag. "Underwear, too. You think of everything."

"Indeed I do." Lisa opened the door. "Toiletries are under the sink. And Viv, seriously. It'll all work out. If it doesn't, we'll take a girls' trip to Amalfi to drown your sorrows in pasta."

"Thanks, Lis."

Lisa lifted a shoulder. "You'd do the same for me."

Lifelong friends were a treasure.

After Lisa shut the door, hope formed a crack in the shell around Vivian's heart.

Please let Lisa be right about John.

Her phone's timer beeped. After a vigorous shampooing, she changed into the jumpsuit, gathered her now-red damp hair into a low ponytail, then slipped into thick-soled cream Hokas.

Legit heaven, like walking on air.

After she emerged from the bathroom, Lisa thrust a coffee at her.

Vivian sighed. "What did I do to deserve a fairy godmother?"

"Never made me feel like an asshole when you taught me how to do basic shit my parents' staff always did for me."

"You could've picked it up from TikTok." Vivian sipped the best cappuccino of her life. "Bitch, there's no way this is your everyday coffee."

"It is." Lisa swiped her card on the storage room door. "I'm a lucky woman."

As they opened the door, John finished buttoning up the short-sleeved collared shirt Lisa had procured. The fit was slim and hugged his biceps, same as his jeans. Those were snug enough that the vague outline of his Zippo in his front pocket was visible.

The clothes weren't the star of the show, though.

Swoon. His beard, much as she'd loved it, had hidden a perfect jawline and cheekbones.

"I like your face," she said. "It's like I'm seeing the real you."

Good Lord. She'd actually said that. If any of her colleagues heard the girlish squeal in her voice, they would tease her more than her siblings had.

"Same. I like the red. It suits you."

Fifty-fifty that he meant the blush blooming in her cheeks.

"Ready to go?" she asked. "Ferry leaves in twenty minutes. You can have shotgun since you've never been here."

True, but also, Lisa drove like a maniac, and she didn't have the stomach for it today.

Ten minutes later, after a whirlwind commute through neighborhoods stuffed with low beige buildings and palm trees, they arrived at the port.

Lisa hugged her awkwardly from the front seat. "Call me when things settle, okay?"

"I will," she said.

"Nice to meet you, Lisa," John said.

"Likewise. Also, *Jane* is great. Stay engaged."

"Lisa," she hissed. "I'm leaving before this gets more awkward."

Vivian escaped the Citroën C3. Cackling, Lisa beeped twice, then careened out of the drop-off area.

"Sorry. See what I mean about her brashness?" She shrugged her backpack onto her shoulders and turned to John.

The shock of his bare handsome face sent an ill-advised sizzle between her thighs.

"I liked her." John scratched at the back of his head. "Listen, about the kiss—"

A boarding announcement played over the loudspeaker, interrupting him and saving her from having this conversation on the streets of Tangier. She wasn't sure *when* they'd have it.

"We'd better go," she said.

Twelve

As they waited for ferry tickets, John slipped the gold-accented designer sunglasses Lisa had provided on his nose. Vivian's hair gleamed copper in the Moroccan sun. If she'd let him talk about the kiss, he would tell her it happened because she'd just listed all the things he tried hard to hide from the world, and she loved him anyway.

She never asked him to change.

"I know how you tick, too," burst from him. "The things you said earlier, about me… I know them about you, too."

The ticket booth agent waved them forward.

"Could we not dissect me here?" Vivian dropped dirham on the counter.

The ticket agent printed their boarding passes and landing cards.

"Merci," Vivian said, then pivoted toward the passport line.

"Then when can we talk?"

"On the ferry, if no one's around." As they shuffled forward, Vivian handed him Jason Jones's passport. "About this next part, don't stress. If there's a problem, I'll figure it out."

Ordering him not to stress was like ordering him to be taller. He swallowed. "But what if—"

"Nope." She squeezed his hand. "No what-ifs, no catastrophizing."

The security officer waved them over.

"You go first." Vivian nudged his back.

His belly dropped like she'd shoved him from an airplane.

"Passport, please?" the officer asked in French.

Blood pounded in his ears. Small win—his hands didn't shake as he slid the passport under the plastic window. When the officer inspected him to compare him to the passport, John smiled a big, toothy, maniacal grin.

Christ, he was bad at this.

The officer returned the passport. "Hurry, sir. Your ferry is departing."

That was it? He'd had more invasive receipt reviews at Costco.

On the checkpoint's other side, he waited for Vivian.

The officer eyeballed her. "Your hair is a different color."

"I wanted a change," she said.

"Why?" the officer asked.

Shit, was the officer not letting her through? If Vivian was denied entry, he'd cross back over the security line. They'd come this far together—he wasn't leaving her now.

"My boyfriend broke up with me," she said.

The officer locked her gaze on Vivian's face. After an eternity, she stamped her passport and handed it back to Vivian. "I've been there. Enjoy your trip."

Relief flooded John as the officer waved Vivian through.

He kissed her cheek and murmured, "I was worried."

"You didn't show it. Gold star." She paused by a trash can. With a sigh, she pulled something from her bag and pitched it in the bin. "Farewell, old friend."

"What was that?"

"My baton. I can't sneak it through the scanners. Shall we?"

The bag check line progressed quickly, and they were on their way to the red-and-white ferry. Before joining the line to board, they showed their passports and tickets to another official, who waved them through.

"I forgot international travel is a pain in the ass," John said.

Vivian scanned the crowd. "Security lines are a good thing."

German tourists wheeled bikes ahead of them. An occasional car drove past them to roll onto the ferry, but most of the line comprised other shambling pedestrians. In the blue straits beyond the marina, catamarans skipped like dragonflies along the water.

An agent scanned their boarding passes at the gangplank.

"I'm dying for a coffee," she said. "Want anything?"

He scratched the back of his neck. "Caffeine sounds good."

She led him up a spiral staircase. Passengers had already claimed half the upholstered seats. The aroma of rich coffee and baked goods overwhelmed the salty tang in the air.

"Bonjour," Vivian said to the cashier at the counter. "Two coffees and a water, please."

The cashier delivered the order quickly. At a table in the corner, John set their coffees down while Vivian withdrew a small yellow box from her bag. Dramamine. She popped two pills from a blister pack and swallowed them with her coffee.

"Do you get seasick?" he asked.

Outside, sunlight silvered the water's hypnotic ripples.

"Big-time. Carsick, too, if the roads are especially twisty. Our jaunt with Lisa upset my stomach, and I'd rather not spew in public. Since my senior prom, I always carry it with me."

"How does a prom cause motion sickness?"

She dropped the box back in her bag. "Mine was on the *Spirit of Baltimore*—it's a dinner cruise ship that can be rented for special occasions. I vomited prolifically during 'Call Me Maybe.' That song still makes me queasy, which is a shame since it's a bop."

Mental note to never play that song around her.

"Where'd you go to high school?"

"Parkville Senior High, home of the mighty Knights. What about you?" She uncapped her coffee and blew on it, then sipped. "Any good prom stories?"

"Nope. We were living in Marseille when I was in high school. No proms in France."

She had a tiny drop of coffee lingering on her bottom lip. He was desperate to wipe it away, but that would be too intimate. Instead, he gestured to his own mouth. "You've got a little..."

The drag of her tongue over her lip sent a lusty zing through him.

"Thanks. Who would you have taken if dances were a thing?" she asked.

He buried his face in his coffee. "My high school girlfriend—Genevieve Alarie."

"Is her last name spelled A-L-A-R-I-E?"

"Yes, why?"

"Wow, you are *blushing*."

He touched his strangely smooth cheek. "No, I'm not."

"Spiritually, I mean." Vivian tapped on her phone, typed a few keys, then twisted it toward him. "Is this her?"

Gen smiled at him from Vivian's phone. The years had been kind to her. Same sparkle in her eyes, same wide smile. And, right on cue, shame gnawed at him like it did every time he thought about his first girlfriend.

"That's her."

"I'm surprised you don't follow her." Vivian scrolled through the social media pics. "Good for teenage you. She's beautiful. And takes lots of shots of coffees and sandwiches."

"Her family runs a café."

Vivian rested her chin on her fists. "Was she your first love?"

"First everything." He thumbed the cleft in his chin. "But we lost touch. Have you ever handled a situation so poorly you wished you could go back in time and redo it?"

"Uh, yeah." She tick-tocked her eyes. Oh, yeah. "I can relate. What happened?"

"Things were great for the first six months, but Gen... I'm an asshole for saying this, but she was clingy. Wanted me to spend all my free time with her. But I don't work that way. I need space. A little solitude."

"Which I definitely gave you." She quirked her lips. "Sorry.

I retract that statement. For the obvious reasons, none of which I can say in an open environment. Continue."

"There's not much more to the story. Let's just say I handled the breakup poorly."

"Is that a pattern of yours?"

The fuck? He leaned back in his chair. "My reaction to your revelation and being strapped to a lie detector was pretty tame, all things considered."

"Shhh." She circled her gaze around the ferry. "Sorry. Also retracted. Let's stop talking and fill out our customs declarations. Just a heads-up—the first time you write a different name feels weird, but you get used to it."

She dropped the forms and some pens on the table.

He picked up the fountain pen.

"Oh, shit. Not that one." She yanked it from his grip. "Here's a normie pen."

She slid a Bic across the table. This was the first time he'd ruffled Vivian's feathers since they started this adventure. It was kind of fun.

"Was the other one a bomb?" he asked. "Switchblade?"

"Jesus." She winced. "Just fill out the damn form, please. And stop grinning."

He clicked the Bic. By the second letter of his first name, he'd messed up the customs card. He was filling this out as Jason Jones, not John Seymour. He turned the *o* into an *a*.

Vivian was right—this was weird, but the rest of the form was easier.

"Done," he said as he signed Jason Jones's name.

"Me too." Vivian's card was filled with the same spiky handwriting as the love notes she left him whenever she went on a business trip. "Let's get our passports stamped. The line'll be longer in Gibraltar."

She rose from the table and descended the central staircase. The short line for customs was near the observation deck.

"Passport and customs form, please." The customs official greeted them with a smile. "What brings you to Gibraltar?"

"Our honeymoon." Vivian handed over the forms and their passports.

A half-truth, the kind she'd said made it easier to escape detection.

"Congratulations." The official paged through the paperwork, then compared passport photos to the people standing in front of him. "How long will you be in Gibraltar?"

"We're only here today, then renting a car and driving to Málaga," she answered. "Do you need to see our hotel reservations?"

John shifted his weight. They hadn't made reservations.

"No need. Enjoy your time in Gibraltar."

The stamp in their passports echoed like cannon fire in his heart. He couldn't say if it was celebratory or more of a firing squad situation since he'd just deceived a government official.

Vivian collected their documents. "We will, thank you."

Off to the side, as his blood pressure returned to normal, Vivian tilted her head.

"You look pale. Want to catch some fresh air on the observation deck?"

He nodded. Outside, they circled to the port side. His heart lifted as they came face-to-face with an enormous mountain peak that seemed to spring straight up from the ocean.

"Holy shit. That's the Rock of Gibraltar." He shaded his eyes. "It's pointy."

Vivian leaned against the railing. "I was expecting awe at one of the world's most famous natural wonders, but I'll take *pointy*."

Acrid cigarette smoke drifted past them.

Vivian wrinkled her nose. "I'd rather enjoy the view upwind, actually."

They rounded a corner, and Vivian stopped cold. As he collided with her, she flung out her arm and pushed him back. "It's her."

"Her who?"

Her brow was cranked low. "Lola."

Vivian palmed her neck. Of all the dumb fucking luck. Hours and hours of internet and dark web research, and they'd ended up on the same ferry as Lola Vorlicek.

"She looks pissed," John said.

He was correct, but they'd never know why. Eavesdropping wasn't possible. Among the ferry's motors, the Straits of Gibraltar crashing against the hull, and the wind, she'd be lucky if she picked up Lola's tone, let alone words.

"We have to follow her," she said to John. "We'll learn more before heading to Monaco. Forewarned is forearmed. Total win."

"You have a strange definition of winning."

"You're not the first person to say that."

The ferry slowed, crawling toward the British colony's pier. Lola descended the stairs. Vivian reached back for John's hand and squeezed.

It was go time.

Thankfully Lola's bleached blond pixie cut was like a neon sign. She must like attention. Unlike herself, who did her best work when people didn't see her coming.

She tugged John to the left.

The ferry docked at a pier where British flags proudly waved. A crew quickly moored the ship and attached a gangplank. Travelers thickened around them, clogging the exit as everyone pushed toward the ramp. Alone, she could slither and slide through the crowd, but this was harder with a partner in tow.

Lola's blond head bobbed through the crowd.

Inside the port building, everyone waited to have their bags scanned and their passports checked. Lola wove through everyone like a ballerina, goddammit, and joined a line.

Vivian chucked her bag in a bin on the conveyor belt.

The security guard waved Vivian through the metal detector.

On the other side, she collected her bag and waited for John. *Come on, come on, come on.* Lola's line was slower than theirs, but Vivian couldn't move until John was through, and…

Fuck. He triggered a loud beep.

The security guard directed him to a separate area. John executed a perfect imitation of the *Vitruvian Man*. The guard's metal-detecting wand squealed over his pocket.

His Zippo.

The security guard pitched the lighter into a bin of confiscated items and waved John forward. Except John didn't move. Nope, he was now arguing with the security guard.

Lola cleared security. Time was of the essence.

"Excuse me?" Vivian used her damsel-in-distress voice, which worked best with security guards. "I'm sorry my husband forgot about his lighter, but it's a precious family heirloom. Is there a fine we can pay to keep it? Would five hundred euros be enough?"

Yes, she was attempting to bribe an official.

But she was trying to make this go as fast as possible, and money was a lubricant. There was no way John was leaving this building without his lighter. She was as certain of that as she was of Rocksy's true identity.

"Ma'am?" the guard asked.

"I'm sorry. The fine must be six hundred euros?"

The guard shifted his eyes between them. "It's actually seven hundred euros."

"Of course it is." She reached into her bag, then handed seven green notes to the guard.

He pocketed the cash. "Next time, don't bring it, or run it through the scanner in a bag."

"Next time?" John murmured. "I'm never doing this again."

Where had Lola—ooh, there—at the taxi stand.

Vivian grabbed John's hand and tugged. "Come on."

Two people stood between them and Lola. Closer than she'd like. They hadn't met, but Lola was bound to recognize her.

Her ego wasn't inflated—any protégée of Jean-Michel's would perform due diligence.

Please let the red hair and sunglasses be disguise enough.

A line of taxis rumbled as they waited to scoop up passengers. If Vivian wasn't mistaken, Lola's cream polo sweater and asymmetric satin skirt were both from Givenchy's spring line from last year.

Lola had money.

The taxi stand operator opened the door to a yellow cab. Lola ducked inside.

Soon the operator opened the rear door of a cab for her and John.

After John and she scooted inside, she addressed the driver. "Hi. What's your name?"

"Nico," he said with a mostly British accent.

"See that cab, Nico?" She pointed at Lola's taxi. "Two ahead of us and on the left? We met a woman on the ferry, and she forgot her scarf."

"You want me to chase her around Gibraltar for a scarf?"

"I'm a giver," Vivian said.

The taxi driver shrugged. "It's your dime."

As they left the port and merged into the traffic, boldly colored high-rises stood in the distance. A red double-decker bus passed them, and people on scooters buzzed between the traffic lanes. Beyond the high-rises, the Rock of Gibraltar dominated the vista.

"Have you been to Gibraltar before?" John asked.

The agency periodically used it as a midpoint meeting location for officers active in North Africa and Europe.

"Once." She held the handle above her door as the taxi sped around a roundabout. Good thing she'd dosed herself with Dramamine on the ferry earlier.

Nico followed Lola's cab toward the airport, but traffic ground to a halt.

"Why are we stopping?" she asked.

"An arriving flight," Nico said.

A huge passenger airplane rolled across the four-lane highway that wound through Gibraltar. As its tail disappeared, the lights turned green.

John craned his neck out the window. "Does that happen whenever a flight arrives?"

"Departures as well, but there are only eight flights per day. The inconvenience is worth living in paradise."

Lola's taxi stopped in front of the small airport's main entrance.

"Can you let us out here?" Vivian asked.

Their taxi driver complied and shared his price.

"You were amazing, Nico." Vivian added a hundred percent tip, then thrust the bills through the window.

"Thanks, love." He handed her his card. "If you need another ride, be sure to call."

Out on the curb, John asked, "Was the cabbie hitting on you?"

"Possibly, but he mostly wants repeat business from a good tipper." Vivian slipped her backpack onto her shoulders. "Let's go."

Among the gleam of polished floors and chrome inside the airport, she spotted Lola in the security line for British Airways.

"Take a selfie?" Vivian slung her arm around John's waist, then pivoted them until Lola was in her view.

She snapped a few in burst mode, then pivoted again to document the departures display. Hmm… All flights went to England or Spain.

"So we're not bulldozing through security to interrogate her?" John asked.

"We can if you want," she said. "I'd like to avoid international security incidents, personally. But if you prefer…"

"Nope, I'm good," he said.

They pushed back through the doors to the warm Gibraltar air.

"You said something about renting a car?" John asked.

"Yes." She paused and withdrew her tablet from her bag, then patted the seat next to her. "We're here, and this is Monte Carlo. The charity auction's tomorrow night, so we have enough time to drive. It's the best way to get there."

The route between here and there lit up on the map.

"Eighteen hours?" John peered at the tablet. "In a car? In one day?"

"There are too many cameras and passport checks in airports. And a road trip'll be fun. I'll get us the most luxurious car on the lot and irresponsible snacks."

"I can always be persuaded with snacks." John tipped his head back as they walked toward the rental car facility. "I think I've been here before. Oh, *monkeys*."

She snapped her gaze to him. "What?"

"Monkeys." He pointed to a poster featuring the pensive face of a Barbary macaque. "I was obsessed with monkeys when I was five, and I'm pretty sure my parents brought me here."

She squeezed his hand. "That's adorable."

Sometimes, playing the besotted honeymooner was easier than she liked to admit.

Thirteen

John's knees ached. By his count, six and a half hours was way too long for a road trip without a break. He shifted in the tiny red car's passenger seat.

"You can move to the back," Vivian said. "So you can stretch your legs? Sorry about the car. I needed an automatic if we're taking turns, and this is all they had."

Because he couldn't drive a manual.

"Nah." He gestured to a blue sign with the image of a person sitting under a tree. "There's a rest area ahead, though. Can we stop?"

Vivian pursed her lips. "Yeah, okay. We need gas anyway."

"And to eat."

She laughed. "Yes, John, and to eat."

As they drove deeper into Spain, picturesque coastal areas had morphed into the grasslands. From there they entered mountains, a desert, and then back to mountains. Windmills sprang like redwoods from the hills, their blades lazily turning in the wind. Over the last hour, John's ears had popped as they descended onto this flat highway.

"We've got snacks in the back if you're desperate." She touched his knee, which sent a jolt straight up his leg.

"If you hand me another protein bar, I'll throw it out the window."

She flicked her indicator and exited the A-4, following signs around a loop that delivered them to the Abades Puerta Andalucía service area.

John laughed as the building came into view. "Popeye's and Tim Horton's?"

"Globalization, baby." She parked at a gas pump tucked next to the rest area.

"Look." He pointed to a kiosk for prepaid phone cards and a bank of pay phones bordering the building. "It's a sign we're supposed to stop here."

"I'll be able to check in with MacColl."

He was happy to see pleasure in her eyes.

"I'll pump." Knees, elbows, ankles—all his joints protested as he unfolded himself from the car. He stretched and twisted as the tank filled. Even the rest areas around here were beautiful. Rolling hills, bright green trees and a sky as blue as the sapphire in Vivian's ring.

After the pump clicked off, they parked under a covered space and entered the building.

As a person who lived on the East Coast and visited friends up and down the I-95 corridor, he'd been to his fair share of rest areas. This one stopped him in his tracks.

"It's like a White Stripes fever dream," Vivian said.

Everything was black, white or red. Besides the quick service restaurants, it contained a self-service convenience store, a gift shop, a live cooking station, a deli, a coffee shop and a tapas restaurant.

Bingo.

"Can we please eat there?" He pointed to the tapas restaurant.

Vivian scoped out the busy scene. "No."

"Are you denying us tapas in *Spain*?" John eyed her. "That's cruel."

"There are too many people in here. But…" She glanced at the robust list of offerings posted at the entryway. "Compromise—carryout?"

He could live with that. "Deal."

At the front of the line, Vivian ordered in halting Spanish.

The cashier lowered her brows. "¿Perdóneme?"

John stepped forward and cleared his throat. In fluid Spanish, he said, "We're on our honeymoon and want to picnic outside. Do you do carryout?"

The hostess's face lit up. "Sí, señor. And congratulations!"

"Muchas gracias." He ordered a half-dozen small plates, all the things Vivian loved, then added three more because he'd hate to leave hungry. After he finished, the hostess stepped away to give the order to the kitchen.

Vivian raised her eyebrows. "When you said you speak Spanish, I thought that meant you took it in high school, not that you're fluent."

Looks like he wasn't the only one who made assumptions.

"Half my crew speaks Spanish. Makes my life easier to keep up with it." He shifted his weight. "Hey, I need to hit the bathroom."

She docked herself outside the bathroom. "Yell if anyone tries to grab you."

He opened the door to the bathroom. "You're not gonna stand there, are you?"

She tilted her head. "We've lived together for six months. I've heard things."

"I could've gone my whole life without knowing that."

She lifted a shoulder. "If it helps, you're the least gross human I know."

Nope, he was still mortified. Game face, though.

"Now there's a vow. 'I promise to pretend to never hear you use the toilet.'"

As she laughed, he disappeared inside the bathroom. Exhilarating as their last few days had been, he understood why Vivian wanted to sleep in after returning from a trip abroad. Always on guard, at risk of missing planes, trains or ferries, literally running from bad guys.

This shit was exhausting.

After washing up, he returned to the hallway to find Vivian leaning against the wall with her eyes closed. Affection thudded through him. This poor woman. Come hell or high water, no matter how much she protested, he'd make sure she slept tonight.

"Hey," he said. "I'll wait for the food if you want to freshen up."

Her eyes flew open. "What? Oh, yeah. Thanks."

A minute later, the hostess beckoned to him.

"Congratulations again." She handed him a heavy paper sack that smelled like heaven. "You make a lovely couple."

"Gracias," he said.

They *did* make a lovely couple. And now that he knew her secrets, they could rebuild trust. He meant what he told Beverly back at the office. Love doesn't shut off. He loved Vivian as much as he had Jane. Possibly more.

Which felt like cheating…but not?

"Is that our picnic?" Vivian said from behind him.

He shook the food in the bag.

"Sorry." She clapped a hand over her mouth. "I always startle you."

"It's fine. There's no reason sudden movements or voices behind me should scare me." He lifted the bag. "Let's go eat."

Most people remained inside because it was easily a hundred degrees today. But it was better for them to stay away from the crowd. On a lonely table in the picnic area next to the building, they spread out their takeaway containers.

This was the best moment of this trip, hands down.

Without much conversation, they gorged themselves on chorizo, Iberian ham, Manchego, deep-fried chipirones with a fresh squeeze of lemon, and piquillo peppers stuffed with goat cheese. Vivian's appreciative moans were music to his ears.

The picnic table provided excellent cover for her effect on him.

"You win." She stuffed a wedge of napkins into her mysterious, potentially lethal Mary Poppins bag. "That was better than a protein bar."

"Hey, I've been meaning to ask—can you walk me through your gadget stash? I don't want to accidentally poison you with an arsenic toothpick."

"I don't carry poison in my bag," she said.

"What about the EpiPens?"

"They aren't poison." She sipped her lemonade. "I'll show you, but you can't mess with any of it. Some of this costs more than your house."

"My parents' house, but point taken."

Carefully, she withdrew items from the bag and laid them in a row.

"In no particular order…" From a velvet envelope, she withdrew a necklace with a quarter-sized pendant. "This is a camera. I get better pictures with this than my camera glasses because frequently, men stare at breasts." She held up a pair of tortoise-shell frames. "And look past a woman wearing these."

"That's sexist."

"I unfortunately have data to back it up. The glasses are also infrared, so they're handy in the dark." She returned the necklace and glasses to the bag, then held up a red piece of metal. "This is a portable door lock for extra hotel security."

His spine stiffened. This woman was all of five-seven and a buck-fifty. She was out there in the world with nothing but this bag of toys and her wits.

Terrifying.

She continued identifying things as she shoved them back in the bag. "Perfume atomizer filled with chloroform. Privacy pen that detects bugs—that's the one I took from you on the ferry. Lipstick from Coco. Vape pen."

He rolled it between his thumb and forefinger. "You said you quit smoking."

"I did." She plucked the device from his grip and tossed it in the bag. "But people say crazy shit on their smoke breaks, so I like to have the option."

"What about this?" He lifted a handkerchief. "Is it a secret gun?"

"Nope. Just a handkerchief." She returned it to the bag. "I *can* handle a gun if I need to carry, but the restrictions in most countries make them a pain in the ass. And I prefer up-close-and-personal defense. Better chance I'm actually taking out the intended target. James Bond, Ethan Hunt, and Sydney Bristow would've been suspended for excessive gunplay."

John popped the last fried baby squid into his mouth. "What else do you have in there?"

"This." She held up a red plastic box with a white cross on the front of it. "First-aid kit. Band-Aids, pain pills, Neosporin, butterfly stitches, et cetera. Those are all the real deal, but the EpiPens are my, uh, special vintage."

"Is that everything?" he asked. He was grateful for the walk-through. If he avoided chloroforming or propofoling himself, he'd be fine.

"I think…oh, wait." Vivian winced. "I lied about the poison thing."

He coughed on the squid. "Oh?"

She lifted the pendant of the necklace she always wore when she traveled. In that first month they dated, she said it had belonged to her dead mother and was her good luck charm. Her story had prompted him to talk about his Zippo.

"This is my L-Pill. It's a cyanide capsule in case I get captured by very bad people."

The blood in his veins chilled. "Jesus, Vivian."

She draped her hand over his. "Don't worry. I'd never actually use it. It's just protocol to keep it handy while I'm in the field."

He wanted to yank it from her neck and throw it in the dumpster.

Based on John's bulging jaw muscles, he wasn't happy about the L-Pill. Fuck, *she* wasn't happy about it and tried not to let her potential capture and demise get to her.

Vivian stood up and collected their trash. "I'll pitch this and make the pay phone call we talked about. Could you keep an eye on the car?"

"Sure you don't want me to come with?"

"I don't know what'll come up in the call, so it's best if you stay here."

He nodded.

The truth was, she didn't want him to hear her be a piece of shit to her family again. After sorting their meal's remnants into the correct trash, compost and recycling bins, she stopped at the kiosk and bought two tarjetas prepagadas.

The first call would be the hard one.

Torrey picked up on the second ring.

"Let me guess," her younger sister said. "Due to your fucked-up priorities, you won't make it to Mom's retirement party next weekend? Alaina'll be pissed."

Vivian leaned against the divider between the phones. "How'd you know it was me?"

"Caller ID told me Spain was calling. While I intend to be courted by a minor Spanish noble in my life, the safer bet was you. Don't dodge the question about Mom's party."

Vivian fiddled with the phone's metal cord. "I hope I can make it."

"You're lucky you can claim you're saving the world," she said. "Otherwise you'd be here with me crafting the macramé centerpieces Mom wants."

Her family knowing where she worked was a blessing and a curse. A blessing because it gave her a pass from family events when she was on mission, and a curse because her brothers harassed her for intel on aliens, Bigfoot, and the JFK assassination.

"Macramé?" she asked.

"Mac. Ra. Mé. It's very seventies-chic. If she knew how much I could charge her based on my current artist's rate, she'd shit a brick. But I'll churn out artisanal table number holders for free like the devoted daughter I am."

"Speaking of artist's rates… Did you read about the Rocksy

auction in London? And do we think the artist has any other stunts up their sleeve?"

"Not today," Torrey said. "Hey, how's John?"

Currently he was perched on the picnic table's bench, elbows resting against the tabletop, head bent back and soaking up the warm Spanish sun.

God, she wanted to lick his neck.

She twiddled the engagement ring. "He's with me, actually."

"In *Spain*? I am chin-hands. Spill."

"It's complicated." Her stomach sizzled. "We got engaged, and—"

Vivian held the phone away from her ear as Torrey screeched.

"Vivian Bernardita Flint, come home and introduce him to the family."

Vivian's heart clenched. "I'll try. The big reveal upset him, so we're…unengaged."

"Wait, wait, wait. Do I hear *doubt* in your voice? Hang on, I need to put down my scissors." A clunk sounded in the background. "Viv, he must be amazing because you picked him. But do not—*do not*—sell yourself short. Who was the valedictorian of her high school?"

"Me," Vivian said.

"And who graduated summa cum laude from Georgetown Fucking University?"

"Also me." Her lips twitched with a grin.

"Who was recruited to work for the sneakiest shadow organization in the US before she could legally rent a car?"

The wobble left her voice. "Me."

"And who, because she was working two jobs, was able to pay her outrageously talented but cash-strapped younger sister's Maryland Institute College of Art tuition, and will therefore always have a ride-or-die hype man in her back pocket?"

"Me," Vivian laughed.

"If you're all those things, can kick ass, crack a joke, and look hot as hell while doing it? I'd leave your doubts behind.

If he's half as smart as you say he is, he'll come around. And if he doesn't, good fucking riddance."

She swiped a tear from her eye. "Thanks, Torrey. I needed that."

"Anytime. Call me as soon as you're home from saving the world, okay? Love you."

"Love you too." Vivian hung up, released a deep breath, then dipped in the second phone card. She dialed the number she'd dialed a thousand times over the years.

"Speak," MacColl barked.

She choked back a sob. After the office attack, she'd feared the worst.

"It's Canvas, Boss. I picked up some palette knives."

"About fucking time." His voice was raspy. "I can't share details while you're on this line. Are you in the vicinity we discussed?"

She hesitated. But this was MacColl. He was a prickly grump, yes, but he kept everyone in her division alive for the ten years she'd been working with him. She trusted him. "Yes, with Brawn."

"Good," he grunted.

From an average person, *good* was faint praise. From MacColl? Angels flourished trumpets.

"Get your asses to Lump by 9:00 a.m. tomorrow. My contacts will expect you. Don't call me on this number until you're in a SCIF and we can VTC."

The line went dead.

Lump was the agency nickname for the US Consulate in Marseille. Video teleconferencing—VTC—in a sensitive compartmented information facility—SCIF—meant MacColl had intel to share.

Which was either good or terrifying.

She pinched the bridge of her nose. MacColl had said *asses*. She needed to bring John to the consulate with her. Which meant the MacColl wanted to question him, use him or both. She marched back to the picnic table.

"I got in touch with my boss. He wants us to go to Marseille tonight."

He lifted his sunglasses. "Any other news? Is everyone okay? And what's in Marseille?"

"A secure line. That's all I know. He'll tell me more once we're there." She covered a surprise yawn. "Sorry."

He rose from the table. "Don't be sorry. You're tired. I'll drive the next leg."

"I'm fine to drive." Another yawn overwhelmed her.

"Agree to disagree. I'd rather not fly off a cliff, and I lived in Marseille, remember? It'll be a sort of homecoming."

When Bossy John showed up, it was best not to argue. After another yawn, she handed him the keys. "Okay, you drive. I have work to do, anyway."

John unlocked their tin can of a car. "Or you could sleep."

"We'll see." She settled into the passenger seat and fired up her tablet. She needed to check her assets' coffee cards. Among the half-dozen accounts, no one besides Amina had bought coffee recently. No news didn't necessarily mean good news.

She rubbed her L-Pill necklace.

What was Jean-Michel thinking?

Bioweapons intelligence was a level of crime for which he was unprepared. Especially since his goons were not top-tier talent. She searched for more information on Lola, but there wasn't much. In the *Vogue France* charity soirée photo currently enlarged on Vivian's tablet, Lola stared at Jean-Michel with cool adoration. Was he grooming Lola to take over his "business" like he once tried to do with her?

John lowered the radio's volume. "Did you love him?"

No point in dodging the question.

"Not at first. Then I thought I did, which shouldn't have happened. The relationship got messy, so I broke it off as unmessily as I could. Then you and I met, and I realized I hadn't known what actual love was."

His hands tightened on the wheel.

Oof. That was too much truth. If she could have disappeared, she would.

"Forget I said anything. Wipe it from your brain."

"I'm glad you told me," he said. "Maybe he's using Lola, too?"

"In all likelihood, yes. But last night's research…wait."

Her synapses flared. Lola's discreet business card had a Monaco number. A pattern was emerging from the messy information swirling around her brain. She added search terms and an intricate combination of quotes and plus signs to narrow the results.

Scan the resulting links, and… Bin-fucking-go.

"Find something?" John asked. "You're jiggling your knees like you won trivia night."

"The Casino d'Or's annual donor report from last year announced a new assistant curator for their gallery. Lola Vorlicek, from Croatia. *She's* his way into the Monte Carlo market."

"He'd use her for access?"

"He'd use his *grandmother* for access. Did, actually. He hocked a few of her lesser impressionist paintings when he flunked out of college. Rather than press charges and be a scandal in the gossip columns, she quietly cut him from the will. People still place stock in his family name, though."

"If that's why Jean-Michel's with her, why would she go after your clients?" John scratched at his jaw.

When he'd had a beard, that gesture made a raspy sound she adored.

Vivian lifted a shoulder. "Because my ex is petty. I can see a universe where he's using her to hit me in the proverbial pocket. Me breaking up with him wounded his pride. My peripheral involvement with the Rocksy prank might've pushed him over the edge."

"Sounds like a prize," John said.

"Which is why I broke up with him. Lola must've had a hand in the Monte Carlo charity auction at Casino d'Or tomorrow night, but she might not know what he's up to with the drives. He's greedy and doesn't like to share."

She searched for the provenance for Jean-Michel's other recent sales.

Nothing shady. Nothing *obviously* shady, anyway.

"Is today only Monday?" John ran his hand through his hair. "It feels like it's been a month since we left the States."

And since they got engaged. Which she would not mention.

"It's the new experience phenomenon." She rubbed her eyes. The midafternoon sun was making her sleepy. "Time seems to slow while our brains log details. Like the sandwich you had this morning. You probably paid more attention to it than you would your thousandth bacon, egg and cheddar from Wisemiller's. First times are exciting because our brains are busy with new information."

"Maybe. I mean, the tosta mista was outstanding, but I still love a bacon, egg and cheddar." Light rain speckled the windshield. He flicked on the wipers. "There's beauty in the familiar, too. That's what contentedness is. Finding the beauty, newness and joy in the familiar. If you can't do that, you might just be chasing a high."

Vivian whipped her gaze toward him. "Are we still talking about sandwiches?"

His Adam's apple bobbed. "The sandwiches are symbolic."

"I need that on a T-shirt," she said.

As they drove around another bend, sapphire water winked at them in the distance.

"Is that the Mediterranean?" John asked.

She glanced at the map on the GPS display. "No, it's the Iberian Sea."

She startled as John groaned and thumped the steering wheel.

"Do you have beef with the Iberian Sea?" she asked.

"No, my parents. I could've been traveling and seeing things like that—" he gestured toward the sparkling sea "—for years."

She'd never put her finger on the problem John had with his parents.

They seemed like lovely people. Friendly, funny, warm. But "Jane" hadn't asked John about his distance with them because that might have encouraged him to ask about her supposedly deceased parents. It had been best to avoid those conversations as much as possible.

But now that he knew everything, she could be nosy.

"Why don't you visit them?" she asked.

"Because I resented the sacrifices their career required of me when I was a kid, so I didn't want to enjoy the perks as an adult. I sort of thought of it as a betrayal of my younger self. Which I now regret." He gestured to the view. "I mean, look at this."

Ah, this she understood. She and regret were good friends.

"Can I offer you advice?" She dug her knuckles into her itchy eyes. "Regret doesn't change the past. It is, however, a kick in the ass to handle things differently in the future. Once you figure that out, the regret has served its purpose, and you can move on. Don't wallow."

"And I need *that* on a T-shirt."

She lifted a shoulder. "Might be too many words."

"T-shirts have two sides." He rested his hand on her upper thigh like he normally did during their road trips. She placed her hand on top of his.

The location was new, but the gesture was familiar, beautiful.

And for now, in the quiet bubble of this car with John, she was content.

Fourteen

The dashboard display glared 12:00 a.m.

Midnight. Officially Tuesday, their fourth day on the run. For the past few hours, Vivian had slept. The quiet had given John a chance to roll her advice around in his head.

Regret *was* a kick in the ass. One he needed.

The woman next to him was all go-go-go, and since college, he was all stay-stay-stay. Then he met Vivian. If her offices hadn't been attacked, he would've stuck with his knee-jerk reaction and remained broken up.

And he would have missed out on the most invigorating days of his life.

As he exited the highway, Vivian stirred.

"Ungh." She scrubbed her eyes with her palms. "Sorry. I didn't mean to sleep for that long. Naps are the worst."

"Incorrect. Naps are objectively awesome."

"Agree to disagree. Where are we?"

"Just arrived in Marseille."

Nostalgia tugged his insides as he threaded through the neighborhoods. Haussmann-style buildings, with their cream-colored stone fronts and intricate wrought-iron Juliet balconies, lined the roads. He'd visited friends in these buildings, gotten his hair cut over there, taken Gen on a date at that cinema. As the tiny Citroën bounced over the picturesque street's cobblestones, his teeth rattled.

"Bet an SUV would be nice on these roads," he said.

"Blending," she answered.

On the circle's other side, the road turned smooth again.

Here, more cars and scooters huddled outside establishments. Despite the late hour, tourists milled about. Inexpensive quick-service joints stood shoulder to shoulder with Michelin-starred restaurants.

The fancy places were unknown to him.

Les Burgers de Papa, though? He could taste their cheeseburgers. His high school best friend, Timothée, had been horrified and impressed by the number he could put away.

"We hang a right at the next light," she said.

They entered another cobblestone circle, then pulled into Hôtel La Residence Du Vieux Port's valet circle. Many flags, including the US's, sprouted above its entryway.

"Bonsoir." John handed the keys to the attendant. "We're checking in."

"Very good, sir." The valet gave John a claim ticket from his booklet. "Enjoy your stay."

They'd enjoy their stay, all right, starting with a full eight hours of sleep in an actual bed. A body couldn't run on adrenaline and coffee forever. Although if Vivian made a move, he'd happily cut back on his sleep.

After check-in, they opened the door to…the tiniest room he'd ever seen.

"Is this a closet?" If he stretched, he *might* be able to touch both ends at the same time.

The view was nice, though. The room's picture window framed the city's famed port, and amber dots of light glowed within the village across the quay. Above it all, on the hill, stood Notre-Dame de la Garde.

"It's all I could get last minute." Vivian shut the door. "Welcome to home sweet-next-eight-hours home. You take the bed."

"And you'll sleep where, the floor? We can both take the bed."

"Okay, thanks." She rustled in her bag and withdrew the not-actually-a-fountain pen, then tossed her bag on the desk. "Help me lift the mattress?"

He joined her side and lifted. "Why are we doing this?"

"To check for bugs." She shone her phone's flashlight between the mattress and the box spring, then ran the pen over its surface. "Both bed and otherwise."

"I don't like either option."

"Me neither, but this isn't a trusted place, so I need to go through the normal checks."

She opened drawers, then traced her fingers along the picture window's edges. Next she took the privacy pen from her bag and carefully scanned walls and furniture like a ghost hunter searching for spirits.

"All clear. But let's still behave as though extra ears are around?"

"Okay," he said. "Need help with anything else?"

"I've got one more thing to do. Then we're secure." She extracted the extra door lock from her bag. After fitting it onto the strike plate, she secured it and flipped the hotel's safety lock as well.

"There." She dusted her hands together, then flicked off the room's overhead light, plunging them into mostly dark.

The city's ambient glow seeped through the window.

Fatigue swamped him. He kicked off his shoes, then sat on the bed. "I should shower."

The bed bounced as Vivian sat on the opposite side. "Me too."

He lay back. "Or at least wash my face."

"Yeah." She curled on her side like a shrimp, her favorite sleeping position.

His joints and muscles throbbed. "Most of me hurts."

"There are pain pills in the first-aid kit."

"Okay." He weighed a thousand pounds. "Do you need any?"

Her soft, rhythmic breathing answered him.

He smiled to himself. A small victory. He *knew* she was exhausted.

As for himself… He'd lie here for five minutes, then dig through her bag for the pain medication. With a Herculean effort, he sat up and pulled the neatly folded red blanket from the foot of the bed and spread it over Vivian and himself.

Five minutes.

Damn. That was *not* five minutes. Sunlight streamed through the window, and he had a warm armful of woman. No wonder he'd slept like a brick.

He always slept better with her by his side.

All he wanted was to wrap his arms around her and hide in the cocoon of this hotel. Let someone stop the bad people chasing bioweapons lab information. But Viv wasn't made that way. If she could do something about a problem, she *would* do something about a problem.

The responsible thing to do was help her.

His stomach growled.

Vivian quaked in his arms.

"How long've you been awake?" he asked.

She delicately twisted out of his grip. "Long enough to decide what I want for breakfast."

"Which is…?"

"Whatever Genevieve's café serves."

"Hard pass." He threw his forearm over his eyes.

Gen was a one-way ticket to a past version of himself he'd like to forget.

"Hard pass noted and disregarded." She peeled his forearm away. A week ago, this would've triggered a wrestling match ending with her naked and him buried between her thighs.

Don't go there.

"Spill," she said.

He'd loved her brown hair, but this fiery red suited her personality better.

"*You* are insisting I can't keep something to myself?" he asked.

"I'm thick with irony." She sat back on her heels. "Come on. You'll feel better."

He sat up. "Okay, but don't think less of me."

"I solemnly swear not to think less of you." She held up her hand the way she must've when she swore her oath to the Constitution. "Now gimme the tea."

"Gen's family's café is near the consulate." He blew out his lips. "I stopped there all the time, and she always threw free macarons in my bag. I asked her out, and we became inseparable. Movies, walks in the park, Sunday dinner with each other's families."

Vivian flipped a palm to the ceiling. "This is wholesome and adorable."

"Haven't gotten to the bad part yet." He tented his knees and rested his folded forearms on them. "Not long after we began having sex, she started talking about how cute our kids would look, that her parents married young, and why wait if you found your person?"

Vivian widened her eyes. "Bet that put some ice in your balls."

"It did not. This is where you'll start to judge me. I knew we should break up, but I liked sex too much. I figured I'd wait it out since college would make us break up."

"This all sounds like standard teenager behavior."

"It was." He sighed. This was his biggest do-over wish. "Until Gen was accepted to UVA, too. When she surprised me with the incroyable news, I panicked and asked my best friend to break up with her for me."

"Oh." Vivian flattened her lips. "That's a weenie move."

He rubbed at the whiskers on his jaw. "It gets worse. I ignored her texts and calls. Figured I could hibernate. When she showed up at our house, my parents got involved and asked her parents to tell her to leave me alone."

Vivian searched his face. "Oh, John. I mean, kudos to you for feeling like an asshole about it, but you were just a kid."

"That's not an excuse."

"No, but it's a reason. And the silver lining is, fucking up a relationship teaches you to be better for your next person."

His gut lurched.

Next person? Was she talking about them, too? He didn't want to be better for someone else.

He wanted them to fix this and be better for each other.

Vivian pushed off the bed. "We're definitely skipping Gen's café. She might stab you with a cheese knife on sight. We'll just grab something after we visit the US Consulate."

John stiffened. "You didn't tell me we're going there."

"Did I not?" She furrowed her brow. "Sorry. That's where the secure line is. We have an appointment at 9:00 a.m. For 'notarial services.'"

He riffled his hair. "Some of my parents' old coworkers might still be there. The local staff, anyway. Will that be a problem?"

"Shouldn't be." She grabbed her bag. "Our appointment's under our real names because I don't fuck with embassy security. So if they recognize you, be your normal pleasant self. Catch up on old times."

Vivian closed the bathroom door.

He thumbed his chin and stared out the window. Despite the confession of his past bad behavior, he was in a great mood. All credit to a solid eight hours of sleep in a comfortable bed next to the woman he loved. Because he did love her. That love had been put under a lot of pressure, but it hadn't gone away. Every second that he'd spent with her since the attack at the office proved that to him.

The bathroom door opened. "Your turn. Do I look okay?"

His heart juddered. Ruby-red lips, the pashmina artfully wrapped around the outfit she'd somehow slept in without wrinkling, and sexy curls. Fuck, he wished they hadn't fallen asleep so fast last night.

"Not okay, amazing," he said. "I'm getting used to the red."

"Me too." She twiddled the wavy ends. "I haven't been red since I started at the agency."

"Why?"

She lifted a shoulder. "Brown blends."

"You think you didn't get a second look with brown hair?"

He paused in front of her on his way to the bathroom. "I looked twice."

She licked her lips. "Just twice?"

"Three times. Twenty. What's the right answer?"

"Twenty is good." She grinned. "Go wash up."

Inside the bathroom, he stared at his clean-shaven face. "You're in over your head."

After he washed up, they gathered their meager belongings from the room.

"Should we drive?" Vivian asked as they left the hotel.

"No, it's close enough to walk. Parking's a pain near the consulate anyway."

"I've never been to Marseille. Will you be my tour guide?" She gestured toward the monument in the middle of the traffic circle up ahead. "What's that?"

The name came to him despite not walking these streets for sixteen years.

"The column of Place Castellane."

"What's its significance?"

"Fuck if I know. But Timothée and I liked the statues."

She bumped shoulders with him. "The *topless* statues?"

"Hey, I appreciated the sculptors' skill." He steered them left again. "Why did you have to come to Marseille to make a secure call?"

"Probably because it's the closest one to Monaco. Most embassies have secure lines. Diplomats and CIA officers need them fairly frequently."

"Not a lot of CIA running around Marseille, though."

"I wouldn't be so confident," she said. "CIA officers are often provided diplomat aliases, and they report to the office just like State Department staff."

He believed her, but he couldn't imagine any of his parents' friends were CIA. They'd started a bowling league and exchanged cookies at Christmas. Across the street, the consulate's American flag flapped in the warm French breeze.

Vivian pressed the consulate gate's button.

A crackling voice answered, "How can I help you?"

"We're here for a 9:00 a.m. appointment," she said.

"Name?"

"Vivian Flint and John Seymour."

After a brief pause, the speaker crackled again. "One of our staff will be out to escort you into the building."

A small woman exited the front doors and greeted them at the gate. He didn't recognize her, but he hadn't expected to. Staff turned over routinely.

"Bienvenue." She opened the gate for them. "I'm Helane Fry."

After following her through the familiar wooden doors, John breathed deeply. The scent of this place was a time machine. Wood soap, linoleum wax and age.

At the security checkpoint, Vivian handed over her bag. Most of the items within were not permitted past security. John, however, was allowed to keep his Zippo.

"Please wait here." Helane gestured to a window seat overlooking the consulate's courtyard. "I'll return momentarily."

This was trippy—like what he was seeing was superimposed over his memories.

He rubbed his hands along his thighs.

"Everything okay?" Vivian asked.

"Yeah, it's just...this was the last tour my family did as a whole. After this one, I was in college. We've never traveled together again." He swallowed the lump in his throat. "Back then, I never stopped to enjoy being with them, and I can't get that life back."

She touched his wrist. "But remember—regret signals a change you can make."

Heels on the parquet floor heralded Helane's return. "Ms. Flint? It's time for your call."

Vivian bumped shoulders with John. "Be right back."

"You'd better," he said.

As Helane led her down a hall, professional jealousy pinballed through her. This was a century-old building with twelve-foot ceilings and barrels of natural light. HQ somehow managed to be both fluorescent-dim and blinding.

Helane opened a door. "We're connected from our end. The other line will join soon. Knock twice when you've finished."

She closed the door behind Vivian.

This was more like her home office. No windows, floor-to-ceiling foam sound absorption panels, and a camera affixed to the monitor dominating the wall opposite a small conference table. A sentence hovered on screen—*Waiting for the host to join*.

She sat and drummed her fingers. Four days on the run took a toll on her manicure.

The screen flared, then resolved on a larger-than-life MacColl.

"Jesus, Boss, are you okay?" He looked like ten miles of rough road. Below a butterfly bandage on his temple, a puce bruise mottled his cheek.

"Nothing a shit-ton of Advil can't handle. How 'bout you? Besides the dye job."

"Bruised and tired. Lawrence and Beverly okay?"

He nodded. "They sheltered in the panic room. I took the brunt before backup arrived. The threat had escaped by then."

"Any clues on who they were? Motivation?"

"Still digging into that. They wouldn't have gotten anything anyway. Why the fuck did you give me a flash drive full of wedding shit?"

Candor had always been the best policy with MacColl. "I mixed up the drives."

"Mixed up the—" He wiped his hand down his face. "Is your head in this, Canvas? Say the word and I'll send Winegrad. Matter of fact, I'll send him anyway. You need backup."

She folded her hands on the table. "Please don't. Winegrad solves everything with his fists. This action requires delicacy. Tact."

"Are you allergic to help?"

"Not at all. I've been calling in favors." Favors from people she wouldn't name. "Which is why we decrypted the London drive."

"What'd you find?"

"Bioweapons. The drive contained BSL-4 lab staff info. Names, addresses, phone numbers. It indicates it's one of three drives, all of which are embedded in artworks to be auctioned. The next one's in Monte Carlo—a charity auction tonight. I plan to be there."

MacColl nodded. "What do you need?"

She had a list ready to go. "Tickets to the event. A new ride—something comfortable. Clothes for me and Brawn. Casino d'Or blueprints, security shift change schedule and a housekeeping security badge. Oh, ceramic screwdrivers."

They were her favorite handy item that would pass through metal detectors unnoticed.

MacColl chewed his cheek. "You don't ask for much. Fiancé keeping up with you?"

She nodded. "Kept us from being nabbed in Casablanca. Twice."

"Use him to your advantage. He's a big guy, and Dilettante's a coward."

Dammit, this was what she was afraid of when MacColl told her to bring John to the consulate. Official involvement put him at risk.

"What if I think that's a bad idea?"

"No lone-wolfing it. It's your guy or Winegrad. You pick."

Under the table, she dug her nails into her palm. She'd be damned if some other agent took down Jean-Michel. She had a hand in making him the problem he was today.

She'd unmake him, too.

"Fine, I'll use Brawn," she said. "But I'll also need a phone connected to his alias's accounts. And, Boss, one more thing. After the scuffle at the office, I contacted Big Boss. She didn't recognize our code word. She wanted me to bring Brawn to HQ for debriefing."

He wrinkled his brow. "Wanted, or ordered?"

"Ordered."

"And you didn't." MacColl massaged his forehead. "Why'd I take a management job? 'It's time to give back,' I told myself. 'Mentor others.'"

"It felt off, Boss. Protocol dictates sending us to a safe house."

"I'll add it to the pile of shit I'm looking into. FYI, I've got a new emergency number. *Emergency* means you're held at gunpoint or have been kidnapped by aliens. Ready?"

He rattled off digits.

"Got it," she said.

"Good. Anything else?" MacColl asked.

Besides MacColl being right about John breaking up with her, and her attempts to win him back while thwarting bioweapons espionage?

"No, that's it."

"Cool your heels for an hour while the staff fulfills your shopping list." MacColl leaned forward into the camera. "And Canvas? Watch your back."

The screen went dark. She stood and knocked on the door twice.

Helane opened it. "Follow me, mademoiselle."

She led Vivian back to John. He stood before an enormous Joseph Garibaldi painting of Marseille's port. This artist deserved more renown. His work fell at the nexus of impressionism, cubism and realism, and evoked a dreamy romanticism of nineteenth-century Provence.

"Bonjour, Mr. Seymour," Helane said. "You like the painting?"

"Yes, but it should hang about three inches higher." He pointed to the empty space above the painting, and Vivian sucked in a breath. He'd rolled up his sleeves. "So it's at eye level for the greatest percentage of people."

From the start, they'd bonded over art. He was the most capable art handler she worked with. Humble, too. He had no idea how attractive competency, art appreciation and muscled forearms were.

"I'll make a note of it, sir." To both of them, Helane said, "In an hour, pick up your car from the hotel. Your new vehicle will contain your requests. May I escort you through the gate?"

"Please." John squeezed Vivian's hand three times.

Yes, indeed. She also wanted to go.

Their shoes scraped against the brick walkway as they followed Helane. After she closed the gate behind them and returned to the building, they strolled from the consulate.

A nice, even pace that wouldn't draw attention.

"How was the call?" John asked.

"Fine." Not many people nearby, but she'd be cautious. "He wants you in the mix in Monte Carlo, too. Nothing dangerous. I'm thinking you can snap photos of beautiful people at the charity soirée. Discreetly. Because Jason Jones is a subtle influencer."

"There's no such thing."

"I'm serious." She pulled up Jason Jones's Instagram and handed John the phone. "They did a fantastic job with his digital footprint. He's all about curated luxury with barely visible hints of himself. You see his hand, his hair, or a shot of his outfit, but never the whole package."

John scrolled Instagram. "God, I hate this guy."

"His followers love him."

They turned a corner down a narrow road ribboning among apartment buildings. In her periphery, she caught movement. A man rounded the corner onto the road as well. A man who, in white New Balance sneakers, aviator sunglasses and a Gore-Tex windbreaker, didn't blend. Maybe in a tourist area of DC, but definitely not in Marseille.

"Lean in for a selfie." She took her phone, snapped a photo of them, then enlarged it to inspect the background.

She'd bet a million dollars New Balance was a tail.

"We've got company. There's a café over there. We'll wait them out there. Plus, we haven't eaten. Two birds, one croissant."

"Okay, but not—"

The bell on the door tinkled. Obviously the best unintended pit stop ever because it smelled decadently of rich coffee and baked goods. A beautiful blonde pushed through the door to the kitchen. She blinked, then shifted her gaze from John, to Vivian, and back to John.

"Johnny?" the blonde said.

"Hey, Gen."

Whoops.

Fifteen

Patronizing his teenage sweetheart's café was *not* on John's agenda today.

Neither was being followed, but here they were.

Gen bounded around the counter and wrapped him in a hug. "It's been a lifetime!"

"You look great, Gen." She still smelled of cinnamon.

"So do you." She leaned back. "Unbelievable. You're a *man* now. And you've got an adorable crinkle between your eyebrows, here."

Gen tapped the delicate bridge of her nose.

Vivian cleared her throat. "Hi. I'm Jane, John's fiancée."

"This is wonderful!" Gen kissed Vivian's cheeks. "How long will you be in Marseille?"

"Just today," he said.

"Then I'm grateful you stopped by. Sit, sit, sit." She directed them to an intimate table tucked beneath the stairs. "What can I get you?"

This was so strange. "Gen, you don't—"

"How about your favorite savory crêpes and a latte?"

Warmth radiated through him. At Lisa's museum, he'd complained about Vivian noticing things about him. But she was right—being noticed was the first step to being known.

"That would be great, yes."

"And you, Jane?"

"An espresso and sweet crêpes, please?"

"Ah, the family specialty. My pleasure." Gen disappeared into the kitchen.

"She doesn't seem mad at you," Vivian said.

He raked his hand through his hair. "This is awkward."

"Sure is." Vivian snapped a napkin onto her lap. "But we can't go anywhere, so let's ride the awkward wave together, shall we?"

He envied Vivian's placid confidence.

Gen pushed through the kitchen doors, then worked the enormous copper espresso machine. After a minute of steam and froth, she brought two mugs and a demitasse to the table, along with a small dish of macarons.

Vivian popped one in her mouth.

Her moan was barely audible, but he caught it.

"The crêpes will be ready in a few minutes." Gen sat at the table with them. "You're in luck. My cousin is magic with crêpes. You remember Pierre, Johnny? You met him at my seventeenth birthday party."

After which they had sex for the first time. His cheeks heated. Ride an awkward wave? More like be swallowed by an awkward tsunami. If he didn't acknowledge the shitty breakup elephant in the room, he might pass out.

"Gen, I'm sorry," he blurted.

She wrinkled her brow. "For what?"

Vivian hid her smile behind her cup. "This is delicious."

He hoped she meant the macaron and espresso combo and not his apology attempt.

"When we broke up, I didn't treat you well."

Gen waved him off. "This is unnecessary. I was sad because you were my first love, eh? But the breakup allowed me to connect with my *true* love. Remember Timothée?"

John sat back in his chair. "My best friend?"

"*My* best friend." She winked. "He was kind when we broke up. Asked me out to cheer me up. And, blah blah blah, we've been married for twelve years and have eight-year-old twins."

A smile bubbled his cheeks. That sneaky little… Timothée had been their third wheel more times than he could count. In retrospect, he'd also been a little too quick to volunteer to be

John's messenger to Gen. His French friend must've been waiting to ask her out for ages. Good for them, because obviously things had worked out for the best.

The bad breakup burden he'd carried for years evaporated.

John lifted his mug. "À ta santé!"

The three of them clinked.

"What're your kids' names?" Vivian asked.

"Léa and Rose." Gen twisted her phone toward them. Two smiling mini-Gens peered at him. "They are different as night and day, but best friends. They've recently declared they are on a teeth-brushing strike."

"France's national sport."

Gen backhanded him gently. "You do not get to joke about France if you do not live here. I wish I could call Timothée and the girls over, but they are visiting his parents. Do you remember Louise and Félix? They retired to the Dordogne. And your parents? They are well?"

"Great," he said.

At least, he assumed so. It had been a minute since they'd spoken.

"Give them my best. Thomas as well. Unless he still likes to pop out of nowhere to startle you, in which case, lecture him on my behalf."

The bell over the door chimed.

"Pardon," Gen said. "I'll return shortly."

Vivian assessed the newcomer, then shook her head. This wasn't their tail.

"You doing okay?" She rested her hand on his.

"Yeah, actually." He rubbed his thumb against Vivian's. "Gen's clearly happy. I guess good things can come from bad endings. Thanks for making me come here."

"Personal growth is not the primary reason we ended up in your ex's café, but okay."

"Here we are." Gen sat a ham-and-brie crêpe in front of him, and a fruit-and-chocolate crêpe in front of Vivian. "You will feel as though you've gone to heaven."

Vivian dug her fork into the sweet folded triangle.

Through her signature moan, she murmured, "My God."

"What did I tell you?" Gen sat with them. "Perfection."

An hour later, they were still chatting. Gen had shared her side of their brief romance, including their first date, which was dinner at home with his parents. His mom and dad had spent the rest of the meal quizzing Gen about her family, her friends and her school.

"I thought they didn't like me," she said.

"They loved you." John finished his second coffee. "They've always asked my friends tons of questions."

Although they hadn't asked much about Jane.

Vivian's phone buzzed on the table. "That's the hotel, John. Our packages have been delivered, so we should go. Perhaps, though, there's a back exit we can use?"

She cast her gaze through the window to a man sitting in a bus shelter.

Was that their tail? Must be. Even he could tell that guy wasn't from Marseille.

"Gen, Jane's got a following in the art world." John started his lie with a truth, like Vivian recommended. "We'd prefer to leave here quietly. Do you still have rooftop access?"

"Where I snogged my boyfriends?" Gen parked her chin on her fist. "Indeed. You are welcome to it. Timothée says he'll board up the hatch when the girls are twelve."

"You go first," Vivian said. "I'll follow soon."

John's shoulders tensed as he stood. He didn't want to leave Vivian with that guy still out there. The man outside looked mostly harmless, but who could be sure? He was also wary of leaving these women in each other's company. They shared an impish streak that would, without a doubt, cost him relationship clout.

But he didn't have much choice.

"Two minutes, and then I come back." He turned to Gen. "What do we owe you?"

"A longer visit." Gen sipped her coffee. "À bientôt, Johnny."

"Yes, Johnny." Vivian grinned. "À bientôt."

Nope, he didn't like this.

Vivian gripped her mug. Tactical procedure required staggering their exits. If she and John both left the table at the same time, their tail would know they'd fucked off into the alley. By the time he clocked that they were gone, they'd have a decent lead.

"How long have you been a couple?" Gen asked.

Vivian returned her attention to Gen's curious blue gaze. "A year."

"Your ring's spectacular."

"Thanks. I drooled over it in an antique shop, and John went back to get it."

Whoops. This was not okay. Officers did not share intimate life details with strangers. She seriously needed to take time off after this operation to clear her head and get it back in the game.

"Johnny's always been sentimental."

Gen's casual nickname for him scratched at Vivian's soul. He wasn't *Johnny*. He was John. Steady, reliable, funny, gentlemanly John.

"So tell me," Gen said. "Is all this sneaking around because of his parents?"

Well, *that* was interesting.

"It could be, but I'm curious why you'd ask?"

Gen lifted a shoulder. "People talk here in the café. There were rumors about them for years after they left Marseille. They traveled frequently. More than others in the same job. They asked many questions, but answered few. Some thought they were spies."

Vivian's stomach squeezed. Sounded familiar.

"But that was impossible." Gen laughed. "They were so

dowdy. Monsieur Seymour was always in need of a haircut, and Madame Seymour wore ill-fitting pantsuits and brooches."

Blend in with the crowd, don't draw attention to yourself.

"She loves those brooches, doesn't she?" Vivian smiled. "Thank you for everything. John told me lots about you, and I'm glad we were able to meet."

Gen waved her off. "May I offer you some advice about John? He was a tenderhearted boy. He must've told you he was often left on his own because his parents were busy solving other people's problems?"

"He has." She nodded.

Gen touched her hand. "It's good to see him with someone who prioritizes him, accompanies him on his walk down memory lane."

Which had been a complete accident.

Vivian drained her coffee. Did she prioritize John? This past year she'd apologetically broken plans, hopped on flights, spent long hours at her computer. He never complained. No, to the contrary, he cheered her on, celebrated exhibit openings with her, brought meals to her desk when she was burning the midnight oil.

She loved him to the point of breathlessness.

But…

If the best that she could love him wasn't the best that he could be loved, was that fair?

"Thank you, Gen." Vivian rose from the table, then shrugged her backpack onto her shoulders. "I hope to return your kindness someday."

To her great surprise, she meant it.

Gen kissed her cheeks. "Now go after your man."

Vivian clambered up the stairs…and more stairs…and yet more stairs.

John leaned over a railing. "Up here."

"When you said 'rooftop,' I didn't think it involved three flights of stairs."

The thick attic air pressed her skin like a steam iron.

"You saw the building from the outside. The roof is usually on the top floor."

"Don't throw logic at me," she huffed. The boxes and furniture stored under the slanted roof looked like they dated to the revolution. "Where's the door?"

John pointed to the hatch directly above them.

"Next question," she said. "Where's the ladder?"

"As soon as Mr. Alarie figured out we were sneaking onto the roof to hook up, he moved the ladder to a downstairs storage area."

She raked her hands through her hair. "Lot of good that does us."

"Joke's on him. We didn't need it." He braced himself against the wall, then climbed onto the banister to fumble with the latch.

"Get down from there." Her heart was in her throat. All she could picture was this ancient French carpentry crumbling under him. "We can stack boxes."

"It's fine. I did this all the time."

"When you were a kid. You need a heating pad after soccer."

"How dare you." He popped the hatch on the ceiling. When he straightened, his upper third disappeared through it. With a slight grunt, he climbed up and through the hole.

"John?" she asked.

He popped his face back through, grinning. "Hey."

Sparkles swirled through her at his smile. "That was dangerous and dumb."

He reached his hands toward her. "Climb up."

Once again grateful for her responsible footwear choice, she braced herself against the wall, then climbed up onto the railing.

She was not afraid of heights.

She glanced into the three flights of stairs' dark maw.

But she was fucking terrified of falling.

"I can't." She edged her foot forward.

"You can," John declared.

Bossy John was back. She didn't mind. She needed his bossiness to beat back the vertigo nibbling at her sense of balance.

"I'm here, Vivian." His arms were like oaks, had picked her up and twirled her easily more times than she could count. She trusted them. "Give me your hands and I'll pull you up."

Trembling, she reached for him.

"That's it," he said. "The strongest hold is by the wrists."

She locked on and felt him clamp around her wrist, too. A week ago, she'd traced hearts on his pulse point, marveling at the solid feel of his flesh.

"Good. Now the other one," he said.

Which meant letting go of the wall.

"C'mon, Gorgeous, you can do this."

The nickname triggered her like it was her sleeper agent activation phrase. Deep breath, let go, then… Shit. She wobbled on the banister until the warm anchor of his hand caught her flailing arm.

"Gotcha. Count of three, push off the banister."

Kink the knees. Get ready.

"Here we go. One, two, *three*."

She was flying. Okay, not flying, but being yanked through the hatch with enough force that she and John tumbled backward onto the roof's hard surface. Actually, John landed on the roof, whereas she landed mostly on John.

"Ow," he said.

"Are you okay?" She tried not to revel in the close, blood-thrumming contact. Fuck the doubt she'd felt while talking to Gen. This intimacy was her normal, and she'd get it back.

"Fine." He tucked her hair behind her ear. "You?"

"Peachy. How horny were you as a teenager to go through all that for some ass?"

"Very. I haven't slowed down much since."

"I'm aware," she said.

Especially since his cock pressed against her hip. Interesting. Apparently a little danger turned him on. She should kiss him. Right here, right now, and damn the consequences. But the wailing siren that stopped in front of the café didn't care what she wanted.

She scurried off him. "How do we get down?"

"You won't like the next part." John reached behind an air vent.

"I already don't like *this* part."

He laid a thick plank across the gap to the neighboring building. "It's just three steps."

"And a forty-foot death plunge to cobblestones."

"You climbed the fire ladder at the riad."

"That was like, twelve feet. Easily survivable."

"Okay." He shrugged. "I guess I win, then."

The cold fear pumping through her veins slowed. "Appealing to my competitive nature isn't fair when plummeting death is on the line."

"Of course it's fair. What's that saying? All's fair in love and war." He glanced at the street as more sirens joined the first. "Look, I'll show you."

She reached for him. "Don't!"

John crossed the plank with nary a wobble.

Easy for him to do. He spent half his life up ladders and on catwalks. Whereas she either hunched over a computer or swanned through fancy parties gathering intelligence. Okay, fine, and occasionally crawling through an air duct.

"You can still tie me," he said. "For facing your fears, you get a hundred points."

Her competitive spirit was a blessing and a curse.

"Fine." She ventured toward the plank. "But if I die, you get minus a thousand."

She put one foot on the plank to test it out. Solid.

"Will you hold it?" she asked.

"Yes." He knelt like he had when he proposed and braced the board with his ropey forearms. "You've got this."

She took a step forward. "People only say that when you *don't* got this but they're rooting for you anyway."

Another step.

"What a dismal interpretation of support," he said.

Almost there. A half step forward. The board wobbled a millimeter, causing her to do the stupidest thing possible—look down. The ground telescoped at her like she was falling.

Her skull would crack like a melon.

Warm arms belted around her, then swiveled her to a solid surface.

"I've got you," he murmured as she pressed her face into his neck.

Her runaway breathing made it impossible to talk.

"You did great."

"Liar. No points for me."

"One hundred points, fair and square." He kissed her temple. "You okay?"

"I will be." She massaged the spot over her heart. "Please don't tell me we need to leapfrog from roof to roof."

He plucked the plank from the gap. "No, this building has a fire escape."

The metal rattled under her feet as he climbed down the fire escape's ladder. Clutching the handrails, she followed. On the last level, he lowered the vertical ladder to the street. Ever the gentleman, he held her waist as she leaped to the sidewalk.

Terra firma restored her confidence.

"We're a couple out for a stroll, okay?" She reached for his hand. "Everything should be ready at the hotel, so we'll get the car and go."

"Got it." John nodded.

Hand in hand, they twined back to the hotel, casually chatting as she scanned for followers. None. As they approached the port area, seagulls' low, piercing calls grew louder. At their hotel's valet stand, John handed their ticket over to the attendant, who quickly disappeared to retrieve their car.

"Excuse me," she said to another attendant. "Do you have bottles of water?"

"Oui, madame." He handed her a chilled bottle of Perrier. Vive la France.

A shiny silver Ferrari Purosangue swooped under the portico. Hot damn, upgrade. She'd asked for a comfortable car for John's sake, but this exceeded expectations. Guess the kind of blending MacColl wanted them to do in Monte Carlo involved luxury and money.

John whistled. "I'm not even a car guy, but can I drive?"

"Be my guest. I want to catch up on research based on what my boss told me."

As John adjusted the seat and mirrors, she popped a Dramamine, half her normal dose.

This was her version of pregaming.

Yesterday, she passed out instead of delighting in sharing a bed with John. She'd make no such mistake today.

Full night's sleep? Check.

Motion sickness pill consumed? Check.

Sexy clothes? She twisted to check out the rear interior. Thick garment bags hung on either side of the car. Probably check.

The house-priced SUV glided and growled as they merged on the highway.

"Let's see what we've got." She sifted through the glove box. "Tickets."

Before tucking them into her bag, she scanned the QR code for the auction's program. The cream-and-gold website opened, and she paged through the listing.

"Sonofabitch," she muttered.

"What?" John asked.

"Amina's painting—the one Lola bought from Mehdi—is being auctioned. I need to tell her. She's not a name here. If it fetches a low price, charity or not, it'll fuck up her bag."

"What if it goes high?"

"That'd be great, but it's unlikely. We haven't built up any excitement around the auction." She continued swiping through pages to the auction's fine print. "Ooh, this is good. The organizers provide insured shipping to the winners. They'll secure the artwork at the casino overnight. That buys us time to search them."

"How?"

"Great question." She drummed her fingers on her knee. "Might need to improvise."

"Not a fan of improv."

"I'm aware," she said. "I've got the casino's blueprints and a badge to get us into employee-only areas. Duct work might be our friend again."

He gripped the steering wheel. "We almost died the last time we crawled through ducts."

"Oh, we did not." A fresh phone lay in the glove box. "Look over here for a second?"

She held the device up to his face and unlocked it.

"Jesus. What is that?"

"Jason Jones's phone." Yep, all his social media accounts were connected. "Didn't make sense for an influencer not to have one."

"They already had my face programmed into it?"

"Yep. It's like I work for a place with advanced tech capabilities." She connected the phone to the car's Bluetooth. "Let's give Jason Jones's music library a spin."

Édith Piaf's expressive voice filled the car.

John snorted. "A sixty-five-year-old song is an odd choice for an influencer."

"Nah, it's perfect. Everything old is new again."

Sixteen

John gripped the wheel.

The approach to Monte Carlo was nuts. Like *Mario Kart* except there'd be no hang glider rescue if they careened off the mountainside. To keep pace with the traffic, he hurtled into the tunnel carved into the rock. It was mostly a straight shot until—

"Holy shit, a roundabout *in* a tunnel?"

Vivian looked up. "At least it's not the Laerdal Tunnel in Norway. That fucker's fifteen miles long. Lighting's better, though."

On the roundabout's other side, the road spit him into daylight.

"We'll be at the Casino d'Or in about five minutes. A piece of advice. Act like money doesn't matter. If they offer us a room upgrade, we take it. Thousand-dollar bottles of wine, no problem. Hundred-dollar cigars might as well be loose cigarettes."

"But I don't like cigars."

"Then don't light it. My point is, we'll exude glitterati." She pom-pommed her fists like fireworks. "Wealthy young tastemakers."

"Ew." His jam was more flannel and discounts at Safeway.

"It's what gets you in with this crowd."

"So if I bragged about working with my hands…"

"They'd hope you were being lewd." She pointed to an ornate building beyond a lush green park. "I think that's the Casino d'Or. I checked in while we were on the road. We can go straight to the room."

He caught her uncertainty. "Is Monte Carlo our first new city together?"

This being a novel experience for both of them made him happy. As much as he loved her expertise, equal footing made him feel like less of a liability.

She quirked her lips. "Yeah, I guess so. Ready for an adventure?"

"Never."

As he eased past a fleet of Lamborghinis, Porsches, Ferraris, Aston Martins and Bentleys, he whistled. The amount of insurance premiums paid among this lineup must be astronomical.

"Pessimist. One more thing," she said. "There's a good chance Jean-Michel will be here. And if not, he'll have eyes at the event. When I ended things with him, I told him I was in love with someone else. So we need to act like a couple."

This he could do.

"What kind of couple? Chastely affectionate? All over each other?"

"Somewhere between an engaged couple on a *Love Is Blind* reunion show—" she wiggled her hand in the air "—and Morticia and Gomez Addams."

This was excellent news.

Since Casablanca, his hands had been eager to skim her skin. True, he'd told her he couldn't get past her job. Then they'd almost died, like, four times, and he decided life was too short to deny himself Vivian.

Which he should probably tell her.

They slipped from the car. Droplets from the enormous water fountains' arcing spray dotted his shirt. After handing the keys to the valet, he grabbed the garment bags.

"Got everything?"

She slung her bag onto her shoulder. "Yep."

"Then let's go." He grabbed her hand and escorted her inside.

In the lobby, tall columns rocketed toward a stained glass ceiling. Curved blue glass panels hung suspended in the air, mimicking the azure sea surrounding the city. At the elevator bank, Vivian held her phone to the sensor, then pressed the button for five.

While they waited for the elevator, he nuzzled her neck.

"Perfect," she murmured. "That's great."

Several vacationers boarded the elevator with them. John slipped his free hand around Vivian's waist and let his fingers play at her hip. When the doors opened, they turned left, while another couple turned right.

After a short walk, she paused at a double-doored entry to Le Suite de Prestige. As she pressed her phone to the sensor, he hovered behind her, not touching, building anticipation. Except for *that* spot, just below her ear. He planted a kiss, then licked her salty skin.

Vivian arched her back and sucked in her breath.

That was her tell that she was turned on.

Good.

The doors unlocked. She held one open for him, then clicked it shut after he crossed the threshold. Contemporary furniture, gleaming fabrics, refined textures greeted them. Beyond their terrace lay the Mediterranean's infinite cerulean cascade. But the only view he cared about was the red-haired spitfire behind him.

He hung the bags in the armoire.

"So," she said. "Let's get down to business."

Hell yes. "Sounds good to me."

When he turned, Vivian had her privacy pen out and was skimming the walls with it.

"You said you didn't like improv—" she ran the pen behind a painting "—but that acting was chef's kiss. Lift the mattress?"

Ah. Her version of *down to business* was different than his.

Ten minutes later, she flung open the terrace doors. As she worked, the Mediterranean sun suffused her clothing, revealing the curves of her body in shadow.

Torture.

She returned to the room and closed the terrace doors. "We're all clear. Come with me."

"Where?" He pushed up from the settee at the foot of the bed.

"Shower."

In the palatial marble bathroom, Vivian spun the dial until water rained from several angles. Maybe her version of *down to business* wasn't different from his after all?

She gestured for him to lean closer.

His cock twitched as he obeyed her command.

"Let's look at the blueprints," she said.

If blue balls were a thing, his would match the sea outside their window.

"Why'd you turn on the shower?" he asked.

"So I can brief you without worrying about listening devices. They can't filter out rushing water easily—it's pattern-less." She shifted her attention back to the tablet. "The gallery is between the casino and the main hotel lobby, here."

Okay, so, this was definitely a logistics meeting.

"This is the service hallway network." She enlarged the schematic's left wing, then pointed to hash marks that symbolized doorways. "Casinos have secret doors everywhere, so security can appear and disappear quickly without disturbing the patrons. Casino d'Or's security team is structured like a police force. Large, intense and fully trained. Cameras are everywhere, and footage is fed through facial recognition software. We should stay as behind-the-scenes as possible. Fortunately, this service hallway runs directly behind the gallery."

She tapped on the screen.

"We're climbing through ducts again, aren't we?"

"Got it in one," she said. "This duct connects the service hallway to the gallery. Since the casino's holding everything overnight, we can inspect the paintings for the drive after hours."

"Which means we need to break into the gallery."

"Correct." She notched her fist under her chin. "I want to

check out the security setup, but we should change into something less bedraggled."

"Now?" he asked.

She nodded, then turned off the shower.

"Okay." He grabbed her garment bag from the armoire. "This one's labeled for you."

After taking the bag, she laid it on the bed and unzipped it. A rich spectrum of colors blossomed from inside. She selected a pale green flowy dress, then stepped into the bathroom.

Without closing the door, she said, "Put on whatever daytime clothing they provided."

"How'd they know my size?" he asked.

A full-length mirror stood across from the open bathroom door. He shouldn't look. But the soft curves and strong muscles of her back deserved admiration.

"There's a system," she said.

"Like a body scan?"

"No," she laughed. "I told them your sizes. When you're an active officer, they want family details in case something like this happens."

"How often does something like *this* happen?"

"They don't tell us when an officer goes black with their families, so I don't know."

With three quarters of her back to the mirror, she dropped her underpants, revealing the bitable curve of her ass. Next, she angled her arms behind her back and unhooked the bra. He tried not to groan as the slope of her breast came into view for a hot second before she slipped the maxi-dress over her head.

Damn.

"Be glad you have clothes." She emerged from the bathroom. "Do they not fit?"

"Sorry. I got distracted by the view."

Let her interpret that how she wanted. Since they weren't being shy, he dropped his pants. Vivian couldn't take her eyes off him. He peeled off his shirt, then slipped on a fresh white oxford. Pink shorts that hit him above the knee came next, followed by boat shoes.

Vivian's gaze scanned him, top to bottom.

"Hang on—a finishing touch." She rummaged in his bag and found several gold chains. Her hands were soft around his neck as she clasped them. "There. Now you blend."

He fiddled with the chains. "I feel like a peacock."

"Lots of men wear them." She withdrew a smaller purse from her garment bag and loaded it with items from her backpack. "Don't forget your phone. We'll need it for photos."

They were about to case a casino's art gallery.

He should have been nervous, but he was with Vivian, so it was actually fun.

In the main gallery, art-covered white panels were fixed to poles and could be spun like tiles to create different artwork arrangements. Vivian and John meandered through the maze of panels to the large exhibition room featuring the pieces to be auctioned.

"'This fundraiser provides vital support toward artists through commissioned exhibition and residency opportunities, incubator grants for Monegasque artists, artist resources and more.'" Vivian twisted her lips. "I bet very little actually makes it back to the artists."

"Now who's a pessimist?" He laid his hand on the back of her neck.

Territorial? Yes, but he'd argue that it fell in the sweet spot she'd described.

"This pessimist has been studying money funnels for ten years." She gestured toward the description. "It's a tax write-off for the collector who donated."

Here, in the smaller gallery, the auction items were more classically arranged. When Vivian paused to admire a piece, he slid behind her and wrapped his hand around her waist.

She palmed his cheek. "Remember to take pictures, Mr. Influencer. Ooh, your face is rough without the beard."

"Haven't shaved today. For the pics, can I go big?" he asked.

She squeezed his biceps. "I dare you to."

He slipped his new phone from his pocket.

"Jane" grinned at him from the lock screen. Vivian's outer wrapping had changed since this pic was taken. New hair color and lighter, looser and more revealing clothing.

But the sparkle in her eyes was the same.

Vivian inspected the placard next to Amina's piece. "Argh, her bio's wrong. It says she trained with her brother."

He snapped pictures of Vivian, hands on her hips, frowning.

"This'll probably fetch—" she squinted one eye and tick-tocked her head "—five thousand euros. But her accurate backstory could bump it up to fifteen. I need to get this fixed before tonight."

Her disappointment was palpable. Even though art brokering was her alias, she sincerely cared about her artists. He loved that about her.

As he moved through the gallery, he snapped pics of the setup. The paintings were hung with simple French gallery hooks, no anchors. Easy enough to lift from the walls. As they progressed, Vivian ballparked what each piece would sell for, giving an accurate mini-bio and sales history for each artist.

She was so good at Jane's job.

Between her sharp sense of humor and irresistible looks, she'd intrigued him from the start. He'd fallen off a cliff for her, though, when she revealed her encyclopedic grasp of art history coupled with her chokehold on the business side.

And it was her second job? He didn't know when she slept.

But when she *did* sleep, he wanted to be the one lying next to her.

Vivian docked her hands on her hips. This would *not* do.

The gallery had hung the Rocksy piece differently than the artist's request to place solid pieces on the floor and lean them against the wall, and to hang flimsy pieces with binder clips.

Instead, they'd framed *Smoking Hon* and hung it on the wall.

In a stroke of luck, though, it was near the vent that capped the duct they'd crawl through. Even better, the Casino d'Or had sprung for fancy Beaux Arts–style vent covers with huge gaps. Easier for anyone crawling through the duct to see through, too. One screw in each corner. Easy enough to kick through.

Vivian tilted her head back. Domed cameras dotted the room's corners.

"Hey, sweetie," she said. "Lie on the ground for a worm's eye view of these pieces."

"Great idea." Without argument, John dropped and fired off shots.

She covered her laughter with her fist. Based on his enthusiastic charades-playing, she should've predicted he'd be a champ at this. As he snapped photos, she encroached on the protective barrier. The thin elastic cord strung through steel uprights was either a visual cue not to come closer to the Rocksy piece or an alarm would be triggered.

"Babe," John said.

She stifled another giggle. Babe? They were not *babe* people. Plus, he'd unbuttoned his shirt down to the middle of his sternum. Much as she liked the view of his pecs, his Hollywood-esque persona was like he'd slipped into a Ryan Gosling-as-Malibu Ken costume.

"Lean in," he said. "Your dress really pops against her cigarette's cherry."

Her shoulder was an inch away from the painting, and…

An electronic squawk interrupted the gallery's hush. Confirmed. Laser curtains protected the painting.

"Step away," the gallery guard droned.

"Sorry!" Vivian held up her hands. "Let's do a selfie, sweetie."

She touched her head to John's, then tilted the camera to view the ceiling. Shit. A fogging system, too? If it detected motion after hours, it would fill the room with opaque fog. Respect to the security team for layered theft countermeasures, but goddammit.

She found his hand and squeezed three times.

"Let's stop at the gift shop," she said as they passed the security guard.

In the overpriced shop, she browsed for toothbrushes, toothpaste, and on a whim, super bouncing balls from the toy section. Ruckus adored them, and they might come in handy.

"Babe, I'm getting this too." He dropped a Formula 1 magazine, a sport he'd never watched, on the pile. And yet another button was undone on his shirt.

After paying, they strolled to the elevators.

John rested his hand on her ass as they walked.

Inside their suite, she flipped the locks and dragged John to the bathroom. Once again, a full blast from the luxurious shower would disguise their voices.

"Let's compare notes," she said.

"The paintings are alarmed but not anchored. I'd guess a minute, maybe two, per painting to remove them, inspect for the flash drive, then return them to the wall."

"Got it. Let me see your phone." She smiled at their goofy selfies, scrolling until she got to his excellent shots of the cameras, then enlarged the pics. "These look like infrareds to me."

Museums lowered the lights at night to save money and preserve the art. But they relied on infrareds to detect thieves' heat signatures.

He nodded. "Me too."

"The fog system might work to our advantage—they won't be able to see our faces. The fog takes an hour to clear, too."

"What's the timeline this evening?" John asked.

Vivian read the event details on her phone. "Gala starts at eight, the auction's at ten, and the exhibit space closes at eleven. Gambling goes until 4:00 a.m."

"When do we hit the gallery?"

"We want to time it with security shift change at 11:30 p.m.

They walk the halls outside the gallery and watch monitors. We want to be in the auction exhibit space by 11:32 p.m. First, we trigger the fog for cover. The infrareds will see that people are in there, but no one can facially ID us. You'll wear my camera glasses—they're also infrared. The paintings carry a light heat signature. We'll locate a painting, you lift it, I'll search it, and we'll move to the next one if we don't find the drive. Ultimately, we'll find it, then blend into the crowd to escape."

This felt good.

There'd be unknowns along the way—there always were—but what she laid out was solid and within her capabilities.

John shifted on his feet.

"Are you good?" she asked.

"Goofing around downstairs was fun, but this is real." His feet slapped the tiles as he paced. "I might mess it up."

The confident persona he showed downstairs was disappearing faster than a watercolor in the rain. She'd seen this with baby agents. If she didn't get him out of his head, he'd spiral.

A brilliant, selfish solution came to her.

With the steam swirling around them, she slid her hands under his shirt. "You won't mess this up. You're with me. My team always wins."

She raised herself on her toes and pressed her mouth to his. John's firm lips, his tongue sweeping her mouth, that quick gaspy breath he took when he was on the edge of losing himself in her...she wanted all that so much she might cry.

"I'm sorry." She pushed away from him. "I shouldn't have kissed you."

"Yes, you fucking should." John hauled her tight against him, clutched a handful of hair and tilted her lips to his. "The kiss in Tangier, and Casablanca. It was hard to walk away."

The trail he kissed from her jaw to the pulse in her neck made words difficult. When he slipped her maxi-dress's straps from her shoulders and the garment dropped in a soft pool around her ankles, difficult became almost impossible.

But she had to ask him. "Then why did you walk away?"

"Pride. Mostly stupidity." His belt, still threaded through the loops of his shorts, clinked as it hit the marble.

An acceptable answer.

"Wait." She stepped back. She had to do one more thing.

He cradled her face. "Is this okay? I shouldn't have pushed. I—"

"Oh, I want you. Desperately. But I'm gross. I haven't showered since Morocco."

"Fortunately..." He hugged her and then dragged her into the Roman shower.

Pulsing heat rained on her from all directions. If they had this shower at home, she'd never leave.

"Turn around," John said.

Anticipation frizzled her nerves. Her nose perked as the scent of delicate flowers mixed into the steam, and John's big, thick fingers scrubbed her scalp with luxurious shampoo. Tingles spiraled from her nape to her back.

"Rinse," he said.

She stepped fully under the water, tipping her head so the suds cascaded down her back. Next he worked conditioner in her tresses. Briefly he removed his hands, then returned them as he gently, so gently she might cry, washed her back with a sudsy washcloth.

"Your bruises are mostly gone."

"Thank God. They would have clashed with my dress."

She sucked in a breath as he pressed his lips to the crook of her neck. While he licked and kissed her ticklish flesh, he dragged the washcloth across her belly and around her breasts. The soap slicked her skin. With his free hand, rolled her nipple between his fingers.

He dropped the washcloth, then dipped his hand between her legs. "Do you like this?"

"*Yes.*" She arched her back, then hooked her arm around his neck, letting him take her weight as he massaged her rapidly swelling bundle of nerves.

She wasn't the only one rapidly swelling. His hard cock pressed firmly against her ass.

Their engagement night felt like a lifetime ago. She'd never had makeup sex before. For the old Vivian, fights meant pulling the relationship's plug. She'd never made up with anyone because she'd barely had time for a relationship in the first place.

But John was worth fighting for.

"I'm sorry for everything." She turned in his arms. "And I need you, now."

He shut off the water, then wrapped her in a towel and scooped her up. In the bedroom, the sun bathed everything in gold. He knelt on the expansive bed and laid her amid the sumptuous linens.

She let the towel's flaps fall open, then reached for him.

With a groan, he said, "God, you're beautiful."

He'd seen all of her more times than she could count. There were no first-time jitters. No questions about the scar on her hip or awkward moments while they figured out each other's bodies. No, this was pure, hot, informed need.

"Turn over," he said.

One secret they shared—John was bossy in bed. He claimed he'd never been this way with anyone else, was worried it might upset her. On the contrary, she *loved* it. Everywhere else in her life, she made decisions, assessed the situation, weighed the options, took charge.

But between the sheets? She did whatever he asked.

John kissed a trail down her back, a reliable shiver-inducing move, followed by a light bite on her ass. He *adored* her ass. Muay Thai training thickened her glutes, and he grabbed a handful any chance he could. Next, he delved between her legs. She gasped as he wheeled her clit with the pressure and speed he knew she liked.

"You're so wet," he murmured. "Because of me?"

She ground her ass against him. "Always."

Thank God for her IUD. The least complicated, most reliable form of birth control for someone who wanted kids maybe someday, definitely not now, and couldn't always predict her schedule or proximity to a pharmacy.

"I want you," she breathed. "Please."

"Too bad." He hoisted her hips up and turned so she was kneeling.

This was also part of their sex life. Playful teasing, denial, capitulation. With his hands clamped to her shoulders, he slid his cock against her folds, a guaranteed turn-on for her.

Desire fully bloomed between her legs.

"Please." She gasped as he gently pinched her nipple. "I need you."

Seventeen

The need John had for Vivian crushed him. Running, fighting and hiding had pounded a truth into him that he only began to realize back when he bought the ring on her finger.

Vivian Flint, in whatever form she took, was a treasure.

Losing her was not an option.

He leaned forward, sealing his chest to her back, and threaded his fingers with hers. "Tell me what you need?"

"You." Her heavy-lidded gaze locked with his. "Forever you."

"I need you too," he said.

His life partner criteria hadn't included *unflinching badass*. Shame on him, because he would've missed out on someone he couldn't breathe without. Her essence was what mattered. The package didn't. What'd she call it? Window dressing.

"Then what are you waiting for?"

She gasped as he eased into her, then met his rolling thrusts. From their first night together, this was how it was. Partnership, shared bliss. As though they were the only two people in the world, locked in love.

This was what mattered.

And he'd learned a powerful, mind-blowing lesson since she revealed herself to him. Their relationship was precious, but it wasn't fragile. They'd fuck up, yes, but they'd find their way back to each other.

They had to, because life didn't make sense without her.

God, he wanted her. Needed her. Needed to touch her everywhere.

As he withdrew, she mewled a complaint.

"Be patient," he said, and palmed her ass.

After dropping to his side, he hugged her to him. With her head pillowed by his arm, he draped her top leg over his thigh, then slid into her tight, wet heat. Their slick friction was magic, like her body welcomed him again, and again and again. Her eager grinding turned him to steel, tightened his balls, made him want to come like a comet.

Not yet, he told himself.

Bringing her pleasure was one of the reasons he'd been made, he was sure of it. He roamed his hands over her perfect skin. Soft on the outside, strong and resilient on the inside. He turned her face to his, then swallowed her whimpering moans with a kiss.

Their tongues found the same rhythm as their bodies.

She was close. The writhing, whimpering, undulating was an unmistakable signal.

A tickle crept through every part of his body, building up into unbearable tension only the woman in his arms could relieve. Soon she bucked and moaned into his mouth.

There she goes.

She arched her back and pulsed around his cock. This was how she came, loud and hard. He usually started kissing her through her climax so they wouldn't wake the tenants at home. When she hit this moment, she preferred him to double down on his strokes, harder, faster, deeper, which triggered his own—

Fuck. It was her turn to swallow his moan as he came.

Bliss blanketed him. On this side of an orgasm, his stacked-up worries disappeared. Criminal that they'd denied themselves this perfection on the run.

Under his palm, Vivian's heart beat a tattoo into his skin.

She turned to him. "Hi. Thank you."

"You're welcome? You've never thanked me for sex before."

"It was for everything this week, not sex." She twiddled his hair. "Did you want me to thank you for sex?"

"Obviously." He eased himself from her.

She giggled, which turned into a yawn. "What time is it?"

He twisted to look at the bedside clock. "Four."

"Perfect time for a disco nap." She slithered from his arms and padded toward the bathroom. "Set the alarm for seven?"

"Nap? I'm not tired." John nudged the clock's buttons. "It's 10:00 a.m. East Coast time."

"You've been away too many days for time zones to matter," she called. "And we need to be sharp tonight."

He sat up. "We could have sex again, then nap?"

"Sounds like a plan." She closed the door.

As the dopamine receded, he braced himself for a possible wave of regret, but none came.

Forgiveness was a powerful thing.

He'd better shut the blackout curtains. After another round of sex, he wouldn't want to get out of bed. He slipped back under the lush covers. The darkened room was the perfect chilled temperature, but he definitely would not be napping.

In the bathroom, Vivian's smile faltered. Officers often used sex as a stress reliever before undertaking tactical actions in the field. It cleared nerves and eased tensions without compromising mental acuity.

No, stop. She was overthinking things. That was bona fide makeup sex.

She glanced at the stubborn ring on her left hand.

She'd been steady in her love for John. He was the one who had doubts. Had he fully forgiven her? She could ask him, straight out, like she did in Casablanca. There was no need to be delicate and subtle. Lives weren't at stake if he didn't love her.

Just her heart.

She washed her hands and slathered herself in the hotel's lotion. She sniffed her skin. Rose, orange and…sage? This job allowed her to try on different lifestyles, but she always came back to her personal favorites.

Like John, and the person she was with him.

Please let them be back together.

She scrubbed her eyes. She needed to talk to him.

She grabbed one of the plush robes hanging in the bathroom. It dwarfed her. In the darkened bedroom, she padded carefully toward the bed to avoid breaking a toe. Nothing blended like hobbling around a fancy soirée.

"John?" she asked.

She veered to her side of the bed. After dropping the robe, she slipped between the sheets. Her damp hair would dry crazily, but she didn't care.

"Hey, John?" She rested her head on her fist. "Can I be vulnerable with you?"

John, who wasn't tired five minutes ago, was asleep.

She sighed. Later, then. Allowing herself an indulgence, she scooted closer to him. Cuddling wouldn't wake him, but she could soak up his warmth.

"Hey, Gorgeous." John's gravelly voice, coupled with the soothing strokes on her shoulders, coaxed her to consciousness.

She fluttered her eyes open. "What time is it?"

"Seven," he answered. "The alarm just went off."

He opened the curtains. The early golds of what would be a magnificent sunset streamed into the room. It couldn't compete with his naked ass, though.

"Time to rise and grind." She stretched against her pillow.

There was something she'd meant to do before falling asleep. What was it? She played back their afternoon. Plans, recon, sex. Ah. Right. A forgiveness heart-to-heart.

She punched her arms into her robe.

"You okay?" John asked. "You just sighed."

"Did I?" She forced a smile. "I'm great. How wild is my hair?"

"It's…" The sun lit him up like an angel from behind. "Big. Large. Cloud-ish."

"*Thanks.*" She twitched back the blankets.

He laughed at her sarcasm. "You asked."

She rolled her neck. It *seemed* like he'd forgiven her. She needed to know for sure, though. But if he still hadn't, it would fuck with her head. That might compromise their operation tonight. She couldn't risk it.

She'd ask later. After they found the drive.

"It'll take me a minute to deal with this." She gestured to her head, then withdrew her clothing and prep kit from the garment bag and dipped into the bathroom.

Oh, holy Jesus.

Half her hair lay flat to her face while the other half stuck up like a cockatoo's crested feathers. She flicked on the shower and grabbed the handheld to douse her hair. After wetting it, she scrunched in gel. Normally she'd tame the waves into sleek, straight, polished strands, but tonight called for a wilder style.

Especially with the dress they'd picked out for her.

When she finished drying her hair, she laughed. This was the biggest it had been since college. Back then her style wasn't so much a choice as it was a consequence of only having time to wash and go. The fresh red color and the curls made her look more like her younger self than she had in a decade.

Now, to get dressed.

The chardonnay strapless high-waisted thong bodysuit and wraparound silk skirt were simple and elegant. Lovely as they were, thongs were her *least* favorite undergarment. Like her job was literally up her ass.

The things she did for her country.

After dusting herself with makeup and applying her new bold Parisian-red lipstick, she emerged from the bathroom. The silk skirt fluttered around her, and the thigh-high split revealed a generous portion of her golden leg.

She poked her head out of the door. "Can you join me in my office?"

John whistled. "Gorgeous, as always."

Words dried in her throat. John's pale blue shirt set off his eyes, and the sand-colored linen suit looked like it had been made for him. Seriously, his *ass* in those tailored pants. The agency's costumer had added a nice touch—John's yellow pocket square matched her dress. If there had been any way to Snap a pic to Thomas and Logan, she would have. They'd never believe John wore something besides jeans.

"Is this suit okay?" he asked as he buttoned a cuff link. "It creases."

"That's part of the charm. Your fit's perfect. All sartorial nonchalance." She turned on the faucet. "Any special instructions come with it?"

"Yep, in my inside pocket." He opened the flap of his jacket, then removed a card.

"Excellent. Carry this for me?" She extracted her ceramic screwdrivers from her bag and handed them to him. "What nifty gadgets did you get?"

"A digital watch and cuff links that have trackers in them. There's a QR code on the card that pulls up a map of where they are."

"So I can find you if we get separated?" She scanned the code, and two dots lit up on an anonymous webpage's map.

"By *separated*, do you mean kidnapped?"

"Not necessarily. Let's be positive tonight." She layered the camera necklace over her L-Pill necklace. "Help me with this?"

His fingers brushed her nape as he fastened it, making her shiver.

"Is that where you want it? There are a lot of loops back here."

The camera nestled directly between her hoisted boobs.

After turning, she said, "You tell me."

His Adam's apple bobbed. "Perfect."

"Good. Are you wearing the swim shorts they gave you?"

He shifted his weight. "*Shorts* is a generous word, but yeah. Why am I wearing them?"

"In case we need to hide in plain sight. Seaside cities are lousy with pools, hot tubs and beaches." She grabbed the instruction cards. "Can I borrow your Zippo?"

"Sure." He fished it out of his pants pocket and handed it to her.

She removed the plastic liner from the metal ice bucket, then opened the door to the patio. The breeze raised goose bumps on her shoulders. She flicked the Zippo and set the cards alight. As they curled to ash, she dropped them in the bucket.

"Thanks." She tossed John's lighter back to him.

John leaned over the terrace's railing. "Why's everyone in matching outfits?"

Below them, people dressed in white-and-red clothing moved through the plaza.

She shrugged. "First-timer, remember?"

John searched on his phone. "It's the St. John's festival. The Roman Catholic church co-opted a solstice celebration that includes a procession, folklore groups, traditional costumes, songs, dance, a church service and a bonfire."

"Spectacle's always handy." She doused the cards' smoldering remains with Perrier, then dumped the muck into the liner. "That should do it."

Back in the room, she loaded up her oversized clutch with everything they might need during this action. Passports, the drive, Ruckus's super bouncing balls, her trusty index cards, camera glasses, vape pen, euros, atomizer, EpiPen, two N95 masks and surgical gloves from the first-aid kit, and a few lady essentials.

The tablet wouldn't fit, though.

"Can you grab a pillowcase?" she asked John.

They couldn't risk leaving it for anyone to find. After tapping a few buttons, she erased all content. Not done yet, though. She took the pillowcase from John and slipped the tablet inside. Unfortunately, her narrow heels were useless for this next part.

"What kind of shoes did they give you?" she asked.

He lifted his pant leg. "Italian loafers, I think."

"Perfect. Stomp on this, please?"

The device crunched under his heel. After several more direct hits, she bundled the pillowcase and shattered remains into the ice bucket liner.

"You've got your phone?" she asked John. "Money clip?"

"And my lighter. I'll take that." He accepted the bag of sodden ashes from her. "This color's amazing on you, by the way."

She ran her hand down the bodice. "My handler must want me to stand out. They normally put me in dark pantsuits."

"And what do you want?" he asked.

"This, actually." The flowing silk siphoned heat from her body.

On the way to the elevators, they passed their floor's trash chute. Vivian opened its golden door, then nodded toward the bag. After John deposited it, she let go, and the busted tablet clunked toward the dumpsters.

Now they could go to the auction. Butterflies fluttered in her belly.

Good—excitement kept her alert.

She threaded her hand with John's. "Still okay?"

He nodded. "I'm Jason Jones, lifestyle influencer. In my charmed life, nothing goes wrong, so this'll be a macaron."

"A macaron?"

He lifted a shoulder. "We both like them better than a piece of cake."

"True." They stepped into the mirrored elevator.

She cleared her throat. One last thing to disclose about the way tonight might unfold.

"We're still playing the hopelessly-into-each-other couple this evening, but I may also need to be flirty tonight. With others. Café Americain taught me people are more agreeable and loose-lipped if they think they have a shot at sex."

"Define flirting?" He nuzzled her neck.

Unfair. He knew this buckled her knees.

"Touching. Dancing. Maybe light groping."

"Noted." John pinched her chin and raised her mouth to his. "Flirt away, as long as I get to take you to bed tonight. But if your ex is here and crosses a line, I might throw hands."

She palmed the back of his neck. "When's the last time you punched anyone?"

"Fifteen years ago. Thomas donated my lucky jersey. He said it was too small and he couldn't trust me not to wear it in public."

"No fighting." She kissed him again. "We can't get kicked out. Just understand that everything I do tonight is designed to be coercive. It's all an act."

"All of it?" John rubbed his thumb on her cheekbone.

"Yep." She grinned. Tonight would be fun. She could feel it.

The doors opened to the Casino d'Or's glittering lobby.

Eighteen

John chewed the inside of his cheek.

He was ninety-nine percent sure he wasn't included in Vivian's *it's all an act* declaration. That one percent sliver of doubt? He was working on it. Until he tweezed it from his heart, his only strategy was to ask open, honest questions.

And hope they didn't piss her off too badly.

"Bonjour," the casino host said. "The entry fee is twenty-five euros."

Vivian nudged him. "Could you pay, sweetie?"

"Yes, babe." John peeled the appropriate number of bills from his money clip.

"Merci," the host said. "Et bonne chance!"

On the other side of the door, the volume was instant and intense. Amid the humming crowd, the gaming tables produced clicks, whirs and rustles, while croupiers and dealers called out results. People cheered or groaned, depending on how they'd placed their bets.

"What game should we play?" Vivian asked.

An obvious choice came to mind. "Baccarat."

"Really?" she asked.

"Nope. Saw it in a Bond movie."

She laughed and squeezed his biceps. "How about blackjack?"

"Love it, babe. That one?" He gestured to an empty table with a view of the room.

"Perfect," she said.

The dealer greeted them. "Bonjour! This table is twenty euros per hand, minimum."

"A bargain." Vivian slid into the chair John held out for her.

After he helped scoot her under the table, he took the seat next to her. Casually she surveyed the room with her intelligent, information-gathering, beautiful gaze. He palmed her nape, caressing the column of her neck.

How she carried the world on her smooth shoulders was beyond him.

The dealer exchanged their euros for a stack of chips. After they placed their bets, the dealer distributed cards—an ace for Vivian, then a seven on the second round. John received a nine and an eight. The dealer showed a king.

Vivian tapped the table.

Another card? She had eight or eighteen, and the second was a good score. The dealer flipped over a deuce. Now she had twenty, but Vivian tapped for *another* card.

"Seriously?" he asked.

"Go big or go home," she said with a gleam in her eye.

The dealer flipped over a card. Another ace. Twenty-one.

"Lucky," he said.

"Not luck. Fortune favors the bold."

He waved his hand to signal he didn't want more cards. They weren't competing with each other—just the dealer—and his seventeen might be enough to beat the house. The dealer flipped over his second card—a five. He drew another and...seven.

Twenty-two in all, which meant John and Vivian both won.

"Congratulations," the dealer said as he paid out their winnings.

Vivian placed the ante for the next round. "Thank you."

As the cards were dealt, Vivian received a pair of jacks, John got a four and a five, and the dealer showed a seven. Vivian added chips to the table adjacent to her first bet, but outside the betting circle. The dealer laid her top jack parallel to the other.

"What are you doing?" he asked. "You have twenty. Take the win."

"Splitting my pair so I can win bigger." She tapped the table.

This was her take-no-prisoners game night personality.

"The odds of you winning again are infinitesimally small."

"I've been in tighter spots," she said.

"I have seen those tight spots," said a smarmy voice behind them. "Bonsoir, Jane. Two encounters in one week means luck is on my side, no?"

John clocked the slight stiffening of Vivian's neck, but her smile conveyed joy.

"I'd hoped you'd be here. Let me introduce you to my boyfriend, Jason Jones."

John turned to find a disarmingly handsome man. The pictures Vivian had shown him didn't do justice to his chin-length blond waves, aristocratic nose, and full mouth.

Jean-Michel de Gramont.

"Pardonnez-moi," the dealer interrupted. "Allow us to finish this hand?"

"But of course." Jean-Michel slid into the seat next to Vivian. "Please, continue."

The dealer laid down Vivian's next cards. An ace for one of her piles and a ten for the other, which meant blackjack and twenty, respectively. John tipped his lips up in a smile. The way life worked out for this woman should be studied.

"Mon dieu," Jean-Michel said. "Truly, they should attach a cooler to you."

John placed a second chip in the betting circle. He was doubling down on his cards.

"Ah, a man of chance yourself, I see?" Jean-Michel asked.

He lowered his brow. "That's me, Jason Jones, man of chance."

"This could go well for you, Jason Jones," Jean-Michel said. "Unless the dealer is greedy and attempts to best you both."

The dealer flipped over a six. John's total was fifteen. Easily beatable by the dealer, who'd just turned over a ten. He'd collect John's chips if he stood on those cards. Instead, he dealt himself another card and—busted with twenty-six, total.

Vivian had won one hundred thirteen euros. Not bad for ten minutes' work.

Jean-Michel twisted in his chair. "Tell me, Jane, what brings you to Monte Carlo?"

"Tonight's charity auction," she said. "One of my artists has a piece in the show."

"A masterpiece, no doubt." Jean-Michel dropped a black hundred-euro chip on the table. "For this next hand of cards, shall we enter a side bet?"

"I'd be delighted." She placed four twenty-five-euro chips atop Jean-Michel's. "I've been meaning to ask—how did things work out after the piece self-destructed last weekend?"

"I admit, I was worried the buyer would be angry."

The dealer laid out their cards.

"Who was the buyer, again?" she asked.

"Undisclosed. Come now, I taught you better than to ask those questions. But suffice it to say, they were happy the painting's value increased significantly."

John would love to punch the smarm off Jean-Michel's face for the way he talked to Vivian. Like she was a dunce and he was an indulgent teacher.

He obviously had no sense of self-preservation. Vivian would rip him to shreds.

She lightly touched Jean-Michel's wrist. "Congratulations. I'd hoped it would."

John flared his nostrils. What the fuck?

"I understand you're responsible for the Rocksy in tonight's auction?" Vivian asked.

"A last-minute addition, yes. I convinced a client to part with it. With a starting bid of five million euros, it should fetch quite the fortune for the princess's charity."

"That's wonderful, Jean-Michel. Only you could pull something like that off."

The dealer finished distributing their cards. Vivian showed fourteen, John sixteen and Jean-Michel seven. Against the dealer's eight, Vivian hit, then stayed at nineteen. John stayed. Jean-Michel hit twice before busting with twenty-three.

"Merde," Jean-Michel said.

John covered his grin with his palm.

"How are your business dealings, Jane?" Jean-Michel asked. "Ending our arrangement and striking out on your own was naive. I won't be surprised if you're struggling and would like to return to my enterprise."

She grinned like Jean-Michel complimented her. "Things are not exactly where I'd like them to be, but my client list is growing. And Rocksy authentications keep me busy."

That's not how she talked about her clients at home, but he kept that info to himself.

The dealer's hand totaled twenty-two, which meant he lost to John and Vivian.

Definitely not this guy's night.

"It's just as well we parted ways." Jean-Michel beckoned to someone. "It opened up the opportunity to mentor an incredible creature with lucrative connections."

Vivian placed her hand on his thigh, and John looked up from his cards. Lola Vorlicek sauntered behind Jean-Michel and set her hands on his shoulders. The crystals on her gunmetal-gray dress shimmered under the chandeliers.

"You needed me, mon beau?"

"Meet your predecessor. Jane Davis, this is Lola Vorlicek." Jean-Michel lifted Lola's palm and kissed it. "Lola shares your taste for new artists but purchases their work directly rather than through broker sales. Artists often prefer cash in hand."

"Thank you for the advice," Vivian said. "It was lovely to run into you. I assume we'll see you at the auction?"

Jean-Michel nodded. "You will."

John rose to ease her chair from under the table, then deposited most of their winnings into the purse Vivian held open for him.

"Before you go," Lola said. "I understand you're personally acquainted with Rocksy?"

Vivian had never mentioned that to him.

With a *Mona Lisa* smile, Vivian said, "It was good to meet you, Lola."

She squeezed John's hand three times.

Vivian *knew* a face-to-face with Jean-Michel would rile John up. As they walked to the cashier line, he said nothing. He eyed her bunches, though, as though he didn't know what to make of her.

Through a smile, she murmured, "I told you flirting might be required to gain intel."

"It wasn't the flirting." John folded his arms. "And we didn't learn anything."

"Untrue," she said. "He bragged that he convinced a client to donate the *Smoking Hon* Rocksy painting and that he expects it to bring in an amount similar to the sale price of *Boy Playing Trombone*. Now we know which painting to check first. And he doesn't know *I* know the provenance. It's been sold once, directly from the artist, so I know who donated it. Might not be the person we're ultimately after, but it's a lead."

John leaned in. "Back up. Do you *actually* know Rocksy?"

Jean-Michel wasn't the only one slipping up.

"Well?" John pressed.

"Bonjour!" the cashier called to them.

Oh, thank God.

She advanced to the cashier's booth. "We'd like to exchange these for euros, please."

The cashier nodded, counted the chips, then handed over a receipt and a slim stack of colorful notes. Vivian slipped them into her clutch.

As they left the cashier's counter, John asked, "So, what about Rocksy?"

She veered toward the hotel's lobby. "I can't talk about it here."

"We can circle back to your ambiguously employed ex, if you prefer?" John riffled his hair, which only made him hotter.

She dragged him behind a potted plant. "Out with it. We were fine upstairs. What changed between the suite and the lobby?"

"He was obnoxious to you." John crossed his arms. "I wanted to punch him, but you told me not to, so now I'm just pissed that you had to be around that for years."

She never needed a man to caveman-defend her, but it was endearing.

She hooked her hands on his forearm. "That's sweet of you, and thank you for your self-restraint. But we have a job to do. Are you good?"

John's jaw muscle bulged. "Long as I stay away from your ex, I'll get there."

Good enough.

After the gallery host scanned their auction tickets, they entered. Anyone in here, from the man in the tux to the woman in the glossy blue fringe dress, could be the buyer.

As for the donor...nope, she didn't see him here, either.

She and Torrey had sold *Smoking Hon* ten years ago to an exiled Croatian pseudo-prince with ties to the House of Savoy. Dad had racked up medical bills after breaking his arm rebuilding their deck, and they'd needed quick cash. A painting they'd sold for ten thousand dollars might fetch millions this evening. Insane.

But that's how the art industry worked.

John collected two fizzing flutes of champagne from a waitress, then handed one to her. "Here's to blending."

They clinked their glasses and drank.

"Barbajuan?" a passing waiter asked.

Vivian plucked a pastry fritter filled with spinach and cheese from the tray.

After finishing the barbajuan, John said, "Damn. Should've taken two of those."

She sipped her champagne. "More canapés on your six."

This waiter offered mini tomates à la monégasque—stuffed cherry tomatoes. After gulping two, John grabbed three skewers of mini beef cubes and sweet-and-sour baby onions from another passing waiter.

"Is this giving swanky influencer?" He held the skewers between his knuckles, Wolverine-style, then snapped a picture.

"Nope. And it's different from Jason's typical aesthetic."

"I'm pivoting from obnoxious ass to flippant ass." He handed her a skewer, then drained his champagne. He plucked another flute from a passing tray. "Upholding my nepo baby influencer image is more of a challenge than I thought it would be."

"The drink's a prop," she murmured. "Take it easy."

"Distinguished guests, may I have your attention?" A woman stood at a lectern in front of a collection of white folding chairs. "We'll begin the auction in two minutes. Please be seated."

John plucked another champagne from a waitress's tray. "One more for the road."

The seats in the back provided a full view of the attendees and, if she swiveled her chair, the doors. As she tucked the fluid yellow silk underneath her, Jean-Michel and Lola entered the room, followed by a man who looked like an Anne Rice vampire, as well as…holy shit. Winegrad?

She flattened her lips.

She'd *told* MacColl not to send Mr. Solves-Everything-with-Fists.

The L-Pill necklace's pendant was smooth under her worrying caress. This wasn't the first time MacColl had disregarded her advice. Unless…

Maybe Winegrad wasn't here on MacColl's orders. That would be a more concerning reality.

Dammit, she needed more info.

The auctioneer tapped the microphone. "Bienvenue, benvegnüu, welcome to the Casino d'Or's tenth auction benefitting the Prince Georges Foundation! We would also like to thank the artists and our generous donors."

Polite applause followed each name the willowy woman listed.

"Now, it's time to open your wallets and bid generously."

With a spotlight shining on the first piece, the auctioneer provided a detailed narrative. Collectors liked to learn a piece's backstory. Any morsel of information, gossip or legend that stoked the imagination potentially increased their willingness to bid.

Vivian cut her gaze to Jean-Michel, Lola and the Mystery Vampire, but they showed no interest in anything on the auction block. John busied himself with snapping photos.

Soon the willowy auctioneer gaveled a win.

Amina's painting was next.

"This piece by Amina Hassan is entitled *Women's Work*," the auctioneer said. "It was donated by our very own Lola Vorlicek."

As the auctioneer continued to introduce the piece, Vivian let out a relieved breath. The bio changes she'd emailed to the event organizer—and to Lisa, on whom she relied to relentlessly follow up—had made their way to this evening's script.

"Let's start the bidding at one thousand euros."

A sea of hands rose, which warmed Vivian's heart. As the number climbed with each round, hands dropped. Next to her, John shot his arm in the air to confirm a bid.

"What are you doing?"

"I'm a nepo baby." He snapped a selfie. "I've got cash to burn for a good cause. You said it should go for fifteen, and I'm bumping it up there."

"Do I have fifteen thousand euros?" the auctioneer asked.

All but John and the blue fringe lady dropped out.

Her heart rate kicked up. "I don't like the way you're embracing this identity."

He raised his hand again. "I bet you do."

The auctioneer scanned the crowd. "Fifteen thousand two hundred?"

John held her hand. She held her breath. Vivian could pay if he won, but she'd have to wire money from Vivian Flint to Lisa, who would wire it to Jane since she was friends with both identities. But it would be an unanticipated administrative pain in the ass.

The blue fringe lady raised her hand.

They were off the hook. Bonus—Amina's profile would rise overnight.

"I was hoping that lady won," John said. "I image-searched her. She's Simone Crovetto, the head of a lifestyle brand called Pied-à-Terre. Should be good for Amina."

"What would you have done if you'd won?"

"Hocked a kidney to pay for it."

Vivian shrugged. "I mean, why else do we have two?"

"Next," the auctioneer said, "we have Rocksy's *Smoking Hon*. Originally sold ten years ago, this stenciled and painted plywood had been used to board up a row house in Baltimore's Penn North neighborhood. The donor wishes to remain anonymous. I assure you we've inspected this piece, and no self-destruct devices have been located. Bidding wars will be the only theatrics tonight. Let's begin with a conservative five million euros?"

Vivian gulped as a dozen hands went up.

She wished she'd kept more of Rocksy's early pieces.

She fixed her attention on Jean-Michel, whose ear was pressed to his phone. As the prices spun up in a whirlwind, his hand remained in the air. His vulpine smile meant he was about to get *exactly* what he wanted.

Jean-Michel shouted, "Twenty-one million euros for my bidder on the phone!"

The crowd silenced itself.

That was more than twice the last bid.

"I have twenty-one million euros! Any other bids? If not, going once, twice…" The auctioneer smacked her gavel against the wooden block. "Sold to Jean-Michel de Gramont on behalf of his client for twenty-one million euros."

The room erupted into applause.

The Mystery Vampire shook Jean-Michel's hand. Interesting.

"Her Serene Highness invites all of you to the ballroom for dancing and refreshments to celebrate raising fifty million euros!"

Mystery Vampire dipped from the room, leaving Jean-Michel, Lola and Winegrad behind. Hmph. So Winegrad was with Jean-Michel and Lola, not Mystery Vampire.

She threaded her fingers with John's, then rose from her chair. "We need to go. Quickly."

Outside the gallery, she picked Mystery Vampire out of the crowd. He was among the people climbing the grand curved staircase to the ballroom. She and John followed on the crowd's fringes.

"I need to take up-close-and-personal pictures of one of the people from the auction," she whispered. "There will be flirting. Stay fifteen feet away at all times."

John squeezed her hand. "I'd rather stick with you."

"We're in a crowded place. I'll be fine."

"As if nothing bad ever happened in a crowded place?"

Eurodance music blasted them as attendants opened the ballroom doors. Despite the dimmed room, she clocked Mystery Vampire standing at the bar.

"Stay over there." She jerked her head toward a pillar, then nudged the tiny button on the back of her camera necklace. "Remember—fifteen feet."

"Got it." He nodded. "But I don't like it."

Neither did she, but this was the job.

At the bar, she shimmied into the spot next to Mystery Vampire. Christ, this was weird. She'd never played the vixen with a boyfriend...fiancé, hopefully...watching.

"Qu'est-ce que vous voudriez?" the bartender asked.

What she would really have liked was to fast-forward to the

moment she and John could return home to restart their lives, but duty called.

"Pink Vesper, s'il vous plaît." She was more of a red wine girl, but she ordered the signature cocktail while she was on the job, both to blend and avoid traceable preferences.

The bartender nodded.

A different bartender delivered a tulip-shaped glass of amber alcohol to Mystery Vampire.

"Merci." Mystery Vampire's voice was deep.

She needed to get him talking to better suss out his accent. One word was not enough.

Her bartender delivered her drink in a chilled coupe glass. It was bubblegum pink.

"Merci." She turned to Mystery Vampire. In French, she asked, "Pardon me, but did I see you at the charity auction?"

"Yes." He peered over her head toward the doors.

Chatty.

She raised her glass. "Cheers to a successful auction!"

He did not reciprocate.

"What's your drink?" she asked. "Looks yummy."

She hated her word choice. But studies showed straight men were looser-lipped around women they perceived to be less intelligent. Madame Curie probably never said *yummy*.

"Rakija," he answered, "is like cognac. Made from plums."

Yeah, plums soaked in lighter fluid. The agency held a course on booze from around the world because it was bridge-building knowledge. Mystery Vampire's choice also helped geolocate his elongated vowels. He spoke like he was holding a bubble in the middle of his tongue. So...likely Eastern European, and based on his drink, probably Croatian.

More conversation was needed.

"Can you believe how much someone spent on the Rocksy painting?" She widened her eyes. "I mean, love that for them. But is it, like, as important as Warhol?"

She sipped her Pink Vesper. *Blech*. Vodka was her enemy.

"I love it," Mystery Vampire said. "People pay millions for spray-painted garbage? I admire his grift."

She did not appreciate Mystery Vampire's pronoun assumption.

"You're so smart," she said. "What do you think about—"

Someone jostled Mystery Vampire's arm. Rajika sloshed onto her and darkened her dress at her nipple. Perfect. She glared at the offender over Mystery Vampire's shoulder.

Jesus fucking Christ.

"Sorry, dude," John said. "Let me buy you a drink."

"No." Mystery Vampire thrust a napkin at Vivian. "Take this."

"Oh my gosh, thank you *so* much." She took the napkin and dabbed her breast with as much come-hither finesse as she could muster. This couldn't possibly be alluring, but she had to try. She pointed to the dance floor. "This is my favorite song. Want to dance?"

Mystery Vampire skimmed his gaze over her, then shook his head.

Big fucking ouch.

He dropped euros into the tip jar, then left. Chasing him would be too obvious. Hopefully the camera picked up some clean shots.

"Jane Davis, I'll dance with you." John caught her free hand. She set her drink on the bar. "What the fuck, *Jason*?"

"Dance with me." He squeezed her hand three times.

No choice but to follow him. The music shifted to jazzy salsa. Her agency dance lessons were stale, but it didn't matter. John led with confidence, twirling her, then reeling her back to him. They clasped their left hands, and his right pressed firmly on the small of her back. They moved through the crowd, not lingering near anyone for more than a few seconds.

"Where'd these dance moves come from?"

"My parents didn't want me to be embarrassed if anyone asked me to dance at a state dinner when I was a teenager." He twirled her again. "And the president of Iceland's daughter had the night of her life."

"Why didn't you stay put like I told you?"

"My cuff links."

"Say more, please."

"I dropped one in that guy's pocket when I bumped into him."

Understanding dawned on her. She hadn't considered planting them on a person of interest. But because John had, they could track Mystery Vampire instead of skulking after him.

"You're brilliant," she said.

"I know." He glanced at his watch. "We need to move. It's 11:20."

"One thing first." She raised herself on her toes and wrapped her arms around his neck, coaxing his mouth to hers. As their tongues tangled, he cupped her ass and hauled her to him.

"Is that because of the cuff links?" he asked.

"It's a cover. If anyone's watching us, they'll assume I'm dragging you to bed."

He arched an eyebrow. "We could skip everything else and do that."

"You wish." She patted his chest. "Let's get to work."

Nineteen

John wrapped his hand around Vivian's as they strolled from the ballroom.

"You're surprising today," she said.

Great, more Vivian observations-that-weren't-insults. "How so?"

They descended from the ballroom and entered a hall leading to the lobby level guest restrooms. The hall also led to the housekeeping supply room that, based on the blueprints she'd shown him earlier, contained a duct that would take them to the gallery.

"Friendly in Marseille, helpful on the rooftop, playful during the exhibit preview, and then in our suite…"

"A beast?" he suggested.

"Attentive," she countered.

He'd take it.

"Jealous in the casino, aggressive in the auction, then suave in the disco. I didn't know you had all that in you." Vivian held the staff security badge against the supply room's sensor. Green lights signaled admittance. "It's surprising."

That word could go either way.

"Surprising like finding twenty bucks in your pocket, or—"

"What the hell are those?" Vivian gestured to a collection of shelves with hand cranks on them. "They weren't on the blueprints."

"They're space savers. We've got them at the museum. They must've been installed after the blueprints were filed." He scanned the wall. "Where's the vent supposed to be?"

She stepped down the row, then stopped. "Here."

As he reached for the crank, Vivian shouted, "Stop!"

He jerked his hand back. "Why?"

"Fingerprints." She handed him an N95 mask and surgical gloves. "The mask's in case the fog machine doesn't deploy. Not a top-notch disguise, but it's something."

He snapped on the gloves, then spun the crank on the mobile shelves. They parted like the Red Sea, revealing a two-foot by two-foot register at the base of the wall.

"Perfect. Should be a twelve-foot crawl." She presented the naked column of her back to him. "Get the hook above my skirt's zipper? The skirt's detachable, and I don't want to wreck it."

Courtesy of working with fasteners every day, his fingers found and undid the hook quickly. His reward was an eyeful of Vivian's ass as she folded the silk.

"Thanks. I need the screwdrivers. Oh, and ditch the jacket." She darted her eyes around the room, then handed him her skirt and heels. "Bury everything under that bathrobe stack. They don't get replaced as often as other linens."

While he stripped and hid the clothes, she converted her purse into a backpack with its hidden straps, then knelt to unscrew the vent. After a tense minute, she pried it free.

"I'll go first, and you follow. But go backward so you can position the vent in front of the duct. And set the timer on your watch—twelve minutes. We need to be fast."

No shit.

After she disappeared into the duct, he reverse-crawled into its cold metal embrace, then positioned the vent like she'd instructed. The duct was narrower than the one at her office.

"This'll make me claustrophobic," he said.

"Unlikely unless you experience a traumatic event."

"*Being* here is a traumatic event." His feet bumped into hers. "Why'd you stop?"

"'Cause we're there. I'm getting the vape pen."

"Not a great time for a smoke break."

"It's to see if the lasers are on."

Behind him, a whooshing sound was followed by a gentle crackling and popping. A lemon-mint haze shrouded him.

"Are they on?" he asked.

"On Amina's painting, yes. And that giant ball of string. Tough angle, so I can't see much more." More rustling. "Good thing I brought super bouncing balls."

"I'm confused by that sentence."

"The balls' movement will trigger the fog cannon. Once the room's full of fog, we can enter and inspect the paintings like we planned."

Right, they'd walked through this in the room this afternoon. Then stripped naked and… *Focus*. He'd been horny in a ton of places, but a duct seemed like a not-great location to add to the list. The unmistakable chaotic sound of rubber balls smacking against parquet erupted behind him. He prayed they didn't bounce against the artwork.

"Here comes the fog," she said.

White mist joined them in the duct. She'd assured him it wasn't toxic, but he was glad he was wearing a mask. Nerves buzzed through him. He could do this. For Vivian, and to stop the information on those drives from ending up in the wrong hands.

The vent clattered against the gallery's floor.

"It's go time!"

He scooted backward. As he emerged, feet first, Vivian's hand was on his calf, his thigh, his ass. Her touch was reassuring as he stood in the opaque, breathable fog.

"I feel like I'm floating in space," he said.

"Here." She placed the infrared glasses in his hand. "I'll hold on to your belt."

He put on the glasses. Nothing but white. They fogged with his breath. Dammit, he'd forgotten about that inconvenience with masks. Stress made his vision swim. After a deep, calming breath, he made out the art's faint heat signatures. *Smoking Hon* was the biggest in the room, closest to the vent, and the drive's likeliest source.

"This way." He tugged Vivian to the four-by-eight-foot plywood.

With a grunt, he lifted the hundred-pound framed painting from the wall.

The room remained quiet as fresh fallen snow.

Gently he set the painting on the ground, then swiveled it around. "No alarm."

"She's gotta be the dead drop," Vivian said.

"You go low, I'll go high." As he spidered his fingers along the painting's top edges and corners, she knelt.

"Fuck," Vivian said. "Splinter. Find anything?"

"Not yet. Where was the first one?"

"Wedged inside the frame on the back."

A lightning bolt realization hit him. "This is a floater frame. It attaches directly to the back of the painting. There's no room to hide anything. But there's a gap that borders the front. It's perfect for hiding a flash drive. I'll turn it back around."

"Do it," she said.

Another grunt, and he turned the painting. "Check the gap on the bottom."

Up top, he dipped his pinky into the quarter-inch gap between the frame and the plywood's edge. A third of the way down on the left, something stopped his progress.

"Give me a screwdriver?" he asked.

"Okay." She patted up his body 'til she found his arm, then pressed a flathead screwdriver into his hand. "Hurry."

Working by feel, he wedged the screwdriver against whatever blocked his pinky. Carefully, like he was popping a staple from a Jackson Pollock, he eased what he'd found from the frame.

It felt like a flash drive. "Got it."

"Holy shit, really?" Joy suffused Vivian's voice.

"Yes." He traced his fingers from her wrist to her palm. "Here."

He placed the drive in her hand, then curled her fingers closed over it. If it weren't for the masks, he'd use one of their precious minutes for a victory kiss.

"Give me a second to put the painting back."

He lifted *Smoking Hon* and hooked her back onto the cable. Impossible to return it to exactly the right place, but hopefully security wouldn't immediately notice.

"You go first," she said.

They felt their way toward the vent. Visuals were terrible in here, too. As he army-crawled back to the housekeeping closet, he snagged his pants. The linen shredded along his thigh. At the end, he climbed into the housekeeping closet. The small amount of fog that had traveled here finally dissipated. He removed his mask and the infrared glasses, then helped Vivian up as she emerged.

His fingers shook around hers. "I can't believe we fucking did that."

"Not done yet. We still have to get away with it." She spun the screws back into place. "The fog'll take an hour to clear, but they'll already be looking for perpetrators. You can't wear those pants to the party… So, plan B. We'll lay low at the pool."

She tossed a bathrobe to him, then slipped into one.

"Plan B was in DC. This is more like plan Q," he said. "Let's grab the car and go."

"The valet would have to bring us the car. People who immediately leave after a theft are suspicious as hell. We want to stay, relax." She frowned. "Why are you still dressed?"

"Because the shorts don't leave a lot to the imagination."

They were Daniel-Craig-emerging-from-the-ocean in *Casino Royale* shorts. He wasn't body-conscious, but he also wasn't Daniel Craig.

"Nothing I haven't seen before." She winked.

"Not you I'm worried about." He peeled off his shirt and dropped his pants.

Vivian wolf-whistled.

"Was that necessary?"

"Completely. They look good on you. I'll take the stuff from your suit pockets. My bag has room. The drive, however—" she tucked it into her bodysuit's bra cup "—stays on me."

All he had in his pockets were his money clip, his Zippo and Jean-Michel's poker chip.

"Here." He handed her his money clip and lighter.

The poker chip went into his tiny shorts' zipper pocket. The tips of his ears heated with the idea of explaining to her that he'd kept it as a memento. Every time he looked at it, he thought of beating that smarmy asshole at blackjack and taking his money.

She wrapped a towel around her purse. "Once the noise dies down, we can leave."

He stashed the clothes they'd shed behind a tea service. After they stepped out from between the shelves, he spun the crank, sealing the vent and their clothes within.

"If anyone stops us, act drunk and lost, okay?"

He could use a drink, that was certain. "Yeah."

"Here we go." Vivian opened the door, then swiveled her gaze.

She gestured for him to follow. Soon his nose tickled with the scent of chlorine.

They pushed through the doors.

John's heart *should* be thundering. They'd broken into an art gallery, yanked a piece from the wall, pried a flash drive containing bioweapons data from its frame, escaped, and were now hiding from security.

But this *view*.

Twinkling lights had been draped on the palm trees bordering the pool area. Illuminated walkways guided guests to the bar, hot tub and infinity pool. Mostly empty, the pool glowed blue. Beyond the resort, the Mediterranean crashed to shore. A smoky scent drifted from the St. John's bonfire on the public beach. Above them, stars speckled the midnight sky.

This should have been their honeymoon.

"Hot tub," she said. "It's semishielded by the palm trees."

He held in a groan as they dropped their bathrobes. Being this close to her without touching her was a Herculean test of willpower. As he climbed into the frothing water and sat next to her, the happy bubbles were at odds with the amorous tension in his body.

"You're doing great." Vivian squeezed his knee. "The beach is our escape route. Easy to get lost in the St. John's crowd."

"Unless you're wearing bathrobes and microscopic shorts."

"I'll think of something." Her gaze snapped to the bar through the scrim of trees. "Damn, security's here."

A guard bellied up to the bar. His gruff voice carried in the peaceful night air.

"See anything unusual this evening?" the guard asked the bartender. "We're looking for Americans. A man and a woman. Red hair."

"Well, shit." Vivian handed John the drive. "They're looking for a couple. Fly solo for a few minutes? And hold me under."

Before he could ask for details, she slipped under the hot tub's surface and pulled his foot onto her thigh. Fear spiked through him. Solo? She was the brains of this—

His watch alarm sounded. Ah, fuck. He forgot to turn that off.

As he slapped at the button, the security guard swung his attention toward John. That wasn't good. If he came over here, he'd see John holding a redheaded American under water.

Wait. *American*.

He hadn't endured endless French accent corrections in high school for nothing.

He ignored his galloping pulse and shouted in Marseille-accented French, "Bonsoir? Je suis là depuis vingt minutes. Devez-vous prendre ma commande de boissons?"

They hadn't been there twenty minutes, and he definitely didn't need a drink. What he needed was for the security guard to fuck off. Or for Vivian and him to be helicoptered out of here. Either would be great.

"Désolé, monsieur," the bartender answered. "Je viendrai bientôt."

The security guard moved on to the beach.

Yes. John tapped Vivian on the shoulder, and she emerged between his legs.

"Security's gone," he said. "You really can hold your breath for five minutes?"

"Why would I lie about that?" She placed her hands on his thighs and pushed up 'til she stood between his legs. Her nipples pebbled the bodysuit. "Drive?"

After he handed it to her, she climbed out of the hot tub.

John, on the other hand, needed a minute. "How are you so calm?"

"Practice." She winked. "Now get your ass out of the hot tub."

Vivian tied the robe's belt at her waist. That had been way too close for her comfort.

"Why'd the security guard move along?" she asked. "All I heard was bubbles."

"Because I shouted to the bartender in perfect French. The guard must've decided I wasn't the American he was looking for."

"That was smart," she said. "Good job."

Unlike MacColl, she believed in positive feedback.

John slipped into his robe, which was a shame. She adored his tiny shorts. But it was for the best—his physique would attract way too much attention.

She had to get them out of here. With her eyes closed, she pictured the blueprints. Specifically the service hallways. There was one across the pool area that led to the waste and recycling bins. Unglamorous, but that was true for a surprising number of operations.

"This way." She tugged him with her.

"Aren't you worried? Security's everywhere."

"Yes, but no?" She pushed through the doors. "I don't think the resort's security team is in cahoots with Jean-Michel or Mystery Vampire."

"Who?" John laughed.

"The guy from the ballroom. I give people code names to keep track in my head. Anyway, Jean-Michel wouldn't bribe a huge security team. Too expensive and risky. If word got out that he had a special arrangement with the resort's—and the auction's—security, people might ask questions he'd rather not answer. No, he's working around the security team, too."

"But they're specifically looking for an American couple. Where'd that come from? Do you think they ID'd us from security footage?"

"Anything's possible." Vivian rubbed her L-Pill pendant. "But I think we can chalk that up to Jean-Michel being a spiteful asshole. Since his painting was targeted, they would've spoken with him. And if he knows the drive is gone, he'll want to take his anger out on someone. I'm a convenient target. Whether he thinks I had anything to do with the break-in, he would've been happy to fuck up my evening."

She peeked around the corner. Clear.

"Charming," John said.

"Yeah, well, sweethearts don't succeed on the black market."

The tang of garbage thickened as they approached the doors marked Sortie.

On the other side, among the neatly organized blue and green dumpsters, a young man flicked the ash from his cigarette. "Bonsoir?"

"Excusez-moi," Vivian said. "Quel est le chemin le plus rapide pour se rendre aux magasins?"

The kid loosely gestured his cigarette toward the sidewalk. "At the end of this path, turn left. But most stores are closed for the evening."

"Merci." After they rounded a corner, she said, "I feel judged when French people switch to English."

John laughed. "Don't take it personally. If their English is better than your French, they'll answer in the language that's more comfortable for you."

"But I could be Icelandic."

"Your accent's American. And it's adorable."

She turned left per the kid's instructions and sighed. "Why is *everything* uphill here?"

"Because we're in the Alps?"

Beyond a lush public park, shops lined this street. Ah, shit. Nothing usable. Lingerie, fountain pens, real estate, mobile phones, Rolexes...

Ooh, that souvenir shop might do the trick.

"Bingo." She gestured to the collection of beach clothes displayed outside the shop.

"Can we leave euros?" he asked. "I feel bad about stealing."

"Yes, of course." After checking for security cameras and police officers, she tucked two hundred euros through the shop's mail slot, then snatched clothing and flip-flops.

They ducked into an alley to change.

She'd scored a white eyelet sleeveless tank. John buttoned a slouchy striped shirt over his chest. After stepping into a purple maxi skirt, she wiggled her feet into slightly-too-small flip-flops that'd give her more blisters than her Jimmy Choos.

"We've got a problem." He held out the cabana shorts. "These don't fit. I need something to cover this banana hammock."

"Everyone wears them." She stuffed her hotel robe into a trash bin. When she looked up, she bit back a laugh. His swimsuit *was* tiny.

"Vivian, come on."

"No time for shyness, Mr. Seymour." She opened her phone's map app. "There's a hotel–slash–youth hostel with a business center at Larvotto Beach. It's an oceanfront walk up the Promenade Prince Jacques. We can get to it via the public beach."

He popped his hands on his hips. "You're really making me do this?"

"Try to make lemons out of lemonade."

"Lemonade requires a shit ton of sugar, which we do not have. Just lemons."

She tried not to stare at the outline of his junk. He had lemons, all right.

"Come on." She grabbed his hand. "Resent me while we walk."

She hurried them along the shop-lined cobblestone streets toward the bonfire-lit section of the public beach. The still-warm sand slipped between her toes and the flip-flops. Some stragglers wore traditional folk outfits—red-and-white-striped skirts and pants, white shirts, black vests—but most were dressed like her and John. In the flickering dark, they blended as they worked their way through the crowd to the promenade's entry.

As a chain of dancers passed them, a drunk teenage girl at the end grabbed Vivian's hand and tugged her into the circle with them.

Shit.

She tried to extract herself without causing a scene. The circle brought them toward police monitoring the scene from the beach's edge.

Double shit.

Close to the bonfire, the circle broke apart. People fell to their knees, laughing. John reeled her to him, then pinned her against the base of a palm tree. His laughter faded, but the fire remained in his eyes. They should run, but she was powerless against the desire whisking through her. He covered her mouth with his, then slid his hand up her shirt and palmed her breast. A second too late, she felt him steal the drive.

Ice replaced the fire in her veins.

Was John an agent who had slipped past the background checks? Her instincts?

He broke the kiss, then nuzzled her ear.

"Cop," he whispered. "If we get caught, diplomats' kids are extracted pretty fast."

Near them stood a baseball-capped woman in a white polo shirt emblazoned with red diamonds between stripes—Monte Carlo's police uniform.

Guilt tightened her chest. He was protecting her, and she'd suspected him for it?

Christ, she was *losing* it.

Vivian nuzzled him back. "We won't get caught. Let's go."

She led him to the promenade, smiling, trying to look like a lover out for a romantic stroll. Which…she supposed she was.

After a quiet minute, John cleared his throat. "I get why you do this work. It's important."

"Hang on." She surveyed the promenade. "Okay, we're alone. But be vague as needed?"

He nodded.

"At the end of the day, you protect people. But why do you put yourself at risk?"

She'd never been brave enough to tell anyone her main motivation. John, though…she should have been vulnerable with him. He was supposed to be her safe space.

She took a deep breath.

"This work makes me feel like I belong. My brothers and sisters all went to the same schools, ran in the same circles. I got left out a lot. The people I work with, though—when they recruited me, I finally felt like I belonged. And there's meaning in what we do. If that comes with some risk, it's worth the trade-off to me."

"You also belong with me." John squeezed her hand.

Those were the words she wanted to hear. But they didn't fit his pattern.

Be brave, Flint. She had to point out his inconsistency.

"Except you…" Her voice cut out. She cleared her throat. "You broke up with me when I told you the truth about who I am. What I do."

"I did, and I'm sorry." He sighed. "It took me a beat to catch up. I mean, you kept me in the dark for a year."

"I know, okay?" She threw her hands in the air. "But I don't have a time machine, so all I can do is do better. Can you be comfortable knowing I can't tell you everything I've done, what I'm doing, where I'm going?"

Silver leaped and bounced on the sea's dark current. The gentle lapping against the promenade was the only sound between them. She wanted to scream, but she'd wait.

He kicked a rock. "I'd like to try."

Twenty

John felt like an anchor from one of those yachts in the marina had thumped him in the chest. He could tell that confession had cost Vivian. One trait she and "Jane" shared—they shied away from vulnerability. Both versions of her preferred for the world to see her as a strong, independent person who needed nothing from anyone.

It might be the most successful of her lies.

And one he'd never believed.

"While I'm trying," John said, "I need to do a better job of making you feel like you belong with me and Ruckus."

"No," she said. "I love you, but fixing me is not your job. This is a me thing. I filled my self-esteem hole with my career for years, but it's not working anymore. I would, however, love you to stick with me while I figure it out."

"And how will you do that?"

She shrugged. "Probably therapy, yoga, meditation. After running from this for so long, I'm scared the solution is to sit with it for a long time in the woods."

"I like sitting in the woods," he said. "Can I come with you?"

She bumped shoulders with him. "You'd better. Hey, I think that's the youth hostel."

Plate glass walls revealed the lobby's exposed brick-and-neon decor.

"Hang on." John opened the door for her. The yeasty scent of fresh-baked bread greeted them. A mohawked man sitting at the minuscule check-in station at the bar, however, did not. Above him, a menu listed alcohol and snacks.

"Let's get something," Vivian said. "Six appetizers is not enough to tide me over."

"This is the best order you've given me this week." To Mr. Mohawk, he said, "Bonjour, monsieur. Could we order the focaccia and…crispy panisses?"

He'd loved chickpea flour fritters as a kid.

"Ouais." The man entered logged their order. "Forty-three euros. What's your name?"

"Jason," he answered without hesitation.

Vivian paid the bill in cash. "You have a business center, yes?"

"Around the corner." The man gestured in a vaguely left direction.

Vivian departed almost before the man finished speaking. Rudeness was another sign of her exhaustion. John followed her to a nook dominated by an enormous Warhol-esque screen print of Prince Albert. His scratchy eyes did not appreciate the visual assault.

Vivian dropped into the seat in front of the computer.

She stifled a yawn. "I can't muster the energy to show how exciting this is. But it is."

He caught her yawn. "I get it."

She disconnected the computer from the internet. When she inserted the drive, the screen showed the same code entry prompt that had flashed at Anjali's house. Vivian flipped through her index cards until she landed on the one with the code, then gave it to John.

"Read that to me?" she said.

As he read the digits, Vivian typed them in. Before hitting Enter, she read them back, and he confirmed the sequence was correct. The screen resolved into two neat files.

"Hot damn," Vivian said as she double-clicked the README file. "It worked."

The simple text file revealed their next destination—Maison Moreau in Paris.

Vivian groaned. "Maison Moreau is a hotel-slash-museum—

slash night club. I curated a show there with Jean-Michel. The owner, Serge Moreau, is an asshole. I swore I'd throw a baby out a window before I returned to that viper's nest."

"Should I go get a baby?" John asked.

She giggled, then palmed her eyes with a groan. "The shit I'll need to eat to be permitted within those walls is incalculable. But I suppose global security is worth my dignity. And if my instincts are on point, I know where they've stashed the drive. Let's see what's on this file."

As she removed her hands, the man at the front called, "Jason?"

"Be right back." He pushed back from the table.

Outside, some tourists had gathered. Good thing they'd gotten here first or they might've had to wait longer for their food. The warm, fried scent of thyme, rosemary and olives wafted from the panisses, just like he remembered.

He rounded the corner. "These smell incredi— What's wrong?"

The color had drained from Vivian's face.

She gestured to the screen. "Security details for the same places as the other drive."

He handed her a hunk of focaccia. Even if she'd lost her appetite, fresh baked bread should never go to waste.

"How far is Paris from here?" he asked.

"Ten hours by car?" She munched the focaccia. "And eight by train."

"What about flights?" he asked.

She sipped her water. "About ninety minutes, but it's a no-go. The thing I said the other day about cameras, IDs and scanners is still true."

An hour and a half would be easier on their exhausted bodies than the other options.

He picked up a panisse and dipped it in the garlic aioli. "Can your pilot friend help?"

"I can't go back to the well too often or they'll block my number."

"What about your boss? Any love there?"

"He offered me backup, but I turned him down. I need to see this through, not hand the baton to someone else."

"Why not take him up on it? You don't need to do this alone."

She winked. "I'm not alone."

He tucked a curl behind her ear. "No, you aren't."

He'd still try to talk her around to getting more official help, though.

"We'd better get going." She withdrew the drive, then cleared the system's recent history.

A sound outside caught Vivian's attention.

"Shit." She squinted at the tourists he'd seen earlier. "Goons. Six, at least."

"Goons?"

"It's what I call hired muscle. Once you've been in the game long enough, you can pick them out of a crowd." She withdrew a tampon from her purse, removed the tampon from its wrapper and hid both BSL-4 drives in the packaging, then resealed it.

He'd purchased that brand for her back home. *I like the kind with the resealable packaging.* He hadn't questioned the preferences of a woman suffering through menstrual cramps, even though he'd had to go to a second store to find them.

She pushed back from the table.

He followed, no hesitation.

Inside the lobby's bathroom, she flipped the lock, then knocked over the metal trash can and scooted it under the lone clerestory window. As she climbed onto the can, he braced it with his foot.

"Damn, no latches. We're trapped." She hopped down from the can.

"Should we hide in the stalls?"

"We'd be sitting ducks." She dug through her purse. "And

our arsenal is...lacking. I've got a nail file, the ceramic screwdrivers, one propofol EpiPen, and..." She looked around the room. "There's a plunger in the corner."

"I could bash people with the trash can?" he suggested.

She snapped her fingers and pointed at him. "Do that. If they force their way in here, hit them, then run if you can."

He lifted the trash can. "I'm not leaving you."

The door thunked as someone tried to push their way inside.

Vivian's heart beat faster than a speedbag at the Langley Field House. John, standing with her, ready to tackle the world by her side, felt *good*. For years, she'd hungered for a loved one to know, *really* know, what she did for a living.

They might both be obliterated in a minute, but at least she got to taste that feeling.

Another thump at the door.

"Somebody's in here," she squeaked.

Christ, what was *that* tone of voice?

"Flint, I'd like to speak with you."

Vivian lowered her hands.

"Who's that?" John still clutched the trash can.

"My boss's boss."

Her gut still insisted something was off with Vandenburg. MacColl hadn't agreed—merely said he'd look into her. Now that Vandenberg had apparently saved them from a losing battle with goons...her gut said to play along.

"Put the can down," she said. "This might be okay."

"Might be?"

"It's better than being outnumbered in a fight."

She flipped the lock and opened the door. Vandenberg was stunning. Silvery hair cut into a loose-waved bob, perfectly applied makeup, and a blue slim-cut Italian suit. Versus Vivian, in wrinkled clothes and too-tight flip flops that had blistered her feet.

"Ma'am," Vivian said.

"Flint. And the fiancé." Vandenberg crossed her arms. "Come outside. We don't talk business in a shitter that hasn't been swept."

Warily, Vivian followed. They passed two agents inspecting the computer she'd been using and the food they left behind. Her stomach grumbled. She should've eaten more focaccia and panisses.

Outside, Vandenberg pointed to a van. "That's our ride."

They walked past four police motorcycles and a patrol wagon. The goons, Winegrad among them, were cuffed and kneeling on the ground. Winegrad winked. Typical. When agents ran into each other in the field, they weren't supposed to acknowledge each other, but he treated protocols like suggestions.

Vandenberg gestured to the seats that faced the back of the van. "Sit there."

Oof. Riding backward might trigger her motion sickness.

John followed her, then Vandenberg. The door slid shut. As the van growled to life and departed the plaza, Vandenberg dragged her gaze between them.

"Someday—" Vandenberg crossed her legs "—you'll have to explain how you left the States after I put you on the no-fly list."

Vivian raised a shoulder. "I know a trick with palette knives."

Vandenberg pinched the bridge of her nose. "That sentence doesn't even make sense. You can't jam 'palette knife' into a normal conversation and keep a low profile. You know MacColl's code words aren't official agency protocol, right? His whole career, he's overcomplicated things with his spy-versus-spy bullshit."

She *did* know the code word. Maybe Vivian could trust her?

"Once we get to a secure location, I'll share more of his… peculiarities." She gestured for Vivian's bag. "First we need to find the tracker that led your friends straight to you."

Insulting. She'd taken great care to avoid detection. Unless she meant John's remaining cuff link? But that was buried under a tea service at the Casino d'Or.

"There's no tracker," Vivian said.

Shit. She hadn't checked the drive for one. But she wouldn't admit to having the drives to Vandenberg. Not yet.

"Uh, there might be," John said.

She swiveled toward him. "What?"

He lifted his hips and dug into his tiny shorts. Shorts she regretted not replacing since Vandenberg got an eyeful of what he was packing.

"I kept the poker chip your ex lost to us at blackjack."

He handed the black chip to Vivian, who passed it to Vandenberg.

"Why?" she asked.

"Because I like it when he loses to me."

Aw, that was sweet. A huge mistake, but a sweet one.

"Blunders from civilians are expected." Vandenberg opened her rugged plastic briefcase and unfolded a black cloth. "Which is why we don't involve them in actions, Flint."

From the briefcase, Vandenberg withdrew a radio frequency detector. It lit up as she passed it over the chip. With brutal efficiency, she crushed the chip in the jaws of a stainless steel nutcracker, then lowered the window and tossed the pieces into Monte Carlo's night hills.

"There," she said. "While I'm at it—phones?"

Not much choice here. Vivian handed them over. Vandenberg swept the radio frequency detector over them. Nothing. Vandenberg nodded and returned them to Vivian.

"Rodriguez? We're good to go to the airport."

The driver U-turned, then twisted under, over and through the mountainous Monegasque streets. Between his driving style and sitting backward, queasiness overtook Vivian.

New rule—never leave the Dramamine behind.

After a nauseating eternity, they arrived at a nondescript location.

Well, nondescript for Monte Carlo. The elegant buttercream building with lush flower boxes in its arched windows would attract attention in any other city, maybe serve as the setting for a Nora Ephron movie. The driver cut the engine, and the van door opened. Two officers escorted them to the second-floor apartment.

"Sit." Vandenberg gestured to the couch. "Can we get you something? Coffee? Wine?"

"Water, thanks," John said.

Vivian nodded. "Same for me."

"Want something stronger, kiddo?" Vandenberg asked. "You won't like this briefing."

Not with this woozy stomach. "Ginger ale?"

Vandenberg smiled. "Hall, check for ginger ale, please?"

A pantsuited woman left the room.

Vandenberg sat across the coffee table from them. "I'll get straight to it. MacColl is a European organized crime asset."

Hot bile rose in Vivian's throat. "Impossible."

Vandenberg folded her hands. "I get it. This is a bitter pill to swallow. He and I have known each other for thirty years, and I didn't see this coming. But I didn't like his answers during his debrief of the office attack, and his notes on the drive you found in London were incomplete. So I started digging."

"Here, Flint." Hall handed her a freezing can of ginger ale.

"What did you find?" She popped the top and guzzled the spicy bubbles, determined to settle her storming stomach.

Vandenberg leaned forward. "It boils down to this. Mac-Coll lost his shirt in his divorce. His career stalled at GS-14, and he felt unappreciated and underutilized by the agency. The operation he works for—that *you* work for—isn't the apple of the directorate's eye. From what we can discern, he's working with Dilettante."

As Vivian slumped backward, John rested his hand on hers. A week ago, she would've shaken him off, mortified at any hint of her inner softness in front of her coworkers. Now? If John made a move to cradle her like Michelangelo's *Pietà*, she'd let him.

"Between them, they cooked up the scheme to use auctions

to pass intelligence to the highest bidder. But MacColl didn't expect Dilettante to use an unauthenticated Rocksy piece for the dead drop. That, of course, required your alias's expertise. And here we are."

Vivian rolled the cold can against her pounding forehead. "MacColl's grumpy. Sometimes an asshole. But treasonous? No."

"I get it. It's a shock when one of us turns. But I have proof."

Vandenberg opened her briefcase and tossed glossy photos on Vivian's lap.

MacColl, half in shadow, and Jean-Michel.

"Ever wonder why MacColl squashed your recommendation to turn Dilettante over to local police? This is why. MacColl skipped town two days ago, and intel shows he's on his way here. That's why *I'm* here. To catch him and clean up this mess." Vandenberg clapped a hand to Vivian's shoulder. "He fooled all of us."

Vivian turned the intel over in her head. Everything Vandenberg said was plausible.

Except… After they broke up, Jean-Michel swore off running jobs with Americans.

"I need your help to fix this." She smiled at Vivian. "You know, you remind me of myself at your age. Doing whatever it takes to complete a mission. Using your wits to leverage the tools and people you have at hand. I applaud your hustle."

Ew. Full-body cringe. Hustle?

"Thanks," she said diplomatically.

Vandenberg leaned forward again. "All this cat-and-mouse, I bet you don't trust anyone."

Not true. She turned her hand over to lace her fingers with John's.

"I promise," Vandenberg said. "I'm not the bad guy here. Since there was a security incident at the gallery tonight and you used the computer at the hostel, I'll go out on a limb and guess you found the second drive. So tell me—where are we headed next?"

"Paris," John said.

Cold anger burst through Vivian.

She yanked her hand from his. That information was *not* his to share. She needed time to assess Vandenberg's motivations before blabbing everything. Photographic—or possibly Photoshopped—evidence be damned. Plain and simple, Vandenberg gave her the ick.

Always trust the ick.

Vandenberg clapped her hands. "So. Who's ready to go to Paris?"

Twenty-One

John shifted in his seat in the van. The leather stuck to his legs. Vivian hadn't spoken to him since they'd left the safe house with Vandenberg. Who, for the record, struck him as a grounded and dedicated civil servant.

"ETA is zero-three-hundred to NCE," the driver said.

NCE—Nice Côte d'Azur Airport.

"You okay?" he asked Vivian.

Her cheeks were pale in the early morning light. She clutched the handle above the door and breathed in through her nose, out through her mouth. Since Monte Carlo, the streets, tunnels and highways to France twisted with sharp climbs and steep drops in elevation.

Vivian must be dying.

Through clenched teeth, she said, "I've been better."

The car peeled off the highway. The driver slowed to follow the speed limit despite being alone on the road. Signs indicated they were at the airport, but the driver diverted from the main passenger drop-off and circled toward the business aviation terminal.

Rodriguez flashed his credentials. "Premier Executive Transport Services. We have a flight scheduled in thirty minutes."

After a cursory inspection of his ID, the guard waved him through.

In the fading dark, their van parked next to a Gulfstream jet.

"Does the government often fly private?" he asked.

"When we need to minimize touch points, yes." Vandenberg unbuckled. "Flying commercial requires seven hundred microinteractions. It's easier to keep a low profile this way."

"Told you," Vivian said.

As they entered the private jet, her color returned. It's plush interior featured creamy leather recliners, glossy caramel wood and flattering lighting that helped them all look more sophisticated. Except for him and his tiny shorts, of course.

"Everyone on board?" Vandenberg asked.

An officer—she'd said her name was Hall—confirmed. "Yes, ma'am."

"Then we're wheels-up." To him and Vivian, she said, "Sit at the table for the debrief."

Minutes later, they were in the air.

Vandenberg positioned a voice recorder between them. "This is Deputy Director Janna Vandenberg debriefing Officer Vivian Flint and her fiancé, John Seymour, on the events that have taken place since 20 June. We are speaking at oh-two hundred on 26 June. Flint, confirm or clarify the following, please. Jean-Michel de Gramont hired your alias, Jane Davis, to authenticate a Rocksy painting. You conducted said authentication in London on 19 June."

Vivian's color was returning. "Correct."

For the next thirty minutes, they volleyed questions and answers.

John stilled his face like he was playing *Clue Conspiracy* and didn't want to give away his identity. After the way she reacted after he let Paris slip, he wouldn't open his mouth unless Vivian told him to speak.

Forget *Taboo, Cards against Humanity, Settlers of Catan*... These two were playing four-dimensional chess. Trying to evaluate what the other knew, how much to give to persuade the other to do the same. He had no read on Vandenberg, but Vivian? She was coolly out for blood.

Never thought he'd find an interrogation hot, but here he was.

"After the video teleconference in Marseille, Rodriguez followed you from the consulate." Vandenberg sipped the water Hall had delivered to her. "How'd you evade him?"

That was him? John glanced at Rodriguez.

Never would have connected the Gore-Tex man to the one sitting over there in a suit.

"The café had roof access. Easy to hop over to the next building and use their fire escape."

Easy? She was selling herself short. But he kept his lips zipped. For all he knew, she'd never told them she had a fear of heights.

"Clever." Vandenberg nodded.

"We drove to Monte Carlo and encountered Jean-Michel and Lola Vorlicek. We learned he donated the Rocksy, and she donated the Amina Hassan."

Vandenberg said, "Any other persons of interest there?"

John sipped his water. Up to Vivian if she wanted to mention Mystery Vampire.

"No one of note," Vivian said.

"Hall, can we pull security footage?" Vandenberg leaned back in her seat. "Since I don't like to assume anything—you two broke into the gallery and triggered the fog?"

Vivian nodded.

John drank more water. If he kept this up, he'd commandeer the private jet's bathroom.

"And you obtained the second drive?" Vandenberg's gaze was like an ice cube.

Vivian said nothing. Therefore, John said nothing.

"Flint. Easy way or hard way?" Vandenberg cast her gaze in John's direction.

What the fuck was that about?

"Easy." She sighed, withdrew the tampon wrapper from her bag and tossed it on the table. "They're in there."

Vandenberg opened the wrapper and shook out the mini-drives. After turning them over in her hand, she pocketed them.

"Good work here, Flint. But I'm surprised you gave them

up without a fight. It's a bitch to hand the work up the line and get no glory for yourself."

Vivian folded her hands on the table. "With all due respect, ma'am, I'm happy to serve the United States' best interests. No spotlight needed. But I'm not sure that's true for everyone."

Vandenberg inspected Vivian's face.

His fiancée didn't flinch.

No wonder he'd never beaten her at poker.

"Glad to hear it." Vandenberg clapped three times. "Gather round, team. Officer Flint will brief us on Maison Moreau, where we'll carry out an action tonight. Flint, the floor's yours."

Something had happened.

He was shit at figuring out what that was, but between these two women, the balance of power was shifting. To whom and to what end, he couldn't say. But it raised the hair on his nape.

"Maison Moreau is a renovated mansion in Montmartre. First floor is the gift shop and event space, second floor comprises the galleries, and the third is offices and special exhibits."

Vivian tucked her curls behind her ears.

He hoped she'd keep the red when this was over.

"That's where the Meghan Shimek exhibit you curated is hung, isn't it?" John asked.

When they first started dating she'd enthused about the artist's textile pieces.

"Yes." Under the table, she gently stepped on his foot.

Message received. Shutting up.

"This deviates from the placement of the other drives," Vandenberg said. "None of the art is for sale this evening. Any thoughts on where it might be hidden?"

Vivian lifted a shoulder. "Could be anywhere. It's an odd museum. It's a gallery and an homage to Serge Moreau, the French pop star. Some rooms are preserved as a time capsule to the day he moved out."

"Sounds like we'll figure it out as we go." Vandenberg sighed.

"Hall, can we confer on logistics? We'll need more space than usual at our Paris safe house."

After they left the table, John asked, "Should I not have mentioned the exhibit?"

She rested her warm hand on his leg. For once, he was glad he was in the shorts.

"Just keep in mind that information is currency. We need to be careful how we spend it."

He tucked his fingers around hers. "Sorry. I wanted to be helpful."

"And I love you for it." She hugged him, then whispered, "You're the only person I trust, okay? Follow my lead, and don't share info unless I ask you to."

He nodded.

Easy enough. He didn't like talking to most people anyway.

Tangerine pink crested the horizon as they landed in Paris.

Vivian stretched on the tarmac of Le Bourget airport, then climbed into another nondescript SUV. As they merged onto the highway, graffiti covered the sound barriers dividing the road from neighborhoods.

Traffic thickened as they got closer to the city.

Rodriguez kept a car length between them and the car in front at all times in this godforsaken stop-and-go traffic. The defensive driving technique was somewhat undercut by motorcyclists zipping around them and filling those gaps.

Complicated Parisian traffic greeted them as they exited the highway. A single traffic signal post was spiked in the multi-lane intersection's center. Rodriguez's quick moves jerked them away from the stalled traffic, but her stomach did not appreciate his skill.

Her fortune for freedom from this van.

"Here we are," Vandenberg said as they arrived at the unassuming Hôtel Chevalier.

Thank Christ.

Maison Moreau was two blocks away, so the proximity was stellar. The other feature of this hotel that made it popular with the agency was its fire escape. Rare in Paris, but vital for officers looking for a hasty exit.

On their way inside, the group feigned work colleague chatter.

The concierge nodded at Vandenberg as the group headed to the elevators. Vivian's chest tightened. Something was off. Their interactions with Vandenberg, this trip... The events did *not* fit her expected pattern. Vandenberg was *way* too casual about John's presence. Also, the agency maintained a handful of safe houses around Paris.

This was not one of them.

At least, not one she'd been to before. As they entered the gleaming Parisian penthouse suite, a bulbous bottle with a flattened bottom waited on the coffee table.

"What's that?" Vandenberg asked.

"For your birthday tomorrow, ma'am," Hall said. "The hotel was kind enough to find it."

Bottles that shape and size contained one thing—plum lighter fluid.

And there were no such things as coincidences.

"Flint, Seymour." Hall pointed to an interior door. "Changes of clothes, toothbrushes etc. are in there. Go clean up. But make it snappy."

Finally, a chance to strategize with John.

"Roger that," she said.

Inside the room, John closed the door. "I want to burn these shorts."

Vivian pressed her finger to his lips and pulled him into the bathroom. The old hotel's pipes groaned when she twisted the shower handle. Once the mirror steamed, she scrawled, *V b-day drink—same as Vampire.*

"Coincidence?" he murmured.

Nope. She shook her head. *Guard up. K?*

After he nodded, she wiped the mirror, then opened the bathroom window to allow steam to unfurl over the fire escape.

"You shower first," she said, then slipped from the room.

She leaned against the closed door. Thank God for John. He had zero training, but his presence calmed her. With him, she had an ally, someone with whom to process things. If she'd left him with a trusted colleague back home and flown to Morocco solo, she might not have made it to Monte Carlo or found the second drive.

And the world might be worse off for it.

Vivian whipped off the tank top and skirt from Monte Carlo, then changed into a black T-shirt dress and blasted her head with dry shampoo. She slung her bag over her shoulder, then grabbed the big sunnies from the dresser's surface.

Vandenberg now knew about the second drive, Maison Moreau, and Jean-Michel's possible connection. If Vandenberg could be trusted, no harm no foul. But *that* was the million-dollar question. The answer was somewhere in her gray matter's fizzing depths. She needed to distract herself and let her synapses do their thing.

Checking on her artists was exactly the distraction she needed.

She entered the main suit. "Any extra laptops?"

Hall withdrew a clunker from the equipment crate in the corner. "Will this do?"

"Yeah, it's just to check email." She sat at the dinette table and logged into Jane Davis's inbox. Nothing urgent. Oh, wait— a reload request for a Costa Coffee gift card.

She logged into the site.

Her Parisienne artist, Camille St. Lucie, had purchased six coffees in the last twenty-four hours. She reloaded the balance on Camille's card to signal she'd seen the request and was on the way to their normal rendezvous point.

John emerged clad in teal chinos and an ivory oxford with the sleeves rolled up. Unexpected heat thrummed between her thighs. An unintended side effect of this trip was learning he looked hot in European-style clothing.

"Ma'am?" Vivian called to Vandenberg. "One of my local assets has requested a meeting. There's a nonzero chance it's related to—" Vivian swirled her hand "—all of this."

"Then you should go." Vandenberg poured water from the electric kettle into a French press. "And Hall? Accompany, but with discretion."

Vivian hid her grimace.

"I'll come," John asked.

"It'll be hard to explain two extra people," Vivian said. "Maybe Hall can—"

"Accompany, but with discretion," Vandenberg repeated. "Take your phones so we can track you."

"Roger that." Vivian sighed. "Time for a field trip."

As she hurried along the narrow Rue Saint-Honoré, birds' exultant chirping filled the morning air. John had no trouble keeping pace with her. And Hall… Well, if they lost her, Vivian wouldn't mind.

"The coffee shop's up ahead," she said. "Remember—I'm Jane to her."

"Who am I, though? John or Jason?"

"John," Vivian answered.

"Did you tell everyone about me?" he asked.

"Why wouldn't I?" she asked. Across the street, Camille occupied a table on the gum-speckled sidewalk. "Sharing personal info is a great way to convince assets to do the same."

"Works with boyfriends, too." John poked the pedestrian button.

"Ha. Glad we can joke about this."

After they crossed the traffic circle, Vivian beamed at her Parisian friend. Her early coffee look was flawless—cropped wide-leg black pants, silver espadrilles, a black tank, and a necklace made of interlocking doll hands. Doll-part jewelry was her signature craft.

"It has been forever, mon amie." Camille rose from her seat and kissed Vivian's cheeks. "And this must be John?"

"Bonjour." He held out his hand, which Camille batted away before delivering enthusiastic cheek kisses.

"We are all friends here, eh?" She returned to her wrought-iron café chair. "Cigarette?"

"No thanks," both Vivian and John said.

"So American." She struck a match to light a Gauloise, but the breeze snuffed the flame.

"Here." John held out his Zippo.

"A gentleman as well?" The tip of her cigarette flared orange. "Jane, you lucky bitch. A handsome American man who speaks like a Frenchman. It's unfair for these gifts to belong to one man. Please tell me he is terrible in bed."

"Alas, Camille, I cannot."

"Then I understand why you've locked him down." She nodded to Vivian's left hand. "You have it good, as I do with my own dear Adélard. Which brings me to my recent purchases. A sacrifice I make for you, friend, as I loathe American coffee."

Camille blew a stream of smoke into the morning air.

"Yes?" Vivian prompted.

"There are rumors about your ex-lover." Another plume of smoke. "Adélard caught up with friends last week and learned Jean-Michel is in deep with the Gang de Brise Fraîche."

A stylish artist didn't typically have connections to the French mob, but Camille's husband was a reformed gangster. They met when she led art therapy classes at La Santé Prison. Upon completing his sentence, Camille picked him up, and they'd been together ever since.

"But the terms of his parole—"

"Pfft." Camille waved her hand. "It's good for him. Keeps him a bit wild yet appreciative of the stability I provide. He'd had a beer or six and returned home chatty. Jean-Michel's new girlfriend—oh, sorry. You knew he had a new girlfriend, yes?"

"Yes, and it's fine." She gestured to John. "Obviously."

"This woman, Lola—she is the mob boss's daughter. She's fresh from Croatia, cutthroat, and doesn't have a record yet. Together, they've reached new heights trafficking goods through price-inflated works of art."

Vivian drummed her fingers. "Why haven't the police gotten involved?"

"It is common knowledge among the *underground*. Honor among thieves, eh? Here's the most interesting thing Adélard shared before passing out—they have an American partner in the clandestine service. An 'angel' who keeps their profiles low and intercedes on their behalf."

Camille sipped her coffee.

Chills dripped down Vivian's spine. Camille's information matched Vandenberg's profile of MacColl. But how could Vivian have missed the signs that the two men she was closest to at one point in her life—Jean-Michel and MacColl—were in international crime cahoots?

"Thanks, Camille. This is helpful."

"You're most welcome." She glanced at her watch. "I must bid you adieu. My class starts at nine, and the public transit workers are once again on strike."

Vivian jiggled her legs. Protocol was to wait a minute before leaving the table, but damn, she wanted to run.

"How could I miss them working together?" she asked.

"Don't beat yourself up," John said.

Her frustration bubbled over.

"I will, thank you." Her chair scraped the asphalt as she pushed away from the table. "This is how intelligence-gathering works. I gather threads, big and small, then weave them together into cogent analysis. Except if I'm distracted by falling in love, adorable dogs and thrilling domesticity, and I miss a thread, I can't save the world."

"Wait up," John called after her. "That's *way* too much pressure to put on yourself."

"Keep up. And agree to disagree."

Hall followed twenty paces behind, per agency guidance. Someone sticking to protocol was oddly comforting.

Vivian ducked into a parfumerie. She was too keyed up to immediately return to the hotel. And while therapy was in her future, retail therapy was in her present.

John sneezed as he entered.

Hall had the decency to wait outside.

"The world's fate is a shared responsibility," John said.

"But I have to do my part." She spritzed herself with the scent she'd abandoned with her car in Maryland. "My part is *noticing* things, extracting patterns to get to truth. I need to be here to do that or I'm useless. There's some shit you can't google."

"You're never useless. But you're bruised and tired. That can't help."

She placed the atomizer on the sales counter. "TL;DR, I should take a nap?"

"No, but maybe yes?" He sighed. "You've got to look after yourself to be your best you. You can't leave it all on the field and bring an empty husk home to me, our friends, our family."

Heat rose in her cheeks. "You've known what I do for six days. You don't understand it well enough to give me advice."

She paid in euros, then flounced outside.

"That's true, Gorgeous. I didn't know what you do, but I know *you*, remember? That's what you kept telling me. That I know you."

She stopped in the middle of Pont Neuf.

Much as Vandenberg wanted to be Vivian's ghost of agency future, she suspected that role was owned by MacColl. Burned out, grumpy and willing to jump on a grenade. Vivian had been resigned to that fate. Content. Because without this job, she was just the middle child of a middle-class family from Baltimore.

Content until she met John.

If another person had walked into John's museum, would his journal entry have been about her? Her heart hurt to think it was possible. But if he could be happy with someone else, why would she shackle him to this mess?

"What if this is as good as I get?" Vivian asked. "What if I never figure out how to slow down? Never have any chill about work?"

"Then..." He cupped her cheek. "I'll take care of you. I'll nag you to take care of yourself, too, but I'll be there for you while you do your thing."

She twisted the paper bag in her hands.

The personal pattern she'd wrestled with since he proposed finally emerged.

The past year, especially the past week, had revealed their biggest relationship problem—John would do anything for her. And she'd be a monster to allow that. She'd disappear, come home injured, angry, worked up. John would leave a light on and take care of everything. House, dogs, possibly kids. She'd burden him while she pursued bad guys.

No. That was selfish. He deserved better.

So she had to throw herself on a grenade.

She stepped away from him. "I love you so much. But we should go our separate ways after we wrap things up here."

Tears blurred her vision.

"Where's this coming from? We love each other." He tried to wrap her in a hug, but she feinted and evaded him.

"And I'm ending it while we still do." She tugged at the ring, but the fucker still refused to budge. "I'm sorry."

"Don't be sorry." His shoulders slumped. "Just don't do this."

"I have to." To save him from misery.

"You don't, Gorgeous."

Tears ran freely down her face. "I'm going to the hotel. Can you... Can you wait a few minutes to follow?"

With a firm jaw, he nodded.

She pivoted and ran.

Twenty-Two

John's heart yelled at him to chase Vivian. But she'd explicitly asked him for space. To ignore what she'd asked would mean putting his needs first.

He wasn't that kind of asshole.

But he'd lose his mind if he didn't talk to someone. Someone who'd be honest. Thomas would happily tell John if and how he'd fucked up.

Not while his shadow could hear him.

"Okay if we go for a walk?" John asked Officer Hall, who'd respectfully buried herself in her phone while Vivian broke up with him.

Officer Hall nodded. "Yeah, sure. That was brutal."

Cool. Someone on the brink of retirement pitied him.

He marched, scanning for ambient, pattern-less noise to prevent eavesdropping. Aha—there. A massive public fountain rose behind a farmer's market. Water cascaded from a sword-wielding angel into a swimming pool–sized bowl flanked by gryphons.

Were gryphons in the Bible?

He shook his head. Not the point.

Fountain droplets moistened his clothes. After a sigh, he dialed the number he memorized while Vivian had been passed out on the train to Tangier.

On the third ring, Thomas answered. "This better be my brother."

He cracked a smile. "It's me."

"Well hello, me. Are you hitched? If so and you've sent zero photos, I'm annoyed."

He let loose a shuddering breath. "She broke up with me."

"I'm getting off the treadmill." Beeps sounded in the background. "What'd you do?"

"Why do you assume *I* did something?"

"Because you self-sabotage like a motherfucker."

He knew Thomas wouldn't pull punches.

"It wasn't me. Well, not just me. She's been working since we left, and I said if she uses all her energy at her job, she won't have much left for me or any future family we have."

Thomas sighed. "Respectfully, what the fuck? You adore her career. What's changed?"

Everything. But he couldn't blow her cover.

"While we've been here, I've met her associates." John leaned against a huge planter. "Her work can be really tense and dangerous."

"Dangerous? Unless you're writing a clickbaity think piece for *The Atlantic*, I wouldn't call art *dangerous*."

"Her line of work is." He could say this without spilling her secrets. "She goes to places and neighborhoods where I wouldn't walk Ruckus. I hate that she puts herself at risk."

A pause.

Finally Thomas spoke. "Big brother, how are you this dumb? Life *is* risk. You can't ask your partner to give something up, to make herself smaller, to dim her light so *you* can breathe easier. If you need that from her, maybe you shouldn't get married."

"Ouch." The planter scraped his spine. "I'm allowed to have concerns."

"Absolutely you do. But if your conclusion is, 'I can't live with this,' then *you're* effectively breaking up with *her*, aren't you?"

"No, I—" Shit. Maybe Thomas was right.

"Marriage is like a foxhole, John. When the world's exploding around you, your partner should make you feel like you're not alone, help you figure out how to climb from the trenches to safety, and make you laugh while you're doing it."

"Like you're so wise? I have shoes that are older than your marriage."

"So dismissive. And throw those work boots out immediately. They're disgusting. But I'm not talking about *my* marriage. I mean Mom and Dad's."

John snorted.

"Mom and Dad? If anything, they prove my point. They were so into work they barely paid attention to us." He paced the fountain's circle. "For what? To process visas faster? Ironic that diplomats aren't better at managing relationships with their own sons."

Thomas was silent.

Ah, shit, maybe he'd crossed a line. He'd always tried to keep his annoyance with their parents under wraps. To protect Thomas from it while he served as a junior dad to his brother.

"Where…" Thomas sighed. "Where do you think our parents work?"

"Uh, the State Department? For thirty-five years."

Thomas sighed again. "Are you sitting down?"

"No." John paused near a gryphon.

"You should."

This kid. "Spit it out."

"They don't work for State, John. They work for the DoD."

Jesus fucking Christ, *what*? Around the DMV, working for the Department of Defense—without any specificity—meant working for an intelligence agency.

If their cover was working for State, CIA was their most likely employer.

"That can't be true," John said.

Thomas laughed. "When you went to college, I had a lot of spare time to snoop through everyone's stuff. I asked several probing questions, and they gave me the broad strokes."

"I'm not surprised they didn't tell me," John huffed. "They barely give me advice. Why would they trust me with this?"

"Boo-hoo. Ever think they don't give you advice because you make good choices?"

Thomas might be right, but letting go of the high ground was surprisingly hard.

"I didn't always make good choices," he grumbled.

"Because you're flawed like the rest of us. But you learned from your mistakes. Mom and Dad interceded on the rare occasions we need them to—like the lock-picking incident, or when they spoke to Gen's parents."

True. He'd been both mortified and grateful when they stepped in. Young enough to know he needed them, and old enough to resent them for it. They'd assured him seventeen-year-olds still need their parents' help and were happy to be there for him. Of course, he'd turned it around on them. If they'd been paying attention, he wouldn't have gotten into trouble.

Teenagers could be self-involved assholes sometimes.

"I guess that's true."

"You guess?" Thomas asked. "They flew in from Europe to check Jane out the minute you said she might be the one."

He scrunched his forehead. "They were in town for work."

"You are such a dope."

John exhaled, long and slow.

If his parents could do this, he could. Vivian wouldn't be able to tell him everything about her job. He'd have to trust her when she disappeared, and remind himself that she might be in danger, but she could handle it.

So her husband should be able to handle it, too.

"I *am* a dope."

"Glad you see things my way. Now go get your woman. I already put a deposit down on the American Visionary Art Museum for next June."

"What?" John laughed. "Why would you do that?"

"Because I *might* have secretly asked Jane what her dream wedding venue would be. While you've been gallivanting through Europe, I called them like a top-notch best man does. They had a cancellation I scooped up. So go grovel."

Thomas hung up.

Time to grovel, indeed.

The walk back to Hôtel Chevalier was fast. He tried to engage Officer Hall in conversation, but she dodged all questions. Just as well. He needed to plot his groveling. At the suite's doors, Officer Hall knocked in a coded rhythm, and Rodriguez let them in.

There she was.

A beam of sunshine arced through the window and lit up Vivian at the kitchenette table like an angel. He couldn't wait to tell her about her parents. But wait…could he? That would be blowing their cover. Vivian, of all people, could keep that secret.

Vivian, who had just crooked her finger at him.

Something was wrong. She looked like she'd gotten the final bar trivia question incorrect and lost all their points.

He edged behind her. "Hey, Gorgeous."

She jerked her head toward the screen. Based on the angle, the photo was from the camera necklace. Mystery Vampire. She'd run it through facial recognition software, which indicated it was a seventy-two percent match with a grainy photo of someone named Dragomir Mihailovic.

Vivian held her thumb sideways and wiggled it—their game night signal asking if he was keeping up.

He double-tapped the table. *Yes.*

She alt-tabbed to a report naming Dragomir what's-his-name as a person of interest in a raid on the Marseille-Fos Port ten years ago. She pointed to two names on the report's header.

Analyst: James J. MacColl
Redacted by: Janna Vandenberg

Black lines obscured half the text. From what he skimmed, Dragomir was born in Croatia on December 25, 1986, was adopted at two years old, and had worked his way up to underboss in an organized crime syndicate.

She wiggled her thumb, and he tapped the table twice.

Hall swiveled her gaze in his direction.

"Sorry," he said. "Nervous habit."

Vivian loaded a map on her phone—the same one she'd

scanned with the QR code from his tux in Monte Carlo. The map showed two pulsing dots, six hundred miles apart. One in Monaco—the one he'd left behind. The other…

She pinched and zoomed, and a pulsing dot appeared in Hôtel Chevalier.

He faced Vivian. Dragomir was here. The same Dragomir about whom Vandenberg was hiding information. In one glance, they had a full conversation.

Vivian widened her eyes. *Act natural.*

John furrowed his brow. *Natural? Your boss's boss is involved in this.*

Vivian nodded, then folded her hands. *True, but we have an advantage.* She *doesn't know* we *know any of this.*

The door across the suite swung open. Vandenberg, dressed in a red suit, clapped three times. "Okay, people. Game plan for tonight."

Vivian wiped her search history and closed all applications.

"Coming?" she asked John.

The quiver in her voice was like the time she'd asked him to accompany her to urgent care, where she'd been diagnosed with walking pneumonia.

She was exhausted and afraid.

And he'd be there for her. He sat next to her on the couch. Hall and Rodriguez perched in the wingback chairs, and Vandenberg paced the room.

"Tonight at Maison Moreau, American actor Bradley Westwood is celebrating his recent divorce," Vandenberg said. "We were able to get Jane Davis and John on the list because of her pre-existing relationship with the museum."

"Does John need to be my plus-one?" Vivian asked. "That puts him in harm's way."

"Because of Monte Carlo, he's known to be your romantic interest," Vandenberg said. "Hall, Rodriguez—you'll be on the museum's perimeter. Specifically, the café across the street. Flint, you're in the museum with John. We're relying on you."

She swallowed. "I won't let you down, ma'am."

"Good. Now get some sleep. Ten hours 'til the doors open."

Vivian hated how comforting John's grip on her hand was in the taxi. To survive their breakup, she couldn't rely on him. It was unfair to them both.

And her heart.

She'd tried to rest but tossed and turned until she opened her borrowed laptop and scanned all the systems she had access to. No additional intel nuggets to be gleaned. She'd exhausted herself, and her emotions were about to snap.

Not a great combo for an action in the field.

Hall turned down the narrow street occupied by Maison Moreau. "In and out as fast as you can. We'll be at the café across the street if shit goes sideways. And look like you're having fun. It's a party, remember?"

Fun. Sure.

Partying with the man she'd just broken up with, while facing down her ex and his new partner who was possibly an organized crime underboss, not to mention trying to find the final piece to a bioweapons lab security breach and operating under the direction of a possible double-agent boss.

Good times.

"Roger that," Vivian said.

As Hall idled, John slipped out of his side, then opened her door. She used his steady grip to balance in another fucking pair of stilettos as they joined the security line.

"Do you go to a lot of parties on your trips?" John draped his hand over her nape, rubbing his thumb along her neck.

Her spine hummed with pleasant, unwelcome shivers.

"Some." She leaned into his caress. For a second. To keep up the ruse. "But not lots."

She felt Hall's and Rodriguez's binocular gazes on them.

The security guard gestured for them to step forward. The Swarovski crystals covering the flap of her purse sparkled in the party's rotating disco lights as the guard flipped it open. He poked his baton through its sparse contents. Phone, wallet and perfume atomizer. She'd also uncomfortably tucked the code index card into her underwear.

Back at the suite, Vandenberg, Hall and Rodriguez insisted most of Vivian's gear would trigger suspicion. True, but they'd made her more vulnerable. Which might actually be their plan, considering John wasn't much better equipped with a propofol EpiPen and ceramic screwdrivers. Vandenberg kept everything else they'd brought, including their passports.

Which gave hostage vibes.

After the security guard waved them through, the bouncer opened the door. With bass thumping her chest, her eyes adjusted to the crowded, black-lit event space. Servers wearing black pants, white shirts, and neon glow-in-the-dark glasses circulated drinks and canapés.

Vivian leaned toward a server who wore a fabulous scarf knotted at her neck. "Tell me about your glasses?"

"Mr. Westwood, through the darkness of his marriage, now 'sees' his ex was terrible." The server rolled her eyes. "So we symbolically wear these disasters. Care for another bouchée?"

The server lifted the tray, and she and John grabbed another appetizer.

"What's your name?" she asked the server.

"Elif," she answered.

"Thanks, Elif, you're a goddess. And I love your scarf."

As they threaded through glittering attendees, John's hand grazed the exposed small of her back. *Unfair.* That was her secret erogenous zone. Not so secret for John, though. He'd discovered it on their fourth date.

He caught her hand and leaned to her ear. "Can we talk?"

Tension simmered under her surface.

"We have a job to do first." She squeezed his hand.

"Promise we'll talk later."

"I promise." She had no intention of living up to her promise.

Instead, she'd focus on the operation.

"Let's check out the gift shop, sweetie." She ambled into the shop adjacent to the museum's entrance. "What do you think of this?"

She unfurled a large scarf, then twirled with it and scanned the walls. Two security cameras, opposite corners, like she remembered. Damn.

"It's large, babe," John said.

She dropped it back on its table, then gestured to a locked acrylic display case. "How about this?"

Within the case stood a fashion doll who'd been turned into a Baltimore Hon, complete with cat's-eye glasses, cigarette and a generous beehive hairstyle. No artist credited, but there was no doubt she was a Rocksy and had served as the model for the *Smoking Hon* portrait in Monte Carlo.

John wrapped his arms around her from behind. "What am I looking at?"

The party's dance music gave her cover to brief John on what she'd held back from Vandenberg, but she wanted his ear closer to her mouth.

"Nuzzle my neck," she said.

"Yes, ma'am."

The frisson his lips caused made it hard to concentrate.

"I'd bet an eyeball it's in there," she murmured. "Rocksy loathes Serge but adores his daughter, who's the museum's exec director. Rocksy gifted her this doll to celebrate the museum's opening. But with Rocksy's blessing, I refused to authenticate it until Michelle's ready so her toxic father can't sell it out from under her."

"There's a hefty price tag now, so someone's selling."

The tag had been scribbled in hasty marker. Twenty-one million euros.

"Can you call in a favor?" John whispered. "Since you know the exec director."

Vivian shook her head. "I tried. She placed herself in the

psych ward at Sainte-Anne two weeks ago. Told you her father's an asshole."

He hugged her from behind. "Sorry to hear that."

She allowed herself a second to sink into his comfort.

"Which means we're on to plan R—you can pick locks, right?"

He rested his chin on her head. "Not without lock-picking tools. Wouldn't work anyway. See that sensor on the door, the white one? If it's moved out of detection range, an alarm's triggered. The whole thing's battery-powered, and those batteries last forever."

"Well, fuck."

Tension banded her temples. She wanted this mission over so she could go home and sob in her bathtub with a pint of honey graham ice cream. And *batteries* stood in her way?

"So I guess we're on to plan S." John's voice made her insides quiver.

Focus, she told herself.

"Can't pick the lock or move the case, so we'll go through it. The acrylic vitrine they used is pretty thin, and my lighter's basically a blowtorch. We can remove her that way."

She relaxed against him. "You can do that?"

"I do it at work all the time. Should take two, three minutes."

From behind them, a voice called, "May I help you?"

Vivian thumped her head against John's chest, then turned to find a sales clerk. "Sorry, we thought the shop was closed because of the party."

"That would have made sense, no?" The clerk smiled. "They usually do. But for tonight, they decided to operate with reduced staff."

Her shimmering peacock-blue chandelier earrings picked up faint light from the shop's neon Serge Moreau quotes high on the wall.

"Your earrings are *amazing*," Vivian said.

Earrings the shop displayed with the scarves, and she could use to distract the clerk.

"We actually sell them here." The clerk gestured toward the display table.

"Oh, *fabulous*. But do you have any in the back? I'm a germophobe, and I'd prefer a pair no one's touched."

"Certainly, madame." She nodded. "I'll be back in a moment."

As the clerk disappeared, the DJ in the event space announced, "Ladies and gentlemen, the guest of honor has arrived!"

A cheer erupted from the crowd. Success was talent plus luck, and tonight, she was leaning hard on luck. She couldn't have planned better timing if she'd tried.

"Now or never, John," she whispered. "I'll keep watch."

He flicked his Zippo, and the sharp smell of burnt plastic filled the air. Vivian generously sprayed her new atomizer to cover it. Well, not so much cover as confuse anyone who walked into this pungent cloud. During the longest two minutes of her life, he melted the top of the display case, then carefully widened the hole with a ceramic screwdriver.

"Can you get her?" he asked. "My fingers are too big."

John grabbed the abandoned scarf she'd been twirling like Stevie Nicks and held it up to shield her from the camera. With careful fingers, Vivian pinched the doll's beehive and lifted her from the case. She unzipped the doll's housecoat. No drive. Next she squeezed the doll's beehive. *Yes*. Adrenaline sizzled through her. She winkled the drive from the doll's hair, then returned Baltimore Hon to the display case.

As she zippered the drive into her purse's secret pocket, the clerk returned.

"Madame? I have the earrings." The clerk wrinkled her nose. "What's that smell?"

She blanked.

"Fog machine from the party, I think?" John said. "I'm surprised they'd use that in a museum."

The clerk looked like she bought it.

As she scanned the earrings, she asked, "Anything else?"

"This." John dropped the scarf on the counter.

Vivian raised an eyebrow but didn't question it.

The clerk folded the scarf. "Would you like a bag?"

"No thank you." Vivian touched her credit card to the payment terminal.

The clerk slid their purchases across the counter. "Merci. Please come again."

If Vivian never set foot in this museum again, she'd die happy.

"Why'd you get the scarf?" she asked.

"Thought you could use another weapon. Just in case."

Why hadn't she thought of that?

"Can you carry these?" She handed him the earrings. "They won't fit in my purse."

John slipped the box into his tweed jacket's inner pocket. "Did you like these?"

"A lot, but I could never pull them off." She tied the brightly patterned scarf into a classic French knot. "I might give them to my sister. All her jewelry is artsy-dangly-jingly. Built to grab attention, whereas I—"

The lights and music shut off.

Black descended on the half-drunk crowd. Vivian reached out, hoping to collide with John, but came up empty. A hand clamped over her mouth, and an arm belted around her waist. She bucked and twisted, but the arms tightened.

"Keep it up and you won't see your boyfriend again."

Fear iced her veins, but she allowed herself to be dragged to another location. Soon she was shoved into a chair. The lights popped on. She shielded her eyes until they adjusted to the sudden brightness.

Well, fuck.

Twenty-Three

John blinked against the blinding lights.

He'd smelled Vivian's perfume when they shoved her into a chair next to him.

"Are you okay?" she asked.

He winked. "Never better."

From the other side of the Louis XIV desk, Jean-Michel slow-clapped. "I must applaud you, Vivian Flint. Frankly, I'm flattered to be your target."

Goddamn, this guy had a punchable face. Lola stood behind him, placid as a frozen lake.

"All this time, Jane Davis was an American spy. Unbelievable, but that's the point, no? I never would've suspected had my inside connection not tipped me off."

Jean-Michel set three wineglasses on the table.

"I don't want to hurt you." He poured crimson wine. "All I want are the drives, and then I shall disappear."

Vivian said nothing, so John followed her lead.

Jean-Michel swirled a glass, then buried his nose in it. "Luscious notes of black cherry balanced by hints of chocolate and baking spices. I'm sure you'll love it."

He withdrew an eyedropper bottle from the desk.

"You're quiet tonight, ma petite." He squeezed clear drops into the glasses set before Vivian and John. "This will help. Drink up."

"Not much of a drinker," John said as Vivian muttered, "No thank you."

"That was a direction, not a suggestion. It's perfectly safe. If I wanted you dead, you'd be dead." He gestured to the goons standing behind him and Vivian. "Pétain and Laval are quite capable. But perhaps they should encourage you?"

One goon—Laval?—took a step toward them.

John tensed, ready to fight.

"Stop." Vivian lifted her glass. "We'll drink."

Goddamn, that was delicious wine, which only made John resent him more. Vivian finished her wine first, then set the glass on the desk.

"Now what?" Vivian demanded.

"I have questions," he said. "Where and when did we first meet?"

"The one you remember is the MOMA's Rocksy exhibit in New York five years ago. Our *actual* first meeting was at your grandmother's funeral a year earlier. You'd learned she'd disinherited you and were drowning your sorrows in cognac. I attempted to seduce you, and we got as far as talking about the weather before you passed out. My initial failed honeypot attempt is the stuff of legend at work." Vivian widened her eyes. "What did you put in that wine?"

"A sort of truth serum." Jean-Michel tilted his head. "What's your middle name?"

She sighed. "Bernardita."

"Not Marie?" he asked.

"Nope. Bernardita. She was my great-grandmother, and she was named for her father."

Jean-Michel glanced over his shoulder at Lola, who nodded.

"That is an unfortunate name. One more question to confirm the serum is working. Where did we have sex for the last time?"

Vivian wrinkled her forehead. "You're awful."

"Agreed." Jean-Michel trailed his fingers on the desk. "Answer, please?"

"Stop." John clutched his armrest to keep from launching himself at Jean-Michel. "This has nothing to do with the drives."

The bastard smiled. "Speak again without my prompting and Laval will break her knees."

"On that desk." Vivian glared at Jean-Michel. "Can you ask about the drives already?"

He wagged his finger. "Patience. Lola, do you have questions?"

"Do you love Jean-Michel?" Lola asked.

"No," shot from Vivian like a cannon.

Lola gestured to John. "Do you love him?"

John felt like canvas being stretched on a too-big frame.

"Yes." She turned to lock gazes with him. "I love him. Adore him, actually. He's the best person I know. But I worry I'll break his heart eventually."

His heart shifted. "You won't."

Jean-Michel rolled his eyes. "I may vomit. What's your real name?"

"John Seymour." That was a strange sensation. He usually ran what he was about to say through a filter, but the truth slipped from his lips like a pleasant burp.

Lola checked her notes and nodded.

"What annoys you about Vivian?" Jean-Michel asked.

"Her interpretation of her employer's policy about sharing her identity was overzealous, but I get it. So, there's nothing."

"Truly?" Jean-Michel asked. "Not her loud laughter, appreciation for food, or the way she constantly craves physical affection?"

"Dude." John leaned back in his chair. "Way to tell on yourself."

"*Why* are we talking about this?" Vivian asked.

"Because it amuses me." Jean-Michel rose from behind the desk, then parked his ass against its front. "When my client went to the gift shop to purchase that ridiculous doll, someone had tampered with the case. The salesgirl identified you as the last customers."

"Is she okay?" Vivian asked. "You didn't hurt her?"

"I'm not an animal. Where's the drive?"

"In a secret pocket in the top flap of my purse."

The goon behind Vivian rifled through her bag. "Got it."

"Parfait." Jean-Michel smirked. "And the others?"

"My boss has them," she answered.

Jean-Michel pushed off the desk. "I'll hold on to your boyfriend while you retrieve them. Before you go, though, a final question. Who is Rocksy?"

John's heart quickened. Did she know?

"John, I'm sorry." Vivian locked gazes with him. "I'm Rocksy."

Another lie of omission. But to his surprise, he didn't fucking care.

Vivian's head pounded. What had she done?

"You?" Jean-Michel shook his head and smiled. "*Another* secret identity? My God, how do you keep track?"

Yes, her. But not just her.

Thank God the serum was wearing off. Had he asked that question first, she might not have been able to keep Torrey's name to herself.

"Ah, but this is a genius arrangement. Produce the paintings, designate Jane Davis as the artist's authorized authenticator, then charge obscene rates for authentication *and* the art itself? Brilliant. I'm certain you'll be happy to allow me to exclusively broker Rocksy's sales going forward, eh, ma petite?"

Lola cleared her throat. "If *we* exclusively broker, correct?"

She should watch herself. Jean-Michel never let anyone get between him and his wallet.

He patted the hand she'd draped on his shoulder. "Of course. But first, we must resolve this issue with the drives. My buyer is unhappy. If my buyer remains unhappy, people will die. Pétain, Laval, escort Ms. Flint out to recover our property. Her boyfriend stays with us."

Vivian's stomach squeezed.

She was outnumbered, without weapons and without friends. Her wits had been enough to save her skin before, and they'd come through for her again.

For now, all she could do was comply.

"Fiancé," she said.

"Pardon?" Jean-Michel asked.

"John's my fiancé." Vivian rose from the chair. "There'll be hell to pay if he's harmed."

Jean-Michel nodded. "I have no doubt. And congratulations on settling for someone."

Christ, what an asshole. "I need my bag. It has my room key."

"Laval, find the key, but keep the bag." Jean-Michel steepled his fingers. "I'm sure our spy friend has weapons within it."

Joke's on him. Vandenberg had already stripped her of them.

The beefy goon dipped his sausage fingers into her bag. "Here."

She took the key card, then bent to kiss John. "I'll be back for you."

"Take your time," John said. "Any wine left, J.M.?"

God, she loved him. He was the best in a crisis. Inconveniences received outsized reactions from him, but any time something terrible happened—hot water heater dying, walking pneumonia, Ruckus eating a Levain chocolate chip cookie the size of his head—John was a rock.

"Tick-tock," Jean-Michel said. "I prefer not to be in your fiancé's company any longer than necessary."

"Back atcha, J.M."

Her insides chilled as the goons marched her down the stairs, through the back, past frenzied caterers, and into Jean-Michel's limo. Its tinted windows shielded her from Hall and Rodriguez, who were sipping wine on the café's sidewalk.

Vivian's stomach churned like it did when she was a kid and she couldn't force the letters to make sense. The more she focused, the more of a jumble her brain created. So instead of thinking, she'd breathe like those long-ago teachers had taught her. Slow, in-two-three, then out-two-three. A fear-clouded mind wouldn't help her or John.

At Hôtel Chevalier, they flanked her as they entered, one at each elbow with their hands obviously on their guns in their pockets. After a tense elevator ride, they arrived at the penthouse.

At the door, she said, "Wait here."

Laval snorted. "Non."

"Armed American agents are in the penthouse." Technically, that was true. Between her and Vandenberg, there'd be more than one agent. "Stay here. It'll turn into a firefight if you enter. Just let me go in and get the drives. It'll take ten minutes, tops."

The three of them contemplated each other.

Finally Pétain nodded. "Ten minutes, then we're coming in. And don't close the door."

Great. Like she needed more constraints.

She slipped into the penthouse suite, then flipped the steel mortise latch to prevent the door from fully shutting. Quietly she kicked off her shoes.

Fucking Jimmy Choos.

The spy gear they'd sorted through earlier still lay on the coffee table, along with her bag from Monte Carlo. She swept most of it into the bag but pocketed her chloroform atomizer and handkerchief. The door was open to the room they'd converted into their command center.

She knocked. "Ma'am?"

Vandenberg swiveled from the monitors that received a feed from Hall's brooch. "Where's John? And why didn't you signal Hall and Rodriguez?"

Vivian closed the door. "The action went sideways. Dilettante has John. I need to borrow them to rescue him."

"Borrow?" Vandenberg crossed her arms. "What are you thinking? You'll run back to the party, rescue John, then fight for the drives?"

Adrenaline pounded in Vivian's ears.

"You say that like it's a bad plan. Wanna come with?"

"Flint." Vandenberg shook her head. "I can't let you endanger the world to rescue your boyfriend."

"Fiancé," she corrected her. "We don't have a choice. We can't leave an American civilian in criminals' hands."

Vandenberg shrugged. "Yes, we can. Sometimes there's no

good decision. Just the least bad one. And in this case, that means sacrificing one American for many."

For an embarrassing moment, Vivian's mouth gaped like a fish out of water.

Then she remembered who she fucking was and closed it.

"Was the mission successful?" Vandenberg asked. "Did you locate the third drive?"

"Yes."

"Give it to me." Vandenberg held out her hand.

"Jean-Michel took it from me." In her pocket, she sprayed the handkerchief generously with the atomizer. "I'm sorry."

"Sorry?" Vandenberg frowned. "Not good enough, Flint. I'll alert—"

Vivian leaped at Vandenberg and clamped her chloroform-soaked handkerchief to her nose and mouth. Ugh, of course Vandenberg was feisty. Vivian slithered behind the older woman, then tugged her down on the bed. She pretzeled her free arm and legs around Vandenberg, tightening, tightening, until the older woman went slack.

She didn't trust it.

Vivian kept the handkerchief pressed to her nose until Vandenberg's body slumped into unmistakable unconscious weight. Gasping for her own breath, she rolled the woman to the side, then slipped out from under her. She left the sodden handkerchief on the woman's face.

If Vandenberg *wasn't* actually on the wrong side of things, Vivian would be fired.

Possibly charged with treason, actually.

But she needed to save John.

"Sorry for the chloroform, I mean. Not the third drive." Vivian rifled through Vandenberg's pockets. "He might be one American, but he's *my* American, and I'm not sacrificing him for anything."

The drives were in her front pants pocket.

Terrible hiding spot.

Vivian dipped them into the laptop on Vandenberg's desk to verify them, and the code screen popped up. Yep, these were the real deal.

After pocketing them and Vandenberg's phone, she eyed Vandenberg's feet.

Business casual sneakers with arch support. Looked like size sevens, too.

Twenty-Four

All things being equal, John should be terrified. He was a bargaining chip amid armed strangers. His secret agent fiancée's ex-boyfriend and a crime boss's daughter had drugged him, threatened him and zip-tied him.

And yet he was fine. Calm.

Because if there was one thing he believed in, it was Vivian Bernardita Flint.

He chuckled. *Bernardita*. Back when they were first dating, "Jane" had joked her parents had picked "Marie" as her middle name because they liked the way it sounded with Jane.

"Why are you laughing?" Lola asked.

"Guess I'm drunk," John answered.

Regaining the ability to lie was handy.

Was this what Thomas meant about being in a foxhole? No, he'd meant it as a metaphor, like when a new hot water heater wipes out your savings. Not literally sitting in a violent situation with his hands zip-tied.

Which was a silly restraint.

He worked with zip ties all the time. They were super handy for art installations. When art handlers got bored, they did goofy shit. Like zip-tie their wrists and see if they could escape.

"Hey." He held up his wrists. "Can you loosen these?"

This was a risk, but he bet Jean-Michel had a sadistic streak.

"Oh, yes, of course." Jean-Michel rose from his chair, then grabbed John's bound wrists. With a smile, he tightened the band. "Better?"

"Ow," John said. "No."

"Good," the Frenchman said.

The ties chafed his skin. Perfect. The more rigid they were, the easier they'd be to break.

Vivian elegantly dropped onto the alley's stone sidewalk from the fire escape. She couldn't let Jean-Michel have the drives. But if she didn't hand them over, he'd hurt John. Or worse? Had Jean-Michel leveled up to murder, too?

Panic gripped her throat.

As she walked in Vandenberg's shoes, her words circled her brain. *Sometimes there's no good decision. Just the least bad one.*

She didn't accept that. Couldn't accept that.

Her churning thoughts leaped like a frog in a frying pan. Despite feeling like she had zero seconds, she needed to take a beat to stop, breathe and look for patterns in the intel, the people, the history. With her sweaty palms pressed to the building, she leaned against a wall.

Patterns, patterns, patterns…

A carousing group of partygoers stumbled past, singing, "Bon anniversaire, nos vœux les plus sincères…"

Happy birthday, our most sincere wishes.

Something about birthdays snagged her brain.

Above the roofs of Paris, the Eiffel tower's lights began to shimmer like they did for the first five minutes of every hour. Midnight. A week since John proposed.

June 27.

Vandenberg's birthday.

0627.

She pulled the code index card from her underpants. The last four digits were 0627—Vandenberg's birthday. She traced the code with her eyes. Holy shit.

Dragomir's birthdate was one of the limited pieces of intel she'd gleaned from his whisper-thin file. Christmas Day, 1986.

1986122519580627.

Was the full code a combo of their birthdays? Were they in this together?

She had to call Anjali. She pinched her lip when the six-digit code prompt popped up on Vandenberg's phone. She entered 861225 and was almost disappointed when it worked.

Vivian dialed Anjali's desk number.

Calling the agency with a stolen phone at the end of Langley's work day violated several orders of professional and friend protocol, but it couldn't be helped.

"Officer Patel."

"I need you to look something up for me."

"Hi, Anjali, how are you? I'm fine after showing up at your house with a global security risk and then disappearing into thin air. Just wanted to call so you didn't worry."

"Sorry." Vivian stared at the sparkling Eiffel Tower. "Please help?"

"Is it about the buyer from the London Rocksy auction? I've been digging all week, but I've got nothing." Shuffling paper noises came through the phone. "Are there more sales to check? If so, I might be able to pull something together."

"I'll bring you more when I'm back. But there's something else I need. Urgently. Is Vandenberg's birthday June 27, 1958?"

"Hang on." The jokiness had left Anjali's voice. "Confirmed."

"Where does the system say she is right now?"

"Um…" Clicking keys. "Skype says she's on vacation."

If she was on official business, she would've set their internal messaging system to indicate she was on a work trip.

"Where was she operating in the mid-eighties?"

More clicking keys. "Yugoslavia."

Which broke up in the 1990s and became Slovenia, Bosnia and Herzegovina, Macedonia.

And Croatia.

"How long?"

"1982 to 1990. Not continuously, though. Her file says she

took a medical leave of absence in November of '86 and was back on duty by February of '87."

The Eiffel Tower's dancing lights resolved into a solid glow. *Finally* a pattern that tied it all together.

Vandenberg had a baby, and Vivian would bet her ass he grew up to be Dragomir Mihailovic. The redacted reports, limited system info, the tip-off to Jean-Michel. *Vandenberg* must be Jean-Michel's inside person, which made a hell of a lot more sense than MacColl. She was giving her kid top cover while throwing MacColl under the bus.

Vivian and John, too.

In fact, it would be better for Vandenberg if they didn't make it back from this operation.

"Thanks, Anj. Let's get drinks when I'm home? Maybe a double date?"

"Love to. Be safe, asshole." Anjali hung up on her.

Time to arrange for backup. Confident in her abilities as she was, she couldn't tackle this many open switches. Vandenberg, the goons, possibly Hall and Rodriguez, Jean-Michel and Lola, and Dragomir out there…somewhere…

Hopefully the cavalry would pick up.

She dialed the MacColl's number, the new one he'd given her in Marseille.

"Boss? So many palette knives."

"How can I help, Canvas?"

MacColl's gruff familiarity nearly made her cry. No time for tears, though.

"I need help," she said. "Big Boss found us. We're in Paris. Dilettante's holding Brawn hostage at the Maison Moreau."

Sacrilege to use actual place names, but she couldn't afford to be coy.

After a beat, MacColl asked, "Where's Big Boss?"

"At Hôtel Chevalier, penthouse. I chloroformed her."

"Happy to stay ignorant of those details."

"Dilettante wants the drives in exchange for Brawn."

"You can't do that, Canvas."

"I won't let him keep them," she said. "But I need backup. Can you send someone to join the party in the upstairs office at Maison Moreau in ten minutes? Signal word is *mix-up*."

"On it," MacColl answered.

"Also, Boss. The Croatian national you like for the London purchase? I'm pretty sure he's Big Boss's son, and she's covering for him. His birthday aligns to medical leave in her work history. And get this—we slipped a tracker in his pocket at our last location. He's in Paris. Can't be a coincidence."

Silence.

"Boss?" she prompted.

"Haven't we talked about burying the lede? I *knew* something was off. Her interest in him has always gone way too deep. Good work here, Canvas. What's your current location?"

"On the way to extract Brawn, sir."

"A team will meet you there."

"Thanks, Boss. Wish me luck."

The Seine's marine scent hit Vivian hard as she rounded the corner to the Quai de la Mégisserie. Her thighs burned as she jogged down the walkway to the Voie Georges-Pompidou, the riverside walking and bike path.

John is okay, she repeated in time with her pumping knees.

Had to, or the fear would choke her.

Sweat slicked her neck as she crossed the Pont des Arts with the Louvre staring down at her. Hundreds of thousands of padlocks clutched the bridge, symbols of unbreakable love.

Yearning nearly buckled her knees.

She should have been strolling through the Louvre, holding John's hand, not sprinting past it to rescue him from the terrible people she'd brought into his life.

A reevaluation of her work/life balance was way overdue.

At the bridge's end, she hung a right. Three blocks to go. Her lungs screamed, but she ignored them. She paused at the

Maison Moreau's street corner and took Vandenberg's phone from her pocket, then zoomed in on the café across the street.

Hall and Rodriguez were enjoying the same sweaty glass of pinot.

An excellent sign that Vandenberg was still knocked out.

She cut down the alley until she spotted a catering staff on a smoke break. Elif, the waitress she'd met earlier, sat among them. She fired up her vape. Ugh, she picked lemon-mint because it tasted terrible, and she didn't want to get addicted to it.

"Bonsoir, Elif." She blew lemon-mint smoke over their heads. "I think it's cooler out here than it is inside."

Elif politely chuckled. "I agree."

"Pity I need to return, but I left my man inside. Au revoir."

On her way through the kitchen, she grabbed a stainless steel tray and headed toward the back stairwell. If Jean-Michel had bothered to make friends with the people hanging their show's art like she had, he'd know the bedroom/office where he was holding John wasn't secure. Serge Moreau was paranoid and never slept anywhere with a single entry/exit point.

Hence the secret entrance in his walk-in closet.

She ducked under the velvet rope that was swagged between steel stanchions guarding the stairs to the second floor. When she reached the landing, she nipped toward a four-foot-tall built-in shelf laden with a dozen framed articles about the museum, grateful for the thick carpet that hushed her footsteps.

Please still work.

After removing the articles, she pushed the spot the contractors had shown her, and voilà—the shelving unit swung inward. She eased the shelf closed. The closet that once held feather boas and sex toys was now stocked with office supplies.

Serge Moreau would be most disappointed.

Jean-Michel's and Lola's murmuring voices sifted through the closet door. With the steel serving tray tucked between her knees, she untied her neck scarf, then wrapped one end around her fist several times. She peeked through the slats in the door and her heart stuttered.

John looked okay. Actually, he looked annoyed. But she'd take it.

In addition to Lola and Jean-Michel, two new goons occupied the room. Fantastic. And based on the bulges under their jackets, she'd brought a platter and a scarf to a gunfight.

Surprise was a powerful advantage, though.

Deep breath.

Now or never.

She burst through the closet and whipped the tray at the short goon and clunked him in the head. While he was stunned, she looped her scarf around the tall goon's neck and yanked him into the kick she delivered to his chest, knocking the wind out of him.

Short goon regained his senses and was coming for her.

"Little help?" she called to John.

Twenty-Five

"Gimme a minute." John raised his hands over his head and brought his wrists down hard on his knee. The zip ties cracked like crystal.

"Don't have a minute." Vivian kicked the shorter guy in the jaw.

"Stop." Lola trained a gun on him. "Stay where you are."

John held up his hands. "Thought you said there were no guns in Europe?"

"I never said no guns." She ducked Tall Guy's punch, then wrapped the scarf around his neck and twisted. "I said fewer."

With a mighty tug, she slammed Tall Guy to the floor, then took off toward Short Guy. The action distracted Lola long enough for him to snatch the EpiPen from his pocket and jab her. She fired a shot toward the ceiling, then slumped as the anesthetic hit her system. The gun spilled from her hand. He kicked it away.

Hands on his shoulder caught his attention.

Vivian. The ringing caused by the gunshot muffled his hearing. But he read her lips.

Are you okay?

Behind her, Jean-Michel had picked up Lola's gun. It had been a decade or more since John had fired one at the range with his dad, but even he could see Jean-Michel's one-armed sideways aim was more style than substance.

"Yes, I brought the drives," Vivian said.

His hearing was coming back, but she still sounded muffled. "May I have them, please?"

"Since you said please." She reached into her pocket, then held them out to him. "Here. You can see the emblem on the base so there's no mix-up."

She'd kind of yelled that last word. Weird.

"Non, ma petite. Place them on the desk, then back away."

With a sigh, Vivian did as he asked.

After a beat, Jean-Michel skulked toward the desk, then sat at it and opened a laptop. He awkwardly kept the gun trained on them. After locating the symbol on each drive, he slipped one into the port.

"You don't trust me?" she asked.

"I trust no one." One by one, he checked them. "Now, what to do with the two of you?"

"Let us go?" Vivian suggested.

Jean-Michel grinned. "I've always appreciated your optimism."

"I have the code," she said. "You could sell the information to more than one buyer. Promise to let us go and never bother us again—Rocksy included—and it's yours."

Jean-Michel leaned back in his chair. "You could have sold the information as well, made a fortune with the first two drives. And you didn't, to save him?"

Vivian reached for John's hand. "Yes."

"How very pedestrian of you. I agree to your terms." Jean-Michel shifted his gaze between them. "First, I'd like to verify the code is correct."

Vivian nodded. "I'd expect nothing less."

As a goon moaned, Jean-Michel slipped a drive into the port. "The code, please?"

"One, nine, eight, six," Vivian began.

As she fed Jean-Michel the code, John loosened his belt. Vivian could use it since her scarf was still wrapped around the moaning goon's throat.

"Zero, six, six, two," she said.

Jean-Michel typed the keys. On the last digit, he looked up

at Vivian. "Non. Something is wrong. For each number, the screen was green, but the last two digits were red."

"Oh, sorry about that mix-up. Remember I switch things up sometimes? Just reverse the last two numbers."

Jealousy flared in John. He hated that this guy had any personal Vivian knowledge.

Jean-Michel typed again.

After the final click, he cranked his brow low. "Ma petite, what did you do?"

He twisted the laptop toward her.

A grim reaper appeared on his screen.

"Sorry, it was a mix-up."

The goon she'd cold-cocked with the serving tray woozily stumbled to his feet. Scarf Goon was already up, eyes flashing with anger as he moved toward them.

"Goddammit, I said, *it was a mix-up*," she shouted.

A beefy guy burst through the door behind them. Jean-Michel fired a wild shot that thumped into the lintel above the door.

"I've got the gunman." She leaped at Jean-Michel. "Clobber, on your three."

Beefy Guy rocketed toward Platter Goon.

"Gorgeous, catch." John tossed his belt to Vivian. "Zip ties are in the desk."

"Dope," Beefy Guy said.

The remaining goon, with Vivian's scarf dribbling from his neck, lurched toward Vivian.

John slide-tackled him.

Vivian had Jean-Michel in a headlock. "Tie up your guy with the scarf, John."

He wrapped a round turn and two half hitches knot around Scarf Goon's wrists. By the time he finished and removed the guy's gun from his holster, Vivian had strapped Jean-Michel to the office chair, and Beefy Guy had hog-tied Platter Goon.

"What about her?" John gestured to Lola's unconscious form.

"Zip ties." Vivian dusted her hands together, then wrapped the plastic around Lola's wrists and ankles.

"Ma petite, let me go." Jean-Michel fought his restraints. "The sellers are ruthless."

"Not my problem." She picked up the gun she'd stripped from him and released its magazine. "Who were the buyers?"

Jean-Michel lifted a shoulder. "I cannot say."

"You're facing a long couple of days of questioning, Jean-Michel." Vivian sighed as she removed the magazine from the gun John handed her. "It'll go easier if you cooperate."

From behind them, a gravelly voice grumbled, "She's right."

Outside Maison Moreau and seated on the back bumper of an open SUV, Vivian pressed her cheek against John's chest. The slow, steady thump of his heartbeat soothed her.

The job wasn't over.

It was never *over*. Each operation had consequences, loose ends, new plots. They needed to find the buyers, Dragomir, learn how he'd gotten the intel, and how, exactly, Vandenberg was involved. But she could turn the page on this particular chapter.

Over the past hour, local police had cleared the scene.

"You got a minute?" MacColl asked.

"For you?" Vivian asked. "We've got at least five."

"Should I go?" John asked.

"Nah." MacColl crossed his rumpled arms. "You're in this as deep as anyone. After the attack on the office in DC, Vandenberg put me on paid leave and took over the operation because I was 'too lax to run a branch.' No investigation, immediate suspension. That didn't pass the sniff test for me, especially with our history. She had a pattern of doubling back on my reporting, second-guessing my asset allocation. So I went black and headed to Europe."

Vivian leaned forward.

This was a new MacColl. In DC he was a harried grump.

Competent, chock-full of integrity, and knowledgeable, but no one you'd want to bump into at 6:00 a.m. Out here in the field, he was all patience and clear reporting.

"How'd you get here undetected?"

"I have my ways," MacColl said. "Once I arrived, I reconnected with my old network to find out more about Vandenberg. Can't get shit from the system—she's got it on lock."

Which explained why Anjali couldn't get much from it.

"I can confirm your suspicions about the leave in the eighties. She had a kid with one of her Yugoslav assets. By all accounts, Vandenberg loved the guy, but she gave the kid up to protect her career and avoid attention from the secret police."

Vivian shivered. *You remind me of myself at your age.*

"But she kept tabs on the kid—Dragomir Mihailovic. Vandenberg's spent the last decade redacting information about him while trying to stop him."

"But why?"

"We'll ask her, but I have my guesses. For better or worse, he's her kid. She might've thought she could rehabilitate him. Or worried his actions would reflect poorly on her. Or he might've learned about her and blackmailed her into helping."

"But she didn't raise him, and he's grown. His actions are his."

MacColl lifted a shoulder. "Logic doesn't always play into these things. Like Hall and Rodriguez letting themselves get wrapped up in it, too. Those three have been a power clique for the past fifteen years. I'd bet they staged the attack on the DC office to get the drive and hide evidence of Dragomir's involvement."

"Speaking of—where is he?"

"Parts unknown." MacColl scratched the back of his neck. "We found the tracker in a bathroom at the hotel. It's clear he was the seller. Any clues about the buyers?"

"Not on the drives. Accounting forensics on the auctions

might tell us." Vivian yawned and covered her mouth with the back of her hand. "Sorry. It's been a long week."

"You should take tomorrow off. I'll give word to Digger about the forensics. It'll be good to have you back in the office." MacColl turned to John. "What about you?"

"What about me what?" John asked.

"The office. We could fast-track an application, and with your family background…"

Vivian swung her gaze toward him. "What does that mean?"

"I recently got some info about my parents' actual careers," John said. "Remember what you told me about the State Department as a cover story for officers abroad?"

Of course.

Another pattern dropped into place. His parents worked at the agency. They could meet for lunch at Langley and spill *all* the beans. It would be without John, of course, but it might be a bonding experience if she and his parents learned about each other's work exploits.

Unless he got clearance?

"Thanks." John shook his head. "But I love my job."

"What about you?" MacColl asked Vivian. "Since your cover's blown, I'll need to pull you from the field for a while. What US-based jobs interest you?"

"Can we talk about this when we're all back in the States?"

One thing was sure. Staying put for a while sounded like heaven.

MacColl nodded. "And that'll be…?"

"Tuesday. We'll be back on Tuesday."

"Great." MacColl dragged his finger across the surface of his phone. "Which reminds me. A wedding gift for the two of you."

Vivian's phone buzzed. "Two tickets to Copenhagen?"

"Mission here's complete. Go have fun." MacColl returned to the police fray, leaving them alone together.

John squeezed her hand. "Hi."

"Hi." She squeezed back.

"This is quite the elopement story," he said.

She laughed. "I'm sorry."

"About what?" He kissed her temple.

"All of it. The lying, the danger, the fighting, the truth serum."

"I liked that part. You said nice things about me."

"I always say nice things about you."

"Still nice to hear them." John twisted toward her. "But I don't need truth serum to be honest. I love you, Vivian Bernardita Flint. I tried not to for a couple of hours, but it didn't take. And I'd never want you to quit something that makes you feel so alive. So I hope you'll reconsider what you said this morning on the bridge."

"Reconsidered and retracted." She laid her hand on his chest. "But let me clarify something. *You* make me feel alive. I don't want to be like Vandenberg and put the job before everything I want out of life. My mom did too, in a way. And I'm tired of working two jobs."

"Three," John corrected. "Including Rocksy."

"Shit, no wonder I'm exhausted." Vivian squeezed his hand. "My point is, I don't need the job to feel alive. Just you. If you're up for it?"

He slid the earrings they'd purchased earlier from his suit pocket.

"Always." As he gently hooked them into her ears, he said, "Gorgeous, you totally pull these off. Can I please take you to Copenhagen and make you my wife?"

Tears pricked her eyes. "I want to say yes. But I need to tell you three secrets first."

"Finally. Aliens?"

"Fuck off." She bumped shoulders with him. "My sister Torrey is also Rocksy. She creates the stencils, and I spray-paint them around the world. That's why I didn't want to give up my apartment. I store the stencils there."

He blew out his breath. "Okay. What's the next one?"

"Everything I said about the agency covering my expenses was true, but because of Rocksy...after all the donations to children's literacy and art programs in Baltimore... I've got two million dollars stashed away for retirement."

"Okay, cool." He blew out a breath. "I mean, that's life-changing money, and I hope you know I'm not a gold digger, but what's the third one? Secret lair?"

"I want another dog. Ruckus could use a buddy, and if I'm not in the field, I can help take care of them."

He tucked a red curl behind her ear. "But if you *were* in the field, your husband would happily handle things while you're off saving the world."

"I like the sound of that." She kissed him. "Oh, and this isn't a secret, more like a warning. When we get back from Copenhagen, we need to go to my mother's retirement party. My whole family is dying to meet you."

He hauled her onto his lap. "I'd love nothing more."

Epilogue

One year later…

"I, John Carroll Seymour, take you, Vivian Bernardita—" John's lips twitched, and she glared at him "—Flint, for my lawful wife. To have and to hold from this day forward, for better, for worse, for richer, for poorer, in sickness and health, 'til death do us part. I'll love and honor you all the days of my life."

He slipped a platinum band onto her finger.

Her heart was full. As they stood in the American Visionary Art Museum's sculpture garden, the dangly blue earrings from Maison Moreau caught the day's sunshine and dappled John's chest. A collection of friends, family and coworkers beamed at them.

"Now you, Vivian," her friend Lisa said.

On their way home from Copenhagen last year, they'd swung back through Tangier. Lisa had squealed and promised to complete her online ordination.

"I, Vivian Bernardita Flint, take you, John Carroll Seymour, for my lawful husband."

As she listed her vows, she felt them more deeply than the oath she'd sworn to the Constitution.

"Excellent." Lisa clasped *A World History of Art* by Hugh Honour and John Fleming to her chest. "By the power given to me by the American Marriage Ministries and by the State of Maryland, I now pronounce you married. You may now kiss."

The gathering erupted into applause.

"Ladies and gentlemen," Lisa announced to their loved ones,

"it's my honor to present for the first time as a married couple, John Seymour and Vivian Flint!"

The string trio played "La Vie En Rose" as they strolled down the aisle, followed by Thomas and Torrey, Logan and Alaina, Patrick and Lisa, and Timothée and Anjali. John had originally suggested James Bond's theme song, but she'd reminded him that, though she was based in the States these days, she still needed to be discreet.

In the museum's sculpture barn, they led their giggling procession to the upstairs waiting room. As wedding guests filtered into the reception and took their seats, they'd chill with cocktails and wait to be announced.

Not her idea, but her parents had insisted they go old school with the party's events if they were making the guests dine near *Fifi*, a fifteen-foot-tall pink poodle kinetic sculpture.

She tugged John into the bridal dressing room for privacy.

"Hello there, husband."

"Hello, wife."

They'd been officially married for a year, but celebrating their vows in front of a hundred friends and family members made their anniversary an occasion.

A knock at the door interrupted their kiss.

"Torrey, I swear to God, if that's another glass of champagne—"

As the door opened, her heart softened.

"This a bad time?" MacColl asked.

"Always," she said to MacColl. "I'm happy you made it."

Especially since they weren't supposed to fraternize outside work and risk a foreign agent connecting them as colleagues. She hugged him anyway.

"Don't worry. I'm not staying, so I won't mess up the seating chart." MacColl checked they were alone, then closed the door. "I'm on my way overseas."

"Congratulations!" She'd heard through the office grapevine he'd been promoted to chief of station in Croatia.

"Thanks. That business last year reminded higher-ups of what I can do in the field. But my departure means there's a vacancy at Langley. I told them you'd fill my shoes well."

She raised her eyebrows.

Over the past year, she'd been cooling her heels training new officers at the Farm while her profile died down. She'd connected her artists with reputable dealers who'd mentor their careers. Taking over for MacColl would put her back in the game. Late nights, unpredictable schedule and periodic heart-stopping emergencies.

John kissed her temple. "You'd be great."

"I'll consider it," she said to MacColl. "But today's about us, not work. John and I need to stuff ourselves with cake. Call you tomorrow?"

"Looking forward to it," MacColl said as he opened the door. "For the record, I'm happy it worked out between you two."

"Thanks, Boss." She closed the door, then squeezed John's hand three times. "Ready for the rest of our lives?"

He squeezed back. "As long as it's with you, Gorgeous, I'm ready for anything."

★ ★ ★ ★ ★

If you loved M.C. Vaughan's hilarious and sexy spy caper romance, then you'll adore her other titles with Harlequin.

Romancing Miss Stone
and
Destination Weddings and Other Disasters

both feature whip-smart banter, thrilling globe-trotting moments, and sizzling chemistry. Available now wherever books are sold!

Acknowledgments

It's impossible to write a globe-trotting spy caper rom-com without a deep bench of assets to make the story sparkle. Enormous thanks to my editor, John Jacobson, whose enthusiasm for this story and inspiring emojis in the manuscript were a constant delight. Also, my humble thanks to Jennifer Stimson, copy editor extraordinaire, who diligently fact-checked every location name in multiple languages (and so many other things!). I'm so lucky to have worked with both of you!

To Barbara Collins Rosenberg, thank you, as always, for being an enthusiastic reader and supporter of my banana pants ideas.

All the gratitude to my husband, David, an amazing partner who holds down the fort when I'm in the writing cave. And the editing cave. And maybe-if-I-fiddle-with-that-sentence-one-more-time-whoops-its-deadline-day cave. I love the life we have together and I'm grateful it does not involve running away from goons in European alleys.

And to my sisters and besties from all phases of my life—Sheila, Gina, Shannon, Kristin, Kate, Molly, Ruth, Colleen, Dawn, Cara, Mary, Elizabeth, and Christi—what would I do without you? Thank you for years of belly laughs, support, and love. No matter how much life throws at us, girlhood never dies.